SOUL TRAPPER

SOUL TRAPPER
A KANE PRYCE NOVEL

F. J. Lennon

ATRIA PAPERBACK

New York   London   Toronto   Sydney   New Delhi

ATRIA PAPERBACK
A Division of Simon & Schuster, Inc.
1230 Avenue of the Americas
New York, NY 10020

First Atria Paperback edition August 2011

ATRIA PAPERBACK and colophon are trademarks of Simon & Schuster, Inc.

"Donna": Words and Music by Ritchie Valens. © 1958 (Renewed 1986).
EMI LONGITUDE MUSIC. All Rights Reserved. International Copyright Secured.
Used by Permission. *Reprinted by permission of Hal Leonard Corporation.*

"Layla": Words and Music by Eric Clapton and Jim Gordon. © 1970 (Copyright Renewed)
by Eric Patrick Clapton and Throat Music Ltd. All Rights in the U.S. Administered by
Unichappell Music Inc. International Copyright Secured. All Rights Reserved.
Used by Permission. *Reprinted by permission of Hal Leonard Corporation.*

For information about special discounts for bulk purchases,
please contact Simon & Schuster Special Sales at
1-866-506-1949 or business@simonandschuster.com.

The Simon & Schuster Speakers Bureau can bring authors to your
live event. For more information or to book an event, contact the
Simon & Schuster Speakers Bureau at 1-866-248-3049 or visit our
website at www.simonspeakers.com.

Designed by Jacquelynne Hudson

Manufactured in the United States of America

10   9   8   7   6   5   4   3   2   1

The Library of Congress has cataloged the hardcover edition as follows:
Lennon, F. J., date.
    Soul trapper : a novel / by F. J. Lennon.—1st Atria Books hardcover ed.
        p. cm.
1. Parapsychology—Fiction. 2. Haunted places—Fiction. 3. Future life—Fiction. 4. Women
journalists—Fiction. I. Title.
    PS3612.E5426S68 2011
    813'.6—dc22   2010044346

ISBN 978-1-4391-8444-8
ISBN 978-1-4391-8445-5 (pbk)
ISBN 978-1-4391-8664-0 (ebook)

For Laura and Olivia

The supernatural is the natural not yet understood.

—Elbert Hubbard

One man's "magic" is another man's engineering. "Supernatural" is a null word.

—Robert A. Heinlein

SOUL TRAPPER

One

Three things I've learned about a pissed-off ghost. First, it likes to do the scaring. When the tables are turned and it's suddenly the one being scared shitless, batten down the hatches. Second, like pretty much anything backed into a corner, it's going to get frantic. And third, it's not going to look like your kid brother under a sheet or Jacob Marley dragging a chain or a glowing pretty boy like Patrick Swayze in *Ghost*. If you're lucky (or unlucky) enough to see it at all, it'll look like a nasty, zigzagging ball of lightning in a jar. That electrical energy—what I call the z-thing—is the *zizz*, the *zam*. Ben Franklin did not discover this stuff. Whatever it is, it stands you right the hell to attention when it zaps you.

The second I enter the barn, a sphere comes at me like a major-league fastball and I hit the deck. Pop! A lightbulb behind me blows. Then another. Then three more surge, explode, and send a burst of wicked sparks into the air. I'm not in darkness long. Flames erupt and race up the walls. Smoke envelopes me and I'm coughing up a lung. The soul trap vibrates and hums in my hands. The horses that fled circle the barn and whinny frantically.

After a display of electromagnetic manipulation like that, the soul will be spent, at least for a minute or two. In a barn like this, baking in the California sun for fifty years, the timbers are as dry as dinosaur bones. I have five minutes to end this—tops.

"Give it up, Casper! I own your spectral ass," I yell as I throw the emitter switch on the soul trap. A wall of red light—the phantom fence—erupts from the barrel and forms a barrier between me and the barn door. I pivot and throw the switch again. A second fence stretches to the barn wall. It's called a fence, but it's more like a bubble. It pens ghosts in, but also puts a barrier above and below them as well.

Now I have it boxed in.

The flames in the hayloft arc and spiral like a gust of wind hit them. Bingo. I grab the ladder it hurled at me moments before and climb to the hayloft. Both phantom fences close behind me and surround us.

Now I have it cornered.

The flames licking the walls ignite the roof. Heavy smoke fills my lungs. The soul trap vibrates madly, then stops. The monitor on the butt end of the trap flashes to life and the targeting program launches automatically. I try to steady my nerves, but the smoke is too thick. I point the barrel of the weapon at the back wall. The spirit roars, and I don't need a digital recorder to hear its rage. It's desperate, cornered—at last, an easy target. An unseen force pulls the barrel a little to the right, then a hair to the left. I look at the monitor—the crosshairs illuminate and I hear the familiar shrill tone. Locked and loaded. I pull the trigger. Fire.

Dirty Harry had his .44 Magnum. Van Helsing, his crucifix and stake. I have the soul trap, and once again, it delivers. I close my eyes and brace for the noise, a cacophony not of this world—loud and long: a static-charged rip, as if the fabric of time and space is torn in half, a soul's anguished moan, a colossal boom, then the slurp of megasuction like a Dirt Devil on steroids. Mission accomplished.

The smoke clouds my vision. I reach for the ladder and halfway down, my lungs close and I can't breathe. It hits me—I might die. I might end up a ghost. With half a dozen rungs left to descend, I leap off and try to sprint, but collapse. I press my cheek to the ground and start crawling toward the door. When I finally emerge from the barn, I use the barrel of the soul trap to help me stand. Then I hear a thousand Louisville Sluggers being snapped like twigs all at once. Adrenaline kicks in and I manage to run. When I'm out of the fire and into the night air, the barn roof collapses and a column of fire darts into the sky. Somehow I'm still on my feet, and moving fast. I sprint twenty yards to safety, drop to my hands and knees and vomit ash, smoke, and a three-hour-old burrito.

Besides the raging inferno, I hear two other things: sirens in the distance and footsteps coming toward me.

"Christ in heaven, are you okay?" asks Rick Camarillo, the owner of the ranch.

I choke out an "uh-huh."

"Did you capture it?" he asks in a Hispanic accent as thick as his salt-and-pepper mustache.

I struggle to speak. "I got it."

"Thank you. God bless you, Kane."

"It's a nasty prick—powerful. The barn just went up." With what feels like a mouthful of charcoal briquettes, I say, "I'm sorry."

"That devil spirit made the flames. I know it. It has threatened me and my horses with fire before." Señor Camarillo stares sadly at the carnage. "You're sure I'm rid of it?" he asks.

"I'm sure."

I look up. Through burning, watery eyes I see him staring at the flames. "Then the barn is a small price to pay."

The sirens get louder. "Must be the fire department," I say, hacking.

"And the police," says Camarillo.

"What?" Goddamnit. Did I mention I pretty much hate everyone? That includes horseshit shovelers with Magnum P.I. mustaches. Fuckin' A, I'm going to jail over this.

"It's my wife," he says, nervously stroking his pornstache. "She doesn't trust you—thinks you're loco. She called the police—told them you burned down our barn."

"And you couldn't stop her?"

"I'm sorry."

Pussy-whipped rancher. I stand and search the horizon for flashing lights, but everything's a blur. "My eyes are on fire. So are my lungs. I need water."

"There's water in the well," Camarillo says, pointing to our left. "I still draw from it. Better than the mule piss the city of L.A. puts through the pipes."

I dart to the well, raise the bucket, and bury my head in the cold water. Heaven on earth. I yank my head out of the bucket, glance around. The sirens echo off the canyon wall behind the ranch. I have a minute, maybe two. My heart pounds. I pick up the trap, shoot a look right and left. Nothing. I glance at Rancher Rick staring at the fallen barn. I'd like to trust him with it, but I can't. I don't trust anyone.

The police cars and fire engines turn onto Camarillo's property. No choice. I dump out the water in the bucket, place the soul trap inside, and lower it halfway down the well. Maybe I'll get lucky and walk out of here with it. Probably not, in which case Ned will have to come and get it.

I could try to make a run for it into the canyon, but I don't have the wind for it. Plus, they'll bust me harder for fleeing the scene. The best I can do now is put a little distance between me and the trap. I raise my hands and run toward the three approaching LAPD cruisers. The cops are out of their vehicles in a flash, nines drawn.

"Freeze or I'll blow your fucking head off."

"Facedown on the ground. Now!"

I've been through this dance before with the trigger-happy LAPD. One stupid move, I'm dead, and these jackasses are off to high-five each other at the TGIF happy hour in Simi Valley. I bite my tongue and drop facedown. It's like a herd of bison approaching and stomping me. Two swats with a nightstick open a gash in my scalp, three punches to my temple and jaw ring my bell, and a well-placed patrol boot to my kidney makes me piss a little in my jeans. My shoulder ligaments are stretched to the max as they slap the cuffs on me and drag me across rocks and dirt to an awaiting cruiser. I can't breathe. I feel like a goldfish on the floor of a mean kid's bedroom.

Fuck biting my tongue. "Hey, assholes," I groan. "Can't we all just get along?"

The two cops dragging me stop and drop me. The only words I hear are "You have the right to remain—" before one of the cops takes his baton upside my head and sends me to dreamland.

Two

The ten-minute ride to LAPD's Foothill Division is pretty much a blur, but what little brainpower I have seems focused on the number 27 again. Ever since I turned 27 last November, I've had this feeling, not really a premonition, but a nagging suspicion, that I might not live to see 28. A lot of important people—at least important in my world—have crapped out at 27. Kurt Cobain, Jim Morrison, Jimi Hendrix, Brian Jones, Janis Joplin, and Robert Johnson, the bluesman who sold his soul at the crossroads. For the last month or so, I've been listening to their music pretty much exclusively as my preoccupation with their untimely deaths intensifies. Granted, they're all famous icons and I'm a schmo, but I still can't shake this feeling that somehow I'm a member of Club 27 with them. Don't know why.

Yes, I'm a musician, but I'm only good behind closed doors and I have no real desire to stand under a spotlight. While I have a passion for music—pretty much all forms of it—I accept the fact that I'll probably never make it. I'm a half decent piano player and am definitely a good enough guitarist to play in a band, but when I'm playing, the music doesn't overtake me. I never surprise myself. I can't feel it deep enough in my bone marrow, and without that magic, I can't stand out. Hollywood is already filled with enough wannabe rock stars. You need the special sauce. Plus, in today's music scene, I'm like a dinosaur. My heroes are all in the past. I was born the same year Madonna was recording "Lucky Star," yet I'm trapped in '60s and '70s rock.

So, in other words, I'm the misfit sitting alone, listening—over and over—to CDs that peaked as vinyl albums.

Before my head clears, I've already been dragged from the police cruiser, photographed, and printed. I'm led to a pay phone and told to make it quick. The one-phone-call myth seen endlessly on TV is bullshit, at least in my experience. Every time I've been busted I've been given at least ten minutes alone, and in that time I can make as many phone calls as I damn well please, so long as there was someone on the other end to accept the charges. Even with this wild freedom to dial recklessly from behind bars, I only ever make one call. Ned Ross. *Doctor* Ned Ross, he'd be quick to point out. I dial the operator and give her Ned's number. It rings and I tense up. A cop shows up right behind me. I remind myself that it doesn't matter if he's here or not—the phones are bugged anyway. I have to think quick and shut Ned up before he goes off on one of his tangents. Ned grumbles when the operator asks him if he'll accept the charges.

"Kane? Where are you?"

"Look, I've—"

"How'd it go? Did you get it? Did you get paid?" he asks, cutting me off.

This is a man who never shuts his fucking mouth. "Don't interrupt me. Listen to me for a minute. It's important you listen to me, okay?"

"Got it."

"I ran into some trouble. I'm in custody at Foothill Division."

"Shit. For what?"

"Arson. But you're interrupting me again," I say, pissed.

"Sorry. Go ahead."

"Listen to me. Don't worry. I'm doing *well*." I drag out the word. "Very *well*, considering." I pause. "*Well*, I need your help. So go take care of business and then get over here and help me out. Okay?"

Ned pauses, processes. "Okay, gotcha."

I hang up. Ned should figure it out. If anything, it'll be so simple, it might throw him. This is a guy who thinks on a whole different level from most mortals. He worked on the soul trap, which puts him in the technological stratosphere, and he's considered a genius in mathematics circles. But his ego gets in his way and he talks way more than he listens, and in the rare instance he does listen, he doesn't hear. He's equal parts blarney, bullshit, and brilliance. He thinks he knows it all, but if you ask me he knows a little bit about a lot of things and a lot about a few things. But the few things he knows top to bottom remain well beyond the scope of comprehension of most people, me included.

Ned knew my dad a little, and he's a college professor, so he thinks this gives him carte blanche to lecture me like I'm a student and order me around like the son he never had. The classic love-hate thing. He can get on my nerves faster than any human on earth, but, in truth, he's the only person I can really count on.

The cop leads me to a holding cell where a goofy-looking bastard is pacing. Two seconds after the door slams, I peg him as a meth head. He looks sixty, so in Methland, that would put him somewhere in his early to midforties. He's missing some teeth, has scabs on his bald scalp, and looks like a corpse that started decaying but forgot to die first. I take a seat on the bench, cross my arms, and close my eyes. I emanate a single silent mantra: *Fuckin' leave me alone.*

For a few silent minutes, it works. I assess my sorry situation. I'm already on probation for breaking and entering at the Comedy Store on Sunset. That was the time I trapped another pissed-off ghost, a mob hit man from the '40s, who got whacked in the basement of what was then Ciro's nightclub. Before that, I had a couple juvie convictions for assault—not supernatural related. After my dad died, I got bounced around a handful of foster homes and had two different run-ins with foster fathers that turned into all-out brawls. Take all of this, add it up, and it equals one big, fucking black mark on my name. I know I'm not walking out of here today. There's not going to be bail set or a summons to appear. It hits me all at once like the cop's nightstick—I'm going to jail.

I continue my mantra, but the silence is broken by the guy I'm trapped with in the cell. "That fucking Obama."

I don't reply.

"You're not asleep. Don't bullshit me."

I don't reply.

"Faggot, I'm talking to you."

I don't reply.

"Look at you sitting there, with that hair, the goatee, the boots, the Nirvana shirt. What are you—a graduate of the Johnny Depp Fashion Academy?

I open my eyes. "They confiscated my shades and my lucky necklace. They really complete my look."

"I'll bet a faggot like you voted for that fucking Obama. Probably going to vote for him again, too."

"I don't talk politics," I say, closing my eyes again.

"You know about that Obama, don't you?"

He's not going to leave me alone. Let's see what brand of crazy I'm dealing with. "Know what?"

"He's part of the sacred bloodline of the Illuminati." Jesus Christ—a meth head that's also nuttier than a Snickers. I knew a guy like this once. Schizophrenic and most likely off his meds. "Obama's the eighth cousin of Dick Cheney, the thirteenth cousin of George Bush. No shit. Kissing fuckin' cousins."

Did I mention I pretty much hate everyone? That includes tweakers, conspiracy buffs, and loons. This douche bag wins the trifecta.

"He's also related to the Windsors and Winston Churchill. It's all one interconnected bloodline going all the way back to Vlad the Impaler. You know who that is, right?"

"Count Chocula," I mumble. He doesn't even hear me.

"That's right, Dracula. Dragooool, baby!" He's tweaking his balls off, throwing piss-poor karate kicks in the air. "That's how this old whore of a world works. Obama was hand-groomed to be the first black president. There were three black guys the Illuminati groomed, but Obama was the one they chose. I'll bet you don't know who the other two were."

I try not to make eye contact as I glance around for something to hit him with. Cell is empty.

"Arthur Ashe was numero uno, but he wouldn't play ball so they killed him with AIDS. Guess who the second one was?"

"Gary Coleman."

"Don't mock me, asshole," he snarls, planting a back kick on the cell door. "I am speaking words of wisdom here."

The boom of his kick echoes and I hear a cop outside yell, "Cut the shit in there." The meth head just resumes his rant. "The second was Colin Powell, but he lacked the charisma to sway the masses."

Did I mention I pretty much hate everyone? That includes shit-kicking racists. I'll be trapped with this jerkoff for God knows how long, and he's not going to shut up. If I can fuck with him . . . play upon his paranoia . . . get him to take a swing at me, and let him land a clean punch, maybe they'll drag him to another cell. Time to engage. I open my eyes, stare him square in the eye until it makes him squirm. "How do you know this stuff?" I ask.

"Shit, I read. Lots of shit. Icke mostly."

David Icke. Figures. Writes mildly entertaining conspiracy books about the Illuminati controlling the world and a reptilian race in charge of everything. Spins a good yarn. Persuasive as hell. Listen to him speak eloquently about Princess Diana's death for an hour and you'll be ready to storm the castle door and hang the royals for murder. I sit up, uncross my arms, nod at him, and speak slowly and with utter certainty. "I'm part of it all."

"Part of what?" he asks, amused.

"Part of the puppet show. Except I'm not a puppet."

"What does that mean?"

I'm remembering a diagram of Freemasonry from an Icke documentary I watched a couple of years ago. "What would you say if I told you I was a Grand Elect Mason?"

"I'd say bullshit. Bull fucking shit."

"I'm fourteenth degree. Illuminated."

"Bullshit." He's suspicious, a little worried.

"The brotherhood of the Scottish Rite." Now he's alarmed. He doesn't reply. "Come on, you read Icke," I say. "*Children of the Matrix?*" I glanced through that crazy fucking book once at Barnes & Noble when I ducked inside to wait out an El Niño rainstorm. Got so hooked, I ended up shoplifting it. His face goes white. Yep, he's read it.

"You're one of them?"

This is easier than I thought. I nod, roll my eyes up in my head until they're white, start blinking madly, and give him my best Nicholson smirk.

"You're a reptile," he whispers, backing away. "You're one of them."

"Why do you think I'm here?"

He shakes his head.

"You know too much." I stop blinking and refocus on him. I smile and whisper answers to the air as I look at him. I stand up and he decides to sit—at the other end of the cell. "Those voices in your head—that's us. We control you. And millions like you." I walk over, lean down, and let out a spraying hiss. Slowly, I ask, "Now, how do you know about Arthur Ashe? Tell me, fucker, or you won't survive the night."

"I ain't telling you shit." He stands and I shove him back down. He throws both fists in the air, begins ducking and weaving. I could knock his ass cold, but instead I lean in and expose my chin. Just when he's ready to wail on me, a cop opens the door and points a taser his way. "Sit down and shut the fuck up or I will fry your ass," he screams. Then he looks at me. "Kane Pryce?"

I nod.

"Follow me. Charges were dropped."

Christmas comes early. I look at the meth head in the corner, fists still raised, ready to rumble. "See? I'm untouchable. You? You're gonna rot in here."

"Fucking reptilian motherfucker, get back here," he screams as the cell door slams behind me.

Down the hallway from the cell, Detective Cliff DuPree from the Hollywood division waits.

"What are you doing in the Valley?" I ask.

"Your name came up on the arrest database. Meet me out front. I'll give you a ride home." I collect my wallet, iPhone, sunglasses, and necklace, then call Ned and leave a message on his voice mail. I walk out the front door and into DuPree's Volvo.

We fly down the 170 Freeway, but hit a wall of traffic near the Victory off-ramp. I can't take my eyes off the navigation system embedded in the walnut-appointed dash. "Nice car," I say.

"Bought it on New Year's Eve. Best day of the year to get a deal on a new fucking ride. They're creaming to get one last sale on the books."

"So I guess I owe you another one," I say.

"Not this time. Lucky for you the rancher's wife changed her tune," DuPree says. "I couldn't have helped you this time." DuPree looks over at me and I glance back. He's a big guy—fit and forty, salt-and-pepper hair, always a classy necktie. He's right out of Central Casting—could play a police detective, good or bad, on any cop show. "Cover your tracks better, Kane. Remember, I'm the only person on this side of the fence who actually believes your stories. I've pulled a lot of strings for you—"

"Going back to juvie hall," I say. "I know."

DuPree nods. "But you can't count on me to bail you out of every jam." He takes one hand off the steering wheel and points at me. "You're too smart to end up in prison. Get your head out of your ass."

I sigh, disgusted and tired. "Okay, the next time I throw down on a violent, desperate ghost, I'll ask it to go light."

"Just destroy that thing and get on with your life."

"I can't do that."

"Look at you. You're alone. You're afraid to make friends, to get close to anyone. That device is a curse."

"I'm keeping it."

"Why? Because of your father?"

Duh. I don't answer. Traffic starts to flow. DuPree focuses on the freeway again. "You can't beat what's not of this world."

"Who says?"

DuPree drops me off on the corner of Yucca and Highland and gives me a final warning to keep my nose clean. I stop at 7-Eleven, buy a lousy coffee, and cross the street to my apartment building. My iPhone rings. It's Ned.

"Got your message. Where are you?"

"Almost home," I say. "Do you have it?"

"I got a couple of things at the Camarillo ranch. I got your eight grand—cash. And, *well*, the soul trap's safe by my side."

"I'm glad you figured it out."

"Forest Gump could have figured it out. *Well*, Kane, I guess I'll meet you at your place in about twenty, that is if you're feeling *well*. *Well?* . . ." He cracks himself up and I hang up on him.

Home sweet home is the Halifax Apartments on the corner of Yucca and Cahuenga. If you live here, you're either on your way up and out or down and out. No in-betweens. I still don't know which category I'm in. Mainly, I'm cheap. I'd rather spend the little money I make tooling up my ghost-hunting gear than paying a wad on a respectable crib.

At the front door, a lousy day starts to look a lot better. I've seen her before, but I'm not sure where or when. A tall blonde with short hair, a long neck, and eyes so big and blue they look like pools you could swim laps in. She wears white and, for a second, I have the hopeful notion that maybe, just maybe, she's an angel bearing a message. But my thoughts go from saintly to sinful when she smiles and approaches. A designer suit and handbag to go with a rose tatt that reveals itself when she bends to retrieve her BlackBerry off the sidewalk.

"Kane? Kane Pryce? Can I speak to you?"

Alarm bells. "How do you know my name?"

She extends a hand. "Eva Kells."

I don't offer my hand in return. "How do you know my name?"

"I've read about you."

"Read what?"

She smiles, all friendly. "About what you do. You're mentioned on a few Southern Cal ghost websites. You're all over laghostpost .com. Interesting reading."

Goddamnit. I made the mistake of going along on a couple of paranormal investigations with a husband-and-wife team. Dumbass that I am, I got drunk with them a couple of times and shot my mouth off. Told them some things—nothing major, but enough for them to hail me as some kind of expert. Next thing I know, they're writing about me.

The website has no style. Amateur hour. No major traffic— mostly the hard-core L.A. ghost buffs. Not enough limelight to get me into trouble; just enough to keep me on my toes. Shouldn't bitch too hard, though. Shitty-looking site has gotten me most of my clients.

"What do you want?" I ask.

"I work at the L.A. *Times.*"

Strike one. "I don't need a subscription. I get my news online."

She shakes her head. "I'm a reporter. I also have a blog."

Strikes two and three. Did I mention I pretty much hate every-one? That includes reporters, bloggers, and tweeters. But . . . a pre-dicament. Did I forget to mention that I'm also a major-league skin hound? What to do, what to do.

Walk away, Kane, but my feet are inexplicably rooted in the sidewalk. *Don't even glance her way,* but I can't stop looking. I have a theory about my weakness for women in white, or any other color in the 32-bit spectrum. It's lame at best, but here it goes: When it comes to women and sex, I most closely identify with a well-known character. No, it's not Ron Jeremy, though he lives just up the street. It's Spock. Everyone knows he's a logical and levelheaded dude, but every seven years or so, he experiences Pon Farr. That's Vulcan for horny as a chimp with three balls. Out of nowhere, his Vulcan blood boils, his logic and reason get jettisoned out the *Enterprise*'s escape hatch, and the normally buttoned-up Spock goes apeshit on everyone until he busts his Vulcan nut. That's me, except it's not seven years, it's seven weeks, give or take. And according to my mental calendar, Vulcan mating season is upon me again.

Jesus, you can't mingle with a reporter, but here I stand, toying with the notion. Wake up—now! I'm single and decent-enough-looking. I can meet a bevy of hot girls in club lines if I walk a few blocks in any direction. I don't need this. "No comment." I say as I make a fast trek for the front door.

"Listen, Kane. I'm on your side," she says, talking fast. "Ghosts are hot. I believe in them. I want to write about you—get your story out there. Give you a push. Let's just talk."

"I guess you didn't hear me, so I'll repeat: No fucking comment."

"Look, here's my card. All of my digits are on there—home, work, cell. Give me a call. Anytime."

"Keep it," I say, stepping inside the foyer.

"Just think about it," she says, shoving the card in my back pocket. Her hand on my ass—even for an instant: electrifying. She smiles at me, then struts away like a model on a catwalk. When she rounds the corner I walk over and watch her sway down Cahuenga. It's the highlight of my day—maybe my piss-poor year. She's a cut above any girl I'll meet in a club line—and if she were anything but a reporter, I'd have been chasing her like a puppy chasing his tail. But I can't risk it.

Or can I?

She disappears out of sight when she reaches Hollywood Boulevard. It's done and over with. The big head prevailed.

I go inside and wait for Ned.

Three

My apartment—number 216—is off-limits to everyone except me and Ned. It's not your standard Hollywood bachelor crib. Aluminum foil on every window. Can't risk snoops or would-be burglars seeing what I have stored in here.

The most prominent piece of furniture in my living room is a hospital gurney. If you broke in you'd think that the person living here is a hospice patient.

"I can still taste that smoke," I complain to Ned as he carefully connects the soul trap to our Nividia Tesla Supercomputer. He's on all fours connecting cables. The crack of his fat ass is out. "My ribs are killing me, too—I think that cop cracked one of them."

"So? I ache all the time," Ned says with a Brooklyn accent thicker than a porterhouse.

"That's because you're a geezer," I say.

He ignores the jab. "And I've been tasting smoke since I was younger than you. Started smoking my sophomore year at Georgia Tech. Hasn't done me any harm."

"Ever try inhaling barn timbers?"

"Thirty-six years I've been smoking three packs a day. That has to equal at least a couple of barns."

"Fine. You win, bro. You get the Black Lung Award."

"Is there a cash prize? Can I make a speech?" Ned stands slowly and balances his mighty girth. He always looks like he needs a good wash. He's wearing his standard khakis and a brown sweater that fit twenty pounds ago. I always tell him he needs another X in the XL, but he never listens. He looks older than he is. He points out that the pathetic goatee he grew last year makes him look a decade younger. His diet is a train wreck and his mostly gray hair has been getting noticeably stringier lately. I worry he'll keel over before he hits sixty.

"Is this what happens in your fifties? You have to win every argument?"

Ned smirks. "After your thirties—when you actually acquire the mental capacity to win an argument—you get more serious about it."

"No wonder your third wife left you."

Ned winces. "I did lose some arguments to her—God rest her wicked soul." He takes a seat in front of our 32-inch dual monitors and starts typing.

"There's a reporter poking around," I say nonchalantly.

Ned fidgets with the settings on the monitor. "Is he on the up-and-up?"

"It's a she."

"Oh boy."

"What's that mean?"

Ned smirks, shakes his head, and redirects the conversation. "I've given this some thought before." Ned opens his mouth, but swallows whatever he was going to say.

"What?" I demand to know.

Ned says, reluctantly, "Maybe it's not such a bad idea to have a reputable reporter in our camp."

I can't believe what I'm hearing. "You're the one always looking over his shoulder. Now you want to go public?"

"Not for publicity. Fuck that." Ned slumps. "For protection." I wave off the idea. I've heard this spiel before. "Look, for all I know we're free and clear here. But someday, somebody might come looking for this thing. A reporter in the know could add a layer of protection." I give this one some silent thought. "Just a thought."

I don't tell him I've been thinking the same thing.

I crack open a beer and watch Ned launch the Silver Cord program. A 3-D representation of my body appears on the left screen. On the right, my heart, breathing, magnetic brain image, and astral meters each have their own quadrant on the screen.

"Depending on how aggressive she is, you may need to take the trap for a while."

"No way, Kane. Too dangerous."

"What the fuck? If I need you to take it, then just take it. You created it. It's yours." Anger bubbles up.

"Calm down or this is never gonna work," Ned says.

I breathe deep and try to dissolve my irritability. I have to stay calm and balanced or I'll never make it. "All I'm saying is, you should take it."

Ned walks to the gurney in the corner and fiddles with the helmet and the wires and electrodes he'll be strapping to me. "I've told you a hundred times—I designed and prototyped the interfaces for the soul trap and all the interfacing software. Granted, the GUI on some of that software was ten years ahead of its time, but I was on and off the project in eight months. A far cry from creating it. It was your dad and the others who did the heavy lifting. I mean, actually, if you want to get übertechnical, it was Tesla who designed it. We just took his ramblings, turned them into functional specs, and produced something."

My heart rate elevates. "You're not helping me here."

Now Ned is annoyed. "Okay, what do you want me to say? That I'll take it?"

"Yeah," I shout. "What the fuck?"

"Fine," he snaps. "If you get in a jam, I'll take it."

"Thank you," I say sarcastically.

"Probably end up with a bullet in my head," he groans. "I'm ready. Just get me in."

Ned takes a seat in front of the monitors and makes final adjustments. "Get on the gurney, wire yourself up, and get your noggin settled."

I stretch out on the gurney and don the NuMag helmet. Looks a little like one of those helmets babies wear to round out flat heads. Sends magnetic fields directly into the brain tissue behind my forehead (the third eye) and the base of my skull (the cerebellum). Kind of like a mega-MRI, except focused on only these two small targets, the most psychically charged regions of the body.

When the helmet is secure, I apply electrodes to my chakras, the major energy points on the body. Next I don my Alpha IV Ganzfeld Goggles and plug in my Interear soundproof buds for maximum sensory deprivation. Ned then sends currents of steady, gentle electricity through the interior of the helmet, the electrodes, and around the rim of my goggles. Beneath the goggles, my field of vision slowly dissolves from pitch-black to soft white. I'm a spider lost in the center of a blank IMAX screen.

Almost immediately I sink into relaxation. The currents intensify and my muscles twitch involuntarily. The helmet vibrates. Puts a whole new spin on catching a buzz. Alone, in silence, lost in a complete Alaskan whiteout, I focus on my breathing.

The soul trap is more than a weapon. It's a means of communication. With Ned maintaining a constant watch and monitoring my vital signs, I can astrally project my consciousness—my soul—into the device. It's a hell of a trip. You never know who or what you're going to find inside.

Ned touches my right hand and squeezes. That's the sign that I'm wired and ready. Time to take my brainwaves to alpha.

It's like tripping acid inside a lucid dream. Sometimes, when my mind is racing or I'm in an especially shitty mood, it takes hours. Sometimes, a few minutes. It's a combination of meditation, Kriya breathing techniques, prayer, and biofeedback on my part—combined with the magnetic fields flooding my brain from within the helmet. Puts my brain on a wavelength that lets my soul leave my body and travel deep into the soul trap.

The routine is now ingrained. I start by inhaling through one nostril and exhaling through the other and reverse and repeat until my heart rate slows by ten percent. Then I begin exhaling through my mouth, also reversing and repeating until my heart rate and body temperature drop significantly. I surround myself with an aura of white light, reach out to benevolent forces for protection, and recall memories of peace and serenity. My database of memories that fit that bill is pretty light, but I have a few nice moments tucked away for use. These mental images produce a current of aural energy that flows in a steady current around me. When my aura is clear and flowing freely, I concentrate on emptying my mind of all thoughts. If I manage to pull this off, the blank movie screen in my field of vision bursts to cinematic life. A dazzling kaleidoscope of colors erupts in my third eye and slowly gels into a single color—first pale blue, then deep purple. When I'm drowning in a sea of purple and I hear an electric hum and a distant ringing, I know I've arrived.

The more I do it, the easier it gets.

I open my eyes and find myself in the featureless space Ned designed to look like the prototypical interrogation room. There's a metal table and two chairs lit by a single lightbulb with a cage wrapped around it. It's a cold place—literally and figuratively. The steady hum can get to you. Some souls get intimidated here. Some don't. My job is to find out why they won't leave the earthly realm before I send them packing.

One of the chairs is empty; the other is occupied by a soul who looks to be mid-nineteenth century. I size him up from the shadows. He's middle-aged and filthy. His long beard looks like a rat's nest. He's in tattered pants, knee-high boots, flannel shirt, and a beat-up cowboy hat. His eyes look tired and black. I take a step forward and he looks over at me.

"Damnit, what's this all about?" he asks with a twang. His voice, like all voices in the soul trap, has a tinny echo that Ned says is grounded in electromagnetic energy. "Where the hell am I?"

I take a seat.

He studies me. "You're the fella from the barn. You the law?"

"What do you think?"

"Well," he says, glancing around, "you got me locked up in this here freezing room with tin furniture under one of them explodin' kinda lights that doesn't even have a flame."

I always wanted to be in a Western. I eye him up and channel Clint Eastwood. "Around these parts, you could say I'm the new sheriff." He fidgets in his chair, runs his hand through his grimy beard.

"Tell me your name," I demand.

He spits in his palm and extends his dirty hand. "Skeeter Jackson's the name, gold mining's the game." I ignore his grubby paw. "Can't believe I got taken in by a hornswogglin' pup like you."

"Why were you haunting that ranch?"

"I don't know what you're spoutin' on about."

Enough already. Bad cop time. I stand and slam my fists on the table. "Get the gold dust out of your ears and listen, Skeeter. For whatever reason, you didn't want to exit peacefully through your door. So how would you like a nice shove? I have that power. So start talking."

Skeeter slumps. "All right. All right," he says. He ponders for a silent moment, then speaks. "It was 1867. I was tin-pannin' the hills of Tujunga Canyon near the Monte Cristo gold mine. I wasn't makin' a lick of progress, but it seemed like everyone around me was strikin'. One of those miners told me about a surefire way to strike it rich." He pauses, as if remembering with regret.

"Go on."

"You had to light yerself some candles and summon up one of the devil's cohorts—a demon named Berith. For the cost of your soul, that old demon would turn worthless metal into pure gold. Well, I summoned me up that demon and gave him a hunk of iron pyrite the size of a bear skull."

"Fool's gold," I say.

Skeeter nods. "Well, that fool's gold became real gold."

"And you got rich."

Skeeter smiles. "That I did."

"Enjoy your fortune?"

He doesn't hesitate. "Hell yeah—up until I blew it."

"How?"

"Gambled away a lot of it. Made a lot of whores wealthy women. Drank an ocean of whiskey. And got swindled out of the rest of it."

"How did it end?"

"Got desperate. Tried to rob a bank, but botched it. Ended up shooting a deputy in cold blood. A posse tracked me down on the land where you trapped me and hung me from an oak near that barn."

"Why did you refuse to move on?"

Skeeter fidgets. "Aw, go blow it out your cornhole."

"Answer me." I grab him by the collar.

"Go hang yerself."

"You're afraid of that door," I tell him. "Afraid of what's on the other side."

Skeeter spits on the floor. "I'm not afeard of anything." His voice cracks. He's ready to break.

I get in his face. "Why did you terrorize the horse rancher and his family? Why not just lay low if you're afraid to move on?"

"Piss off, Sheriff."

"Tell me now." I look at the door, then back at him.

"That rancher's wife—Esmerelda—does a lot of prayin'. When she starts spoutin' on her rosary beads, my door glows brighter—it calls out to me. I can barely fight the urge to open it."

"Then you should have opened it," I tell him.

"No!" he shouts. His voice quivers. "Something's waitin' on the other side—I know it."

I press a button under the corner of the table. "Well, guess what? We're about to find out."

A lever with a crystal handle materializes at my side. A steel door appears behind Skeeter. He turns, worried. "What do you plan to do there, Sheriff?" He rubs his hands nervously. He knows what it's like to be hunted and lynched and he's getting that feeling again. Yes, even ghosts get scared.

I grab the lever.

"No! Don't!" he cries.

I look into his black eyes and shake my head no. He collapses to his knees, and clutches his hands like an anguished soul praying before a church statue. "You let me go," he says through sobs, "and I'll never bother another dadburn soul. You got my word on that, Sheriff. Listen here—you turn me loose and I'll make you a fortune."

Did I mention I pretty much hate everyone? That includes liars—dead or alive. "Not today." I pull the lever. It sounds like a thousand heavy chains prying the door open. "Sorry, pardner." There's a blast of horrific noise from the vacuum of the hereafter. A rush of moans. Static. Electrified reverberations. A legion of voices—fierce battle cries. Whimpers of starving animals. Growls of animals feeding. Skeeter was right about one thing: Someone was waiting for him on the other side.

A voice—high-pitched and almost supervillain sinister—thunders from the black abyss awaiting Skeeter. "You couldn't hide forever, Samuel Jackson." All I see is blackness—not a speck of light—but I feel the demon's presence.

A forceful blast of hot, foul air hits us square. Feels like a bus-sized hair dryer is blowing straight in my face. Can't breath. Choking on toxic fumes. Smell is nauseating. Eyes flooding.

Skeeter's hat blows across the room. His grimy hair and beard blow wildly in the sulfur-laden wind. An unseen force sucks Skeeter toward the open door like he's a nail pulled by a magnet. He drops to his knees, bear-hugs a table leg, and screams in terror.

The voice of a second demon, also layered with the shrieks of animals, laughs. "We will feed on your soul."

The black abyss glows orange. Two forms take shape behind a veil of ash and smoke. Demons, bathed in murky rust-colored auras. My first look ever.

Holy mother of fuck.

Head and torso of a human dwarf, legs of a horse. Looks Middle Eastern. Cartoon-huge nose, dark eyes, dark complexion, black hair, and beard. He wears a bejeweled crown and a regal cherry-colored velvet robe. Next to the dwarf, a lion with the head of a sickly looking old man. His roar and mad giggle blend into an unsettling reverberation.

One by one, Skeeter's fingers are pried loose. The demons frolic like cats toying with a mouse before the kill. Pure joy as they wave Skeeter toward them, each outdoing the other. Skeeter is helpless. He gives me one last pleading glance. Happy trails, fucko. In an instant, he's yanked loose and sucked in. The lion-human hybrid pounces—tears into Skeeter's throat. The rust-colored aura of the demons envelops Skeeter and his screams go from terror to agony to muffled whimpers of surrender. The dwarf looks beyond the barrier between us and gives me a little nod. Fucker seems to be thanking me. As the beast drags Skeeter away by the throat, the dwarf leaps up onto the lion-man's back and the door slams shut. After the echo wanes, all is silent save for the familiar electronic hum and distant ring.

Fool's gold? Damn straight.

A smaller, kinder, gentler door appears on the wall behind me. I empty my mind and turn the doorknob. It feels like I'm being slingshotted from Oz to Kansas.

This is the bad part. Reentry. Every journey inside the soul trap takes a real toll on my body. The intensity of the helmet's magnetic alignment temporarily realigns some of the protons in the targeted regions of my brain. Some of these protons never go back to their normal alignment. My central nervous system goes haywire for a spell. And I usually end up feeling like I have an immense hangover—cotton mouth, headache, nausea, exhaustion, muscle cramps, depression. Lasts about as long as a real hangover. Considering I drink too much at least three nights a week and am largely a glass-half-empty guy anyway, the side effects feel routine.

Ned says each trip probably shortens my lifespan.

I open my eyes and I'm on the gurney. Mission accomplished.

Ned checks my vitals and I give him a recap. "A tin-panner?" he marvels. "A guy who died over a century ago. Freakin' amazing. Were those demons?"

I sit up, but my heads spins so I reconsider. "Yep. Berith. He turns metal to gold. Big ego. Thinks he's a king. And, based on that," I add, pointing to the black leather-bound book of demonology on the shelf above my desk, "the lion was probably Valefar. He leads thieves to the gallows."

"That book gives me the creeps," Ned says, looking over at the pentagram etched in gold on the book's spine.

"It's one thing to read about them," I say. "But to see them . . ." I shake my head and let it hang.

Ned returns to the desk and powers down the system. "You need to take it easy. Your blood pressure was up and down the whole time."

"I feel like shit," I say.

"Well, there's eight grand in an envelope on your desk. Care of Señor Ricardo Camarillo. Go treat yourself to a meal."

I tear open the envelope. I love to count cash. "Do me a favor."

"Sure."

I shoot Ned an email from my iPhone. "I just sent you the contact info for that reporter—Eva Kells. Get in touch. Offer her information on me. See if she bites."

"No problem."

When Ned leaves, I grab my Blackie Strat, plug it into my Fender '57 Twin amp, and start banging away again on "Layla." The Derek and the Dominos classic has been playing in my head for the past couple of weeks, especially the finale with the piano and guitar solos. Not sure why, but it's relentless. I started listening to it more closely the other day and tried to zone in on the layering. From what I can tell there are at least six different guitar tracks by the band's two guitarists: Eric Clapton and Duane Allman—two equally brilliant guitarists grounded in blues, but with completely different styles. Clapton bends strings; Allman uses a slide. Together their solos blend into this goddamn magic formula dripping in brilliance, the likes of which may never be heard again.

I want to play this song. Scratch that. I want to re-create this song—every note, every nuance—the whole goddamn thing. It's beyond a mega challenge. It's a doctoral thesis in music. The piano solo will be easy. The maddening part for me will be trying to tune into each track and isolate it with my own ears, tear the fucker down note by note, reproduce and record it, and mix it myself. If I can ever pull it off, I'll be a real guitar hero. Fuck the video game.

I grab my glass medicine bottle guitar slide and work a little on my Allmanesque slide playing, but my hands are too shaky to get the intonation right. Shit. I try again—I suck. Shit. I give up for the night.

I'm hungry so I take a handful of cash and make my way to Musso & Frank. After a New York strip with mashed potatoes and creamed spinach, I head to the bar. Feels like I'm coming back to life.

It takes many drinks to take the edge off the sight of those demons. I lose count after a half-dozen Manhattans served by the best bartender in the city, Ruben, who entertains me with stories about his old buddy, Charles Bukowski.

Four

The next morning, with "Layla" blaring in my head, I feel like Bukowski must have felt most mornings of his life. Not sure if it was the Manhattans or the journey into the trap that did the damage—probably a little of both.

I linger in my bed and stare at a signed Chili Peppers poster from a show I saw at the Palladium in '99. I was in the mosh pit and a crowd surfer nailed me above the eye with her spiked boot. Flea caught sight of me bleeding all over the floor and the next thing I know I'm backstage getting stitched up. Not only did I get a good battle scar, I ended up partying with the band. Open bar, food, and Penthouse Pets mud wrestling. That was a good night. The band even sent me the signed poster after—worth every one of the seven stitches.

I feel like shit. Item one on the list this morning is to book an appointment with Master Choi for a prana healing session at his office in Santa Monica. I swear by it. Originated in the Gangwon-do province of South Korea. Found its way to the West in the '50s. It's all about energy balancing, repairing the body's aura. Ned thinks it's a load of New Age bullshit, but it helps me, especially after trips inside the trap.

Item two is Project Layla. I don't feel like playing guitar this morning, but I download and print the piano sheet music and start practicing on my Yamaha electric piano. In less than hour, I have the basics down. I'm on my way.

I drag my ass to my Mac, check my email, and surf a few of my go-to sites: Drudge Report, coasttocoastam.com, perezhilton .com, TechCrunch. Get bored fast and Google Eva Kells. Interesting stuff. Good writer. Smart. Spent a year crafting a story about shit-bag employees at UCLA Medical Center leaking medical records of celebrities to the tabloids. Eva worked with a single source inside the hospital for months. Interviewed Farrah Fawcett before she died. Didn't shoot her wad early. Broke the story only after she nailed it down. Find my way to her blog—mostly obscure and hidden L.A. stuff. A first—a blog I can actually bear to read.

There's a knock. I stand. My feet and legs are stiffer than a dead gangbanger in Compton. My neighbor, Pat Boreo—skinny guy, EMT for an ambulance service in Burbank, killer bassist in a Police tribute band—is in my doorway holding a box. "Dude, this was just sitting down by the mailboxes yesterday. Grabbed it. Wouldn't have lasted long."

Pat's okay, and knows a shitload about guitars, but I don't invite him in. I don't invite anyone in, except Ned. Still, I'm cordial. I take the box. Shipped from Ireland.

"How goes the training?" Pat's on the cusp of graduating to full paramedic.

"Two more classes and a 110 more hours."

"Sweet. You know 'Layla'?" I ask.

"Sure."

"I'm trying to reproduce it," I boast.

Pat laughs. "Get the fuck out."

I have a killer idea. "You interested in playing bass?"

"For fun?"

"Sure as fuck not for money."

"Fucking A," he laughs. "I'd be into it. When?"

"I don't know . . . sometime soon . . . maybe."

"You still want your Strat set up?" Pat asks.

I nod. "If I'm going to try to play like Clapton, I need the action fixed. I'll bring it over one night this week."

"Cool. We'll listen to *Chinese Democracy* again."

"I'll bring the whiskey."

I kick the door shut and open the box on my kitchen table. From my pal Seamus in Dublin. Within a grave of Styrofoam peanuts is a Waterford crystal goblet. A chain of unicursal hexagrams etched around the rim. I know that symbol. I know who created it. It can't be. I find the note:

> *Kane-O:*
>
> *Came across a prize. This belonged to Aleister Crowley. Don't ask me where I got it. Wouldn't want to make you an accessory after the fact. Hope this gets the old IVeR humming. Watch out—it's powerful. Tread lightly.*
>
> —*Seamus.*

Aleister Crowley. British occultist, writer, scholar, hedonist, and drug addict—generally considered wicked and depraved. I take in the goblet, the kaleidoscope of colors in the hand-chiseled facets. This could be the mother lode. The opening riff from "Purple Haze"—my ringtone for this week—breaks the spell.

A guy with a drawl introduces himself as Stacks Fabin, the owner of the C&S traveling carnival that works the Southland. A soul, in the form of a circus clown, is wreaking havoc on his carnival, attacking patrons, maybe even luring a few of them to their deaths. Stacks is about to pitch his tents in Canoga Park and offers me $5K to send Bozo packing. I counter with $10K and we agree on seven plus expenses. I'll have a look, I tell him—no guarantees.

The whole time I'm chatting it up with Stacks, my mind is on Crowley's goblet. As soon as I end the call, I'm at the sink, soaking the goblet in saltwater and polishing it until it gleams. Then I place it atop the IVeR—Interdimensional Voice Recorder. It's a sick machine I built out of magnets, coils, and transistors. When it's working, the IVeR lets me communicate with a spirit named Karl.

Sorry, no last name. I have no idea who or what Karl is—or why he can communicate with me—but sometimes he says something relevant to my work. Call him my ghostly Google.

Like the soul trap itself, the IVeR's based on another of Nikola Tesla's designs that Ned had a look at years ago. That mad-ass Serbian inventor had to be from another galaxy. Invented the radio in 1891, five years before Marconi got credit for it. Largely responsible for electromagnetism, modern robotics, radar, lasers, and X-rays. Obtained over 300 patents (that we know about). Hell, probably 80 percent of the electronic and wireless shit I interface with daily—from any light switch I flip to my cell phone to my remote control to that candy-ass electric Prius I almost rear-ended the other day—came directly from him. And he invented most of it well over a hundred years ago. Had a huge appetite for the occult. Experimented with invisibility. Might have even invented a death ray—a particle beam that could completely evaporate a person. Wherever he was from or whatever it was that powered his mind, thanks to Uncle Nikola, I have a decent job.

Edison tinkered with a device similar to the IVeR, but couldn't simplify it enough to make it work. Leave it to Tesla—he was all about elegant simplicity, basic complexity.

The IVeR was an easy enough contraption to build. Finding the right supernaturally charged crystal to power it is the bitch. Requires definite mojo and lots of trial and error. Last crystal that managed to do the trick was a paperweight from Shirley MacLaine.

Two years ago, she hired me and Ned to clear her Malibu beach house. Turned out to be a former tenant who didn't want to give up his ocean view. Only took about twenty minutes. Shirley sat at her desk and wrote a twenty-grand check. When I complimented the paperweight, she threw it in. Nice lady. Shirley's paperweight turned out to be so powerful it kept the IVeR running until a couple of months ago, when it finally fried out. I haven't spoken to Karl since.

I place Crowley's goblet on the magnetic platform and position the amplifier and microphone above it. I power up the steel coils, connect the oscillator, and send voltage to an electrode on the base of the goblet. The inductor, capacitor, and resistor distort the electric field surrounding the goblet, and it resonates an interdimensional radio frequency.

I rub my finger around the rim of the goblet until it hums. It reminds me of a sound I heard at a New Age conference last summer. Someone had a recording of solar vibrations supposedly from the edge of the known universe. A deep, menacing groan. A bunch of attendees touted this as the voice of God. If that's true, God's not happy.

Once the goblet is humming on its own, I tune the ectometer, searching, listening for Karl. There's a new power emanating from the unit; the signal is stronger than ever—off the charts. I dial a hair to the right and hear a guttural voice—distant and echoey—butchering "I Am the Walrus." I lock on the voice to secure the signal and begin to record.

It's Karl, for sure. He always begins his transmission with a hymn from the Gospel of John and Paul.

"Come in, Walrus—this is Eggman," I reply. "Can you hear me?"

"Yes," comes a static-charged reply. Karl sounds closer than he has before.

"C and S Carnival. Can you help me?"

Karl's reply is fragmented, like an AM radio station cutting in and out. "Beware," he says. "Gravity on . . . Harlequin. . . ." I lean closer to the IVeR, struggle to make out the words. "Tears. . . . All . . . Tear. . . . Terrell."

The transmission cuts out. The hum of the goblet wanes and the IVeR powers down.

That's about as long as a normal IVeR transmission lasts. Quick and dirty. No time for chitchat. Precise questions. To speak to Karl again, I'll need to take Crowley's goblet to an outdoor location with a magnetic vortex and let it charge for a few hours in the midday sun.

I'll probably take it up to the ruins of Houdini's mansion. The place burned up in a Laurel Canyon brush fire in the early '50s.

Houdini chose that spot to build his lavish estate for good reason: There are huge deposits of the mineral magnetite beneath the surface that create magnetic fields aboveground. There are also deposits of native copper and iron. Combine magnetite with certain metals like copper and you'll find yourself standing knee-deep in a highly charged magnetic vortex. Certain people—psychically aware—are sensitive to vortexes. So are certain objects—like leaded crystal. They become charged or energized like astral batteries. But, eventually, they'll lose their power and need to be recharged.

It sounded like Karl said tears—or maybe it was terrible, or the name Terrell. Shit, I don't know. I take out my iPad and launch Google, but stop. What do I even search for? I type in C&S Carnival. There's a link to a website I know—forty comments from visitors who claim to have seen or photographed a phantom clown. Some of the photos are clearly Photoshopped, but two or three look real. I download a photo of orbs outside the fun house and zoom in. They're not doctored, not reflections off dust. Another photo shows a clown on the Ferris wheel. I look for evidence of layering, but nada. Count me in.

I open my closet door and move my decoy—a milk crate full of foul old underwear and socks—from the floor in the corner. I remove a two-foot square of drywall, reach inside, and come back with a gun box. I scan my thumbprint and the electronic lock springs open. I grab the soul trap from inside and shove it in my backpack.

I grab my lucky necklace. It's a homemade piece of jewelry—Ned calls it an artistic statement. It's a rosary willed to me by Lucinda Marquez, my old landlady, a nice Hispanic woman who treated me like a son. Between many of the crystal rosary beads, I've linked religious medals and random talismans I've accumulated—a crucifix from Florence, my dad's Saint Jude medal, a Buddha, a Star of David, a Paramahansa Yogananda medal, a Hindu Om talisman, a Native American amulet, a sword of Allah pendant. A little bit of everything. There are elements of most religions that I dig and others I hate, so I cherry-pick what I like, flush the rest, and mix it all up into one big theological stew.

Before I leave I call Ned and tell him where I'm headed. "Be careful," he warns. "And, oh, by the way, I called that reporter. Offered to meet with her—give her the inside scoop on Kane Pryce."

"And?"

"And she turned me down."

"No shit?"

"Sounds sexy," Ned says.

"Is sexy," I tell him.

I MapQuest directions to the park where the carnival is underway, grab the keys to my shitbox-red '96 Mustang convertible, and head out hunting.

Five

I reach Canoga Park at dusk, just as the Ferris wheel lights blink on. It's a two-bit carnival, but the locals seem to like it. I approach the admission gate.

Dilemma number one: They're searching bags.

Shit. I waste twenty-five minutes circling the carnival, looking for just the right place to jump the fence. Inside, before I can even throw away my first buck on a losing game of chance . . .

Dilemma number two: She approaches.

"Kane, how about that interview?" Eva's casual—skin-tight jeans, a black leather jacket, designer eyeglasses, and Uggs. In this crowd, she stands out like a silver dollar among pennies.

"Did you follow me?"

"Maybe," she says. "Maybe I just love cotton candy." She soaks up the scene and smiles. She's good.

"No effing comment," I say.

She ignores me and starts hammering away. "I want to know about the soul trap. Does it exist? Is it true it was invented by Nikola Tesla? Are you investigating paranormal phenomena here at the carnival?" She definitely poked around online. She knows a thing or two.

"Let me guess, is it the 'effing' part of 'no effing comment' that you don't understand?"

She won't stop. "Is it true you can communicate with spirits?"

I grab the sleeve of her leather jacket, give her a tug, and a hard stare. "Listen, when you're on stage at the Spearmint Rhino, then
I'll pay attention to you. Judging by the way you look, I'll probably
even tip you. But until then, you're shit outta luck."
"I'm not trying to be an asshole."
"You're failing."
"Just keep me in mind, Kane." She glances at the carnival lights
encircling us and smiles like a kid. "I think I'll go enjoy the carnival. See you around."

She walks away and I shout, "Just enjoy it at least a hundred yards away from me." She waves and disappears behind the dunking booth.

It's not easy to say no to that.

I glance around. The smell of popcorn hits me square and I'm helpless. There's a MILF redhead working the food stand. I can see her over the head of a kid in front. I smile at her and she stops pouring the kid's Icee and smiles right back. *Ding, ding*—we have a winner. Eva in those jeans, the smell of popcorn, the smile I just got—I am Spock. Pon Farr red alert. My Vulcan blood fever boils.

"Hey, cutie, nice shirt. Who is that, Bob Marley?"

"It's Jean-Michel Basquiat. Awesome artist. OD'd when he was 27."

"No shit," she says. "What'll you have?"

"Popcorn."

"What's your name?"

"Kane."

She laughs—a peculiar and inviting little giggle. "You're not going to believe it. My name's Candy. Candy and Kane."

"Where do I start licking?"

She laughs and waves me closer. She's got ten years on me, at least, and more miles on her engine than my Mustang, but I like what I see. Smokin' body, green eyes that have seen hard days, and a giggle that puts a bow on the whole skankalicious package. "I get off at nine. Swing by and pick me up." I peg her as divorced—living with her ten-year-old bully son in a valley trailer park.

"I'll be here at ten till," I say.

Somehow this seems *too* easy. She hands me the popcorn. "No charge."

"You're sweet, Candy."

"You're not going to stand me up, are you?" she asks, looking me straight in the eye.

"I'm not that kind of guy," I reassure.

"So what kind of guy are you?"

Dilemma number three: communication breakdown.

A nagging doubt tells me we may have crossed our signals—that I'm talking about the Safari Inn on Victory and she's talking about a church social. I choose the direct route, leaning in. "I'm the kind of guy who'll take you out for a Denny's Grand Slam after I give *you* a grand slamming."

That earns another giggle. "We are going to party," she promises.

A rush of customers hits the stand and I head to the midway. Only an hour until I play Candy Land—just one hour to catch a clown and find a box of extrastrength condoms.

The trap vibrates in my backpack and I reach in for my earpiece—a Bluetooth that Ned tricked out to send me alerts directly from the trap. It beeps in my ear, signaling a paranormal presence is near.

The beeping stops when I reach the games, but I'm distracted by a large eyeball on a mirror at the darts and balloons booth. It's the Nickelback cover *Silver Side Up,* and it'll look sweet hanging on my bathroom wall. I approach the vendor.

"Five bucks, ten darts," says the carney, a kid with a mop of black hair and a Cal State Northridge hoodie.

"No darts. How much for the Nickelback mirror?"

"Gotta earn that prize," he says.

I watch a Hispanic teenager whale darts at a balloon that's thicker than the Goodyear Blimp. His little sister sits in a wheelchair next to him. She looks sad.

"Come on—how much?"

"Make me an offer," he whispers.

Dilemma number four: How much is too much?

"Ten bucks," I say.

He smiles and shakes his head. "Gotta earn that prize," he says, holding up a handful of darts.

"Twenty bucks," I offer. The carney nods. "But," I add with a finger wave, "throw in the bear for the girl."

The carney looks at the girl, then nods. "Sure," he says. "If she weren't a cripple, I'd charge you five more." He pops a dart into a balloon behind him, rings the bell, and shouts, "We've got a winner!"

The kid and his sister look at me like a beacon of hope. "This is for you," the carney says, handing me the Nickelback mirror. It's flimsy as cardboard, but so what? It'll give Ned the creeps next time he stinks up my john. "And this is for you." The carney hands the girl in the wheelchair a small white bear with a green vest and a shamrock on his belly.

The little girl frowns. "What's this?" she demands. "I don't want this. I want the gorilla," she says, pointing to the rafters at a pink gorilla the size of a Rwandan silverback.

The carney winks. "Hundred bucks for Kong," he whispers.

No effing way. "That's a good-luck bear you got there," I tell the little girl. "See the four-leaf clover? Go ahead, take it," I urge. She tosses it in the dirt. Did I mention I pretty much hate everyone? That includes carneys and kids. I snatch the snubbed bear and shove it into my backpack. I'll tickle Candy's ass with it if I have to, but this bear will be appreciated, this sting of rejection will be squelched—one way or another.

I approach the ramshackle rides with caution for fear they might topple over. I can feel the trap vibrating and my earpiece signals another alert. One of the rides catches my eye—the Gravitron. Karl said something, but what? I check the MP3 of Karl's message on my iPad. He said, gravity, but with the static, it could have been Gravitron.

I buy six ride tickets and board the saucer. The view inside triggers childhood memories. This is the ride that spins so fast you get sucked against the wall.

The ride groans to life. Twenty seconds later I'm against the wall alongside four other riders. A teenager flips himself upside down. I'm loopy, the popcorn in my stomach threatens to decorate the walls, and the medals on my lucky necklace tear into my neck. As much fun as a catheter insertion.

Someone laughs—a mad cackle that's out of place.

Dilemma number five: getting a look.

I open my eyes and struggle to crane my neck right. There's someone in my field of vision, but he's not pinned to the wall. Adrenaline races. My head won't budge, but I can see enough to know that a clown stands near the center of the ride. A full-body apparition—only the second one I've ever seen. Though I can't get a direct look, I can make out stringy red hair, runny makeup, filthy red pom-pom buttons on a checkered jumpsuit. My earpiece beeps steadily but I can't reach behind my back to grab the trap. Bozo does a series of ungraceful pirouettes and spins in circles. "Come and play," he cackles before vanishing. I force my head free as the ride grinds to a halt and scan for the reaction of the other riders. No one else saw him.

Even before the ride stops, I'm unstrapped, out the door and following the signal. When I reach the fun house, the trap's targeting software launches and I receive an audio prompt in my earpiece.

Dilemma number six: I need time inside the fun house—alone.

"Four tickets," the ticket collector says with an open hand. I peel off two twenties. "Forty bucks for five minutes alone inside."

"What for?" he asks.

"I want to take some pictures. Photography class project."

"Bullshit—you wanna take a chick in there, admit it."

"Yeah, but only to photograph her," I lie.

"I'll bet."

"I have my camera here in my backpack. Come on—I'll be quick."

The carney snatches the money from my hand, clears out a couple of teenagers from inside, and ropes off the entrance. "Five minutes and counting," he says.

I enter and pull out the trap. Some fun house. It's a rinky-dink trailer with a few hallways of foggy mirrors and a stench worse than a ballpark men's room. No monsters, no trapdoors—just the lame ambient sounds of chains rattling and voices moaning. I pass a row of mirrors and the trap vibrates so forcefully I almost drop it. I look closer. Souls. Lots of them. Trapped in the mirrors. How?

Suddenly Bozo cackles behind me and my heart leaps into my throat. "Here I am. Come and get me." The clown's laugh drops in pitch. I hear the hint of a hungry predator layered in his words. Fuck. I whirl around and Bozo is cornered against an intersection of mirrors. "Dare to follow through the looking glass?" The clown cackles and steps directly into the mirror.

I finally get a direct look at him. He glows in the light of a murky rust-colored aura. I know that aura. I raise the trap and aim, one eye on the clown and one on the reticle, but I already know it's pointless.

Dilemma number seven: This is no ghost—it's a friggin' demon!

Bozo laughs, part human, part beast. The demon Teeraal. That's what Karl was saying. Damn. How could I have been so stupid? I'm way outgunned.

A voice near the entrance startles me from my panic. "Kane, what are you doing in here?" asks Eva, mischievously curious. She enters cautiously, expecting a scare. She's about to get a doozy.

"Eva, get outta here—now!" I shout. But Teeraal pirouettes toward Eva, clutches her arm, and yanks her toward the mirror.

"Oh no, you don't," Teeraal growls. Dozens of voices cry out from the glass.

"Kane? Where are you?" She becomes hysterical. "Kane! He's pulling me into the mirror!"

Teeraal beams with pride at his trophy. "I'll trap this sow like I've trapped these others." Cries of anguished souls pour from every mirror in the fun house. "Help!" they scream. "Save us!"

The clown pulls Eva halfway into the mirror. His aura surrounds her. Her body warps and distorts with the bending glass. She looks deep inside the mirror and shoots me a look of panic. "I see reflections. They're reaching for me."

The soul trap can't handle a demon, but it may stun Teeraal long enough for me to grab Eva. Gotta stay calm, aim true. The trap vibrates in my sweaty palms. I aim at Teeraal and just before he grabs Eva by the throat, I pull the trigger. The blast hits him square and sends him sailing backward into the mirror. I race toward Eva. "Grab my hand." Her left arm is inside the mirror but she reaches out with her right and I grab it. Teeraal sits up and grabs her other hand and I'm suddenly in an interdimensional tug-of-war. I fire again and Eva breaks free of his grasp as he's knocked backward. It feels like I'm pulling Eva out of cosmic quicksand. My ribs erupt with waves of pain like someone is firing a nail gun into me every few seconds. When I yank her free the force of my effort sends her and the soul trap flying across the fun house floor.

I glance around in a panic, trying to eye the trap. A gloved hand reaches from behind me and clutches my throat. "If I can't have the bitch, then you'll have to do," Teeraall whispers in my ear.

I'm down and out, like I took a bullet in the head. But I surprise myself by springing back to my feet almost instantly. Four things tell me that I'm good and fucked. First, I can't see my reflection in any of the mirrors; second, I'm bound in chains that Teeraal is clutching and yanking on; third, I'm looking down at myself—another me—lying on the ground, motionless; fourth, there's a red door with a crystal doorknob next to me—right in the center of the fun house. It wasn't there a minute ago. It's my door to the other side. I know it. A pale blue light pours in through the cracks around the door.

It's a surreal moment. As I try to figure out which me is really me, Teeraal pulls me closer and closer to the mirror behind him. I desperately want to walk through that red door. I struggle, but am powerless against Teeraal's might.

Then I hear a thunderous boom and Teeraal gets hit with another soul trap blast. He flies backward and into the mirror, which explodes in a million shards. I turn. Eva is holding the trap, her finger on the trigger. She drops it and rushes toward the other me on my back. She feels for a pulse. Tilts my head back, opens my mouth, and locks lips with the other me. Wish I were in there to enjoy it. Close enough to a kiss for me. I step nearer, look down. Eva pumps the other me's chest over and over and breathes into the other me's mouth again. I feel like I melt into the floor.

I'm looking up. Eva has my wrist in her hand. "Kane? Can you hear me?"

I nod. Struggle to sit up.

"Jesus Christ," Eva says, relieved but still panting. "You were dead."

Before I can respond, the fun house rocks violently as the sound of Teeraal's voice rages. "Run!" I shout. I somehow manage to stand and grab my backpack and we're out the emergency side exit in a few seconds. The ticket taker stares in disbelief at the topsy-turvy fun house. "Fucking earthquake!" he shouts, ducking for cover.

A crowd gathers and watches the fun house shudder and sway. Teeraal's roars thunder from the shabby building. "How cool is that?" I hear a teenage skater say. "That's fucking sick, dude. Let's go. You got tickets?" his buddy asks.

Eva and I don't stop running until we reach the front gate. "Let's get out of here," I say, struggling for breath.

"Where?" she asks.

"Somewhere with plenty of liquor."

Six

As Eva tails me to Canoga Park, I crank "The End" by the Doors. The Lizard King, one of the founding members of Club 27, knew a thing or two about death. During the long instrumental solo, the reality of it hits me: I died. Only for a minute at most, but long enough for me to see my dead body and to see that clown take possession of my soul. If Eva hadn't been there . . . I feel nauseous. I'm frantic. I need to know I'm alive. I need to touch a beer bottle. See people. Hear music. I need to put my dick in someone . . . or something.

I lead Eva to my favorite watering hole, the Frolic Room, at Hollywood and Vine. You can't miss it. It's the best neon sign in the city, shining like a beacon for drinkers in this mecca of shattered dreams. It's old and grungy and so full of weird energy that I think it has a pulse. Inside, it's a small space—forty feet long, ten feet wide—dimly lit by retro saucer-shaped lamps. Smells as musty as your grandpap's underwear drawer. An Al Hirschfeld mural—depicting caricatures of Hollywood legends—stretches along the back wall. The crowd, a dozen or so drinkers when the place is packed, is always a can of mixed nuts. You're liable to see a skid-row drunk next to a Hollywood agent next to a washed-up rocker rubbing shoulders with a transvestite hooker taking a break between blowjobs. If the bar is mostly empty, you'll feel the presence of spirits. You might even see a face in the mirror behind the bar if you mix the right amount of booze with the right level of concentration.

Did I mention I pretty much hate everything? But I love the Frolic Room. I can stagger home and take a DUI out of the equation. Plus, it has an old-school jukebox, not one of these bullshit broadband versions housing an infinite well of music. This one has a little something for every character that walks through the door. Though I've been coming here for years, that jukebox still manages to surprise me.

Eva and I sit at the front corner of the bar near the door. Though it's crowded, we're tucked in a nook that remains out of earshot. "What the fuck, Kane?" Eva asks pleadingly, still shaky.

I look her in the eye so she knows I'm sincere when I say, "Just forget everything you saw tonight. Trust me."

"Forget what I saw?" she says. "I saw you die."

"Just a little bit." I decide to play all cool and lighthearted. Hope she can't see my hands. They're still shaking.

Eva shakes her head in disbelief.

"Thanks, by the way," I say. "First time you ever did CPR?"

"Yeah," Eva says. "I can't believe it worked."

"Well, it saved my ass."

"And you saved mine," she says. "What happened to us back there, Kane?"

We clam up when the bartender, Gabe, a doughy-looking blond guy wearing a black bow tie and vest, brings me a beer and Eva a Belvedere tonic. He pours me a shot of whiskey and I knock it back before he even walks away. "You inhaled that one. Rough night?" he asks, like he's reading my mind.

I love the bar but hate Gabe. He usually talks my ear off, offers unwelcome advice, and annoys me worse than a John Mayer song. It's crowded tonight, so Gabe's hands will be full and his mouth will be shut.

"Another?" Gabe asks.

"Like Rocky Balboa, I plan to go fifteen rounds. Keep 'em coming. No chitchat." It's not every day you die and still manage to end up in a bar. I'm double fisting tonight—bottles of Harp with Jameson chasers; a pure blend of two soul-warming potions, the combination of which is my muse, my medicine.

Eva plucks the lime from her cocktail, gives it a squeeze, and waits for Gabe to make his way to the other end of the bar before asking, "I'm waiting. What happened to us back there?"

Now I avoid eye contact and stare at the harp on my bottle. "I'm not telling you anything—I can't."

"Why?"

"Because someone might come after me—after the trap—if they read about it in a mainstream rag."

"Who? The CIA? FBI?"

I remain silent, drain half my Harp in a single gulp, and stare at the caricature of Albert Einstein on the back wall.

"Then the soul trap was a government project?" Eva says, already crafting her lead.

I exhale in disgust and wave Gabe over with the Jameson bottle. "I didn't say that." Now I'm pissed off. "See, this is exactly why I can't talk to you. You'll put words in my mouth."

She hones in on my anger and seems to know just how to defuse it. "We need some music," she says. And my anger dissolves. Eva stands and walks to the jukebox where she remains for a long time while I cool down with another round. She's good. I glance over at her every so often while she flips back and forth between page after page of CD covers. This will tell me all I need to know about the lovely Miss Eva. He first choice plays and she sways gracefully while continuing her selections. It's Finger Eleven, "Paralyzer." A good start.

She finishes punching in her numbers and takes her seat. "How many did you play?" I ask.

"Twelve."

"Good song."

"Tell you what, Kane," she says. "I'll make you a deal. You shoot straight with me—tell me your story, and I promise you that I won't print a word until you OK it."

I pretend I didn't hear that. We listen to the rest of the song in silence, then she says, "You have my word on this. All I ask for is an exclusive. You only talk to me."

Second song begins as she finishes her first round: Hole, *Celebrity Skin*. Haven't heard that one in years. Courtney Love belts out something about demonology. Against my better judgment, I entertain her offer.

"Well . . . ?" she asks.

"Well," I say, "Courtney Love is totally underrated."

"Come on," she says, waving to Gabe for another round. "Do we have a deal?"

I make her wait until the song ends before I answer. "How much is my story worth to you?"

She tenses and leans back. She's seething, but remains calm. "You want me to pay you?"

"A good story in this town is worth a bundle."

Gabe brings another round. Eva immediately takes a healthy swig. "How much do you want?"

"How much you got?"

Third song plays: The Doors, "Break on Through." This may be love.

"How's 500 bucks?" she finally answers.

I'm tapping my boot on the foot railing. "Sounds good." She relaxes a little, until I add: " . . . A week."

"Are you kidding?" she says, trying to force eye contact. "You're not kidding. Okay. Deal."

I'm not done yet. "Up front," I demand.

This is one angry, beautiful woman. She plucks her cocktail straw out of her drink and flicks it in disgust. She thinks for a long time. "I don't have that much on me."

I glance over my shoulder. "There's an ATM right by the door."

Her fourth song begins: Sinatra, "The Shadow of Your Smile." Live version. Great choice. I wish I could hear what she's calling me right now in her head. She marches to the ATM. I let her enter her PIN before I finally stop her. "Hey . . ." I call out, laughing. "Sit down. I'm just busting your balls."

Eva returns, relieved but still annoyed. "I believed you," she says with an insincere chuckle. She doesn't take a joke well and that's the first check mark in the con column. Her next song, "Seven Nation Army," by the White Stripes, redeems her utterly. We both rock in our stools to the thumping beat for the duration of the song. Check mark erased. Who needs a sense of humor?

Eva's sixth song—"Spirit in the Sky"—stops the presses. I've told Ned more than once I want that one played at my funeral. A cosmic sign I've made the right choice? When Gabe delivers our next round, Eva raises a glass. "We start being honest with each other—right now." This is it—the point of no return, the shit or get off the pot moment of truth—trust-or-die time. Damn if I'm not talking myself into it: Someday I might want to get my story out. If something happens to me, she can clear my name. If someone threatens me, I can threaten him back. I can't tell if it's the whiskey spring bubbling in my brain or the little head slaying the big head, or the music, or the thought of Eva swaying in the jukebox light, or the fact that I'd be dead right now if it weren't for her, but I take the plunge.

I clink her glass. "I'll drink to that."

"Cheers."

She wastes no time launching her inquisition. "So what was that thing in the fun house? It sure wasn't a clown," she half whispers.

I glance around to make sure there are no solo patrons eavesdropping. This conversation is about to be as crazy as it gets, and that's saying a lot for Hollywood and Vine. "He was a demon. Teer-aal. A genuine A-list badass."

"How did he kill you?" she wants to know.

"I don't know," I answer honestly. "By touch," I guess. "By clutching my throat. It sucked all the air out of my lungs. Stopped my heart."

"He's that powerful?"

"Appears to be."

"Would he have killed me?"

"Appears so. He was reaching for your throat when I stopped him."

"Jesus."

"No, he's on the other team."

Eva looks dazed. She takes a stiff sip of her drink. Out comes the notebook and pen. "And you couldn't trap him?"

"The soul trap only works on souls. A demon like that is way too powerful."

Eva seems confused. "So what's the difference between a ghost and a demon?"

The alcohol is hitting me harder than a Kimbo Slice uppercut. I fight the urge to babble and focus on a succinct reply. "Demons are supernatural beings, not of this world. Ghosts are disembodied souls that hang around after they die."

"Hang around? How?"

As I throw down yet another shot, my words stick to the roof of my mouth. Radiohead's "Karma Police" warms me as much as the Jameson. Gabe nods to Eva to see if she wants another drink, but she shakes her head. Not me. *Bring it on, Gabe.* I can tell Eva wants to take this in with a semisober ear. "Let's say you wouldn't have been there to resuscitate me. Or that I couldn't have saved you. We would have died—for real. Our souls would have left our bodies permanently, right there. That's the point where, under normal circumstances, we'd go through our doors. But, because we were dying at the hands of a demon, Teeraal would have kept us away from our doors . . . took us prisoner."

"When you say door, do you mean door?" she asks. "Like a real door?"

"When we die, we see a door. It's bathed in light, but it still looks like a door. Style, color—it's uniquely our own. A projection of our own soul. No two doors are alike. When you see it, you feel an overwhelming need to open that door and walk through."

"To the afterlife?"

"Right." Gabe brings me another shot and beer. He overhears Eva say "afterlife."

"Heavy discussion?" he asks.

"No chitchat," I remind him. We ignore him and, for once, the jerkoff takes the hint and slinks off.

I take a sip of Harp and continue my thought. "Sometimes, souls fight the urge, ignore their doors, and refuse to pass through them."

"Why?"

"Maybe they've become attached to someone or something and can't let go. Maybe they just won't admit to themselves that they're dead. Or maybe there's a debt waiting to be collected on the other side of their door."

Eva looks at me like I'm playing another joke on her. "A debt?"

I sigh, annoyed that she can't read my mind. We've been here a half hour, tops, and I'm as drunk as Andy Dick at a Chippendale revue. I'm also getting cockier by the second, like I have all the answers in the world. I can either rein it in right now or turn into a flaming asshole. "It's easy to sell your soul, Eva. A lot easier than you'd imagine. You strike a deal with the devil—or one of his legion—and they'll never let you off the hook. Never."

"How would I sell my soul?" Eva asks.

I pause for a minute to listen to the end of the sad song. At least I'm sipping my shots now. "Find the demon who can best serve you and just invite him in. Simple as that. Mentally invite evil to join you and a demon will be on that barstool right next to you before you know it."

"What? In person?"

I take another look around and shrug. "Sometimes. Maybe. Sometimes not. They can take many forms. Or they might just be a voice in your head or an idea in your mind." My thoughts are starting to splinter. "Did you ever have a weird conversation with yourself and wonder where it came from?" I ask Eva.

"Probably. Yeah."

"That's probably them." I take another sip of whiskey and reach the bottom of the shot glass.

Eva's eighth song is a nice surprise—The Killers, "Mr. Bright-side."

"And . . ." Eva demands.

"And it builds from there. But by the time you've cut a deal, you'll know they're the ones behind it. The only way to seal the deal is to do it willingly."

Eva reaches over and pulls my lucky necklace from beneath my shirt. She fingers the assortment of medals and talismans. "Well, if demons exist, are there also angels? Is there a God? Is there a heaven?" she asks, leaning over and studying my angel pendant.

This is a sore spot—one of my open psychic wounds. But the feel of her fingers grazing my neck brings me comfort in the face of this nagging question. "I wish I knew."

"Well, from the looks of this necklace, you sure believe in some-thing."

"Put it this way: I've never seen an angel. Never saw any sign of God on the other side of that door."

"That's too bad," she says, patting my necklace before stirring her lime at the bottom of her empty glass with her finger and tasting it.

"Tell me about it. I've seen my share of evil. I wish—just once—I saw some sign of goodness or mercy." I finish my beer and motion for Gabe, who winks and approaches with the Jameson bottle held aloft. Eva orders a soda water and lime.

"Do you pray?" she asks.

"Sometimes."

"Me, too. Do you think God's listening?" she asks.

No snappy answer to this one. "Not really," I say.

"Me neither." Eva loses herself in a thought, then asks. "You believe in an afterlife, though? You must."

"Yeah," I say. "Based on what I've seen, there's something out there. Maybe it's just more of what we have here—misery and injus-tice, just vibrating at a higher frequency."

Eva smiles and pats my hand. I get a chill. "I don't know," she says. "Life's not so bad." I shrug. "Do you go to church?" she asks.

The booze is stripping the gears of my mind. For whatever reason, this seems like an intensely personal question. Memories spill together. "I liked stained glass," I reply, and it comes out sounding dopey. "About the only time I stop in a church is to have a look at the stained glass." I down another shot. I've lost count. I'm slurring. "I go to a botanical garden up in the foothills. I guess that's my church. That's one of two places I go to clear my head."

"Where's the other place?" she asks.

"This stool."

"Well, this place isn't doing my head any good. Your buddy Gabe there pours a mother of a drink." She stands and saunters to the ladies' room. While she's gone, I take in her next selection "Mr. Brownstone." Guns N' Roses. "Mr. Brightside" followed by "Mr. Brownstone." Clever.

When Eva returns, she looks disgusted. "That bathroom is a national disgrace," she says.

U2's "Vertigo" is number ten. I love that song. The riff is pure and sharp, just like a Tesla design. I can't hold back the compliments. "You, my dear, have chosen some epic kick-ass tunes. I'm impressed." I'm slurring badly. Finito. I wave off another shot and focus on finishing my Harp while we praise the song.

"A couple more," she says.

"Songs?" I ask.

"Yes. And questions."

"Norwegian Wood" follows next. The song feels like an old friend breezing in and giving me a hug. Those lyrics—a guy, a girl, a late-night conversation, alcohol, and most definitely, sex.

Is Eva telling me something or am I just shitfaced?

She asks, "So how far can a soul roam?"

I look at myself in the mirror behind the bar. I'm way drunker than I look. "It depends, but there are always definite boundaries. Sometimes souls are confined to a single room. Sometimes they can roam across a whole city. But that door is always there within their field of view—pulling at them."

"Last question . . . for now," she says. "Where did the soul trap come from?"

I hesitate. I've never discussed this with anyone, except Ned. I'm in unchartered territory, drunk and worried. I take a giant leap of faith and whisper to her. "My father helped build it . . . with a team of eight others."

Eva looks like she just solved a murder. "So was it a government black box project?" she whispers.

"Where did you read that?" I demand to know.

"That website I mentioned when I met you."

This raises my ire. "I know that site. They don't know dick about shit." *Damn, I've killed too many brain cells.* My mouth now flies without a pilot. I shove my beer bottle aside and swear that I'm finished. "I know someone who was involved and even he's not sure. The team was isolated up in Colorado Springs. There's a big military presence there, but it could have just as easily been a civilian operation."

She stuns me with her next question. "And your father disappeared when?"

Dark clouds have gathered in the funky saucer lamps. This is a raw nerve. There's been no mention of it whatsoever on any of the websites I've shown up on. I nod to Gabe to refill my shot glass one last time.

"I don't mean to drum up bad memories," she says.

"How do you know?" I ask.

"Standard background check," she says. "I'm sorry, but I have to ask."

"In 1993," I say. "Something must have happened. I don't know what, but he was there one day and gone the next."

She treads lightly. "Do you think he's dead?" she whispers, leaning in.

I pound the last of my shots. "Yeah. We were tight. He wouldn't have just left me."

"One last thing," she says with a little smile. "Can I see it?"

I smile.

"The soul trap, that is."

I glance down at the backpack at my feet. "In there—just don't take it out here."

Eva reaches down and peers in. She raises both eyebrows. I study her reaction. "So that's it?"

"Yeah, that's it."

She smiles. She has her story.

Eva's jukebox selections end with the Rolling Stones' "Factory Girl." The studio version from *Beggar's Banquet* has a Celtic vibe. All about getting drunk with a cool girl on a Friday night.

"And can you really go inside to meet the souls you trap?"

I nod.

"What's that like?" she asks.

I'm ready to go to sleep on the bar, but instead, I sit up and answer. "It really fucks up my body. I've done it nine times, I think." I try to count but I'm too fucked up to remember clearly. "Sometimes they go quietly. Sometimes they don't."

Eva reaches in the backpack and seems poised to pull the trap out. "Don't," I snap. "I told you, don't take it out here." Instead, she pulls out the stuffed bear with the shamrock on his belly. "What's this?" she asks coyly.

"Top secret," I say with a laugh.

"Hey, there's a broken mirror in here," she says as she shoves the bear back inside.

"Shit, my Nickelback mirror. Must have cracked when I dropped the backpack in the fun house."

"Seven years of bad luck," Eva says.

"I'm used to it."

Eva closes the backpack and places it back carefully at my feet. She takes a drink and pauses before finally asking, "So you hand some of the souls over to demons they're hiding from?"

"Whatever it takes to get paid."

I can tell that her cylinders are firing. She's imagining herself inside. "Can you follow them—the souls?" she asks. "Can you see for yourself what lies beyond?"

"Nope," I say, disappointed as always. "Wish I could. As long as I'm tethered to my body, the door inside the trap is a barrier I can't cross."

"Too bad." This is more than a juicy scoop. Her story is gelling. "One more drink," she says. "This is blowing my mind."

I switch to Diet Coke. For the next half hour we talk about a lot of things . . . not all of them supernatural. After feeling like I gave away the secrets of the kingdom, I put her in the hot seat and she's charming and forthcoming.

I pegged the hint of a Midwest accent and I was right. Madison, Wisconsin. Got her journalism degree from Northwestern in '06 and headed west. A real go-getter. She senses she's tapped into something trendy and relevant with her focus on the supernatural, but she's stuck in a real boys club at the *Times*. Now she's branching out with a blog that's gaining a fan base. She wants to be the first legit journalist to objectively cover the fringe beat of the paranormal.

She's way more than just a pretty face—she's whippy smart to boot. And with that ear for music—I'm way past Spock's Pon Farr. I'm fucking smitten.

Gabe throws up the lights. Last call. Eva steadies herself. "I'm going to pay for this in the morning," she says.

"Call in sick."

"I promise, this is our secret. I won't print a word."

"I know."

"So you trust me?" she asks.

I shake my head and pay the hefty tab with a handful of cash from the Camarillo job. "No. But if you stab me in the back, I'll unleash a demon on you."

Eva stops and looks at me for a smile or wink. "You're kidding?" I ignore her, count out the money, and hand it to Gabe. "You're not kidding."

"Just make sure you never find out," I warn.

"I'll be in touch," Eva says, offering her hand. "Can I call you when I have questions? Or drop by?"

I push aside her hand and give her a hug. "Sure. You can drop by right now and we can keep the party going." Dumb move, shithead. She pulls away. Not tonight, pal.

She throws me a bone. "Listen, not that I'm not tempted, but . . . I'm kind of seeing someone . . . a guy from work. . . . And . . . well . . . let's keep it strictly professional."

Ouch.

After a pause she adds: "For now."

It's a bone and a half—a ray of hope. "Sure thing," I say as I escort her onto Hollywood Boulevard and walk her a block to her car before stumbling on toward my apartment building.

And then I realize Candy was right. I stood her up.

SOUL TRAPPER

Seven

At ten in the morning, my iPhone ringtone wakes me, Nirvana's "All Apologies." I must have downloaded it sometime after I left the Frolic Room and before I woke up at 4:45 AM to vomit. I vaguely remember lying on my couch and trying unsuccessfully to read an email from Ned.

I didn't even begin to treat the hangover until after I puked. Once my stomach was empty and my liver had dumped its bile, I employed my patented cure—three Tylenol Extra Strengths, a quart of water, followed by a quart of grape Pedialyte, created primarily for babies with the runs and secondarily for dehydrated binge drinkers like me. I remember staggering back to bed at five, but I didn't sleep well. Kept seeing the face of that clown in my dreams. Kept thinking about Eva but was too lazy to whack off.

I grab my phone, but I don't recognize the incoming number or the voice on the other end.

"Hello," I say, my throat clogged with phlegm.

"Kane Pryce?"

"Speaking." I sound both groggy and terminally ill. I sit up, hoping my sinuses clear.

"Allow me to introduce myself," a deep, calm voice says. "My name is Father Demetrius and I'm calling from Holy Family Mission Church in Lompoc."

"Okay," I say. "Lompoc. Up the coast." I try to sound awake and aware.

"I must confess that I feel odd calling you, but there's a situation here at the church . . . and . . ." He hesitates.

"Go on," I urge.

I stand and pace, first in my closet-size bedroom and then the rest of my apartment. My head throbs. All the Pedialyte in Children's Hospital couldn't thwart this hangover.

The priest tells me he thinks his church is haunted by a mischievous entity, but not necessarily an evil one. I agree. Demons rarely have the power or balls to set up shop on consecrated ground. The presence of anything holy tends to torment them, kind of like if I were to attend a never-ending John Mayer concert.

The priest sounds honest enough. He seems pleased when I tell him my colleague and I will drive up to the next afternoon. That means I need to do research today—and talk to Karl. But I can't until I recharge Crowley's goblet. I'm way too hungover to drive up to the ruins of Houdini's mansion. That leaves two places within walking distance that have magnetic vortexes with enough chops to power the crystal: the Roosevelt Hotel or Hollywood Forever Cemetery. The Roosevelt is closer, but I'll be too tempted to drop by the pool bar for a little hair of the dog while the goblet soaks up the sun. I'll dry out, suck it up, and walk to the neighborhood graveyard of the stars instead.

I wrap the goblet in bubble wrap, place it in my backpack, grab my iPhone, and hit the pavement. Clouds gather overhead. If the goblet doesn't get direct sunlight, forget talking to Karl.

I don my headphones and listen to Amy Winehouse, but a few blocks down Vine, my forehead thumps and I turn it off. My empty stomach rumbles with nausea. I dry heave. I need grub—greasy and unholy—right now. Behold, another demon clown, one that serves food: Jack in the Box. Two Bacon Breakfast Jacks do the trick and I'm back on my feet, refueled. My headache dissipates with the cloud cover above. I hang a left at Santa Monica Boulevard and cross the street to the cemetery gates.

Hollywood Forever is the Vegas of cemeteries. Parked right in the backyard of Paramount Studios, from the mid-'50s on, it was run down and on the verge of closure. But like other great Hollywood legends, the cemetery made a thrilling comeback with the birth of the new millennium. Only in Hollywood will you find the world's first interactive tombstones, high-def plasma TVs in the chapel, and Blu-ray tributes handed out to mourners as funeral favors. You can even bring your picnic basket and have movie night on Grandpa's grave. No shit. You should see the crowds that gather to watch classic films screened on the side of the Cathedral Mausoleum like a drive-in of the dead.

While it's as over the top as a Kiss concert, the graveyard's also one of the most haunted spots in town. Sits directly on top of huge deposits of magnetite and copper. Take an EMF reading anywhere on the grounds and it'll spike off the charts. For every good person buried here there are at least four selfish, egomaniacal Hollywood pricks wishing they were still making movies. Walk in any direction and you'll feel a flood of angry, restless energy crackling up through the ground.

As I walk toward the back of the cemetery through rows of tombstones, I'm keenly aware of how close I just came to ending up under one. I do a fair job of blocking that further intrusion.

There are a lot of interesting graves in the cemetery where I could rest the goblet for an hour or two—Cecil B. DeMille, or maybe Douglas Fairbanks—but today, I'm here to pay tribute to the Ramones. Even Stevie Wonder couldn't miss the monument to Johnny Ramone. This one's the balls. A bronze, life-sized statue of Johnny from the knees up, strumming his Mosrite in an iconic rock star pose.

I unwrap Crowley's goblet and place it carefully on the platform right under the controls of Johnny's guitar. Sunlight hits the crystal and I read a quote on the plaque:

> *If a man can tell if he's a success in his life by having*
> *great friends, then I have been very successful.*

I sit at the base of the monument and lean my back against two other quotes carved into the marble: *He was a great American and the greatest friend. I love you John—Eddie Vedder.* Another: *A dedicated punk and loyal friend. Thanks for everything. I miss ya, Johnny—Rob Zombie.* In case you're wondering, the key word here is friendship.

I have at least two hours to kill while the crystal recharges. I pay tribute to Johnny by donning my earbuds and launching my Ramones playlist. "Blitzkrieg Bop" starts the show and I play the chords on air guitar.

During "I Wanna Be Your Boyfriend," my mind races back to last night with Eva. I gotta find a way into her buttoned-up life. Getting plastered in front of her was probably a mistake, but my nerves were shot and I was going to drown my tension whether she was there or not. I'll give her a call later to assess the damage.

This being the only cemetery I know of with total Wi-Fi coverage, I launch Google on my iPad and do a search on the demon Teeraal. Not a lot out there. A lesser prince of hell serving under the command of the demon Alastor, one of the monarchs of hell. Teeraal's a trickster, lures souls from life to death, has the power to take even noble souls to hell. I compare the info I find on the web with a book of demonology I keep in my backpack. I bought the book at the Psychic Eye, on Ventura. When I think of how the book was resting on a shelf in the corner beneath a bust of Aleister Crowley, I get a chill. Teeraal only merits a small mention in the dense book. Small potatoes in the hierarchy of hell.

"Pinhead" kicks in. With the music in my ears, I'm singing way too loud for a burial ground. Then it hits me. The bust of Crowley in the Psychic Eye was next to the book that I'm holding next to

Crowley's goblet at the moment and I'm listening to a song that pays homage to the 1932 cult movie about a bunch of homicidal carnival freaks just as I'm digging up info about a murderous supernatural überfreak terrorizing a carnival. A meaningful coincidence? Fucking A right. It's Jung's synchronicity whirling like a cyclone through this psychic minefield smack in the middle of Hollywood. I surrender and leap directly in the tempest's fierce path. It's moments like these—few and far between—that remind me there's way more going on behind the scenes than I'll ever know. Note to self: *chill out, quit trying to figure it all out, and enjoy the cosmic ride.*

I spend a half hour Googling Holy Family Mission Church. Turns out it's a hub for paranormal activity. One Southern Cal ghost site has photos and electronic voice phenomena, better known as EVPs: disembodied voices that have been captured on a digital recorder. The church is definitely worth a look.

When my iPad battery hits red, I stash it and grab the goblet. It's getting there, nice and hot, about halfway charged. When "I Wanna Be Sedated" plays, I take a stroll around the lake to Dee Dee Ramone's grave while keeping an eye on the goblet in the distance. Dee Dee OD'd on heroin in '02. He was sedated, all right. His tombstone is modest compared to Johnny's, but still rock and roll. The Ramones logo and at the bottom: "OK. . . . I gotta go now."

Clouds roll in and it suddenly looks like rain. The goblet hasn't charged long enough, but it's time to go. I'm in no mood to get drenched. I double-time it back to Johnny's grave, where I wrap the hot goblet and hightail it home, sweating out the last of the liquor damming up my bloodstream.

At Hollywood Boulevard, the skies open and I sprint the last few blocks to my apartment.

Inside, I place Crowley's goblet atop the IVeR and throw the switch. The charge is solid enough for contact, but little else. I fidget with the ectometer and wait for a sign.

I hear something and stop. "Karl?" Nothing.

The goblet hums. From the static, a very distant voice sings, "She Said She Said." The Beatles, as usual. It's Karl.

"Speak to me, Nowhere Man."

"Kane?" His voice remains distant. I have to act fast.

"Holy Family Mission Church," I say clearly and slowly. "Lompoc, California. Talk to me."

The static crackles. Across the void, Karl sings like a child: "Ollie ollie oxen free."

"What?" I ask, my hands raised in confusion.

"Ollie, ollie, oxen free," Karl repeats, then he sings, "Oh, Donna, Oh, Donna." It sounds vaguely familiar. I know it from somewhere. Karl repeats the name Donna. "Donna . . . Donna on a . . . Donna on a . . ." There's a pause then Karl adds, ". . . Donna on a *highway to hell*." He sings it like AC/DC—pretty well.

"What the fuck are you smoking, Karl? Is this a joke?" Why does everything with this guy have to be a muddled puzzle?

The transmission trails off and the IVeR powers down.

Karl stuck it to me good this time. I'm clueless. When I Google the name of the church with the name Donna and the children's hide-and-seek call, ollie ollie oxen free, nothing worthwhile surfaces. What a waste. "Glad you have a sense of humor, Karl." Google "Oh, Donna." Ritchie Valens. Should have known that. Local boy—Pacoima native. Died in that plane crash with Buddy Holly.

I grab my iPhone and call Ned.

"What?" he shouts at me. "I'm watching golf."

"Pick me up tomorrow morning at nine. We've got another gig."

"Where?" he asks, chewing something crunchy. He's probably halfway through a bag of Funyons.

"Lompoc."

"I know a good place for lunch."

"Tell me something new."

"You're paying for gas," he adds.

"Fine."

Ned chuckles like a kid with a secret. "Three jobs back-to-back-to-back. See that? I told you. Shirley MacLaine likes to gab. And word got around town after the Comedy Store thing."

"That's because I got arrested smack in the middle of Sunset Boulevard," I remind him.

"We don't even have to advertise," Ned boasts. "The word is out. And if we bring that reporter into the fold, who knows? The sky's the limit."

"You think so?"

"I know so," he says. "We're on a roll, buddy."

Eight

Ned calls at ten after eight to tell me he'll be late. Has a bad case of the runs after a late-night visit to a taco truck. I put the delay to good use. Dive back into "Layla." I don my headphones and listen to the song over and over, zoning in on the different guitar parts. I take copious notes. Download guitar tabs. It's a real exercise in concentration. Starts to drive me a little batty by the time Ned finally arrives.

We load Ned's old camper and finally head up the 101 to Lompoc. I fill Ned in on the carnival, Teeraal, my minideath, and my booze-soaked evening with Eva. Keeping with my "27" fixation, we spend the next hour listening to a cassette of Jimi Hendrix's *Electric Ladyland* on Ned's recommendation. With Hendrix, I'm pretty much a greatest-hits guy. These songs, all new to me, blew me away, especially "Rainy Day, Dream Away." The song just grooves—the saxophone, the funk-ass B3, Hendrix's JB-style comping, and then some vintage Cry Baby wah-wah playing. A masterpiece.

"You can tell Clapton learned a lot from this guy," I tell Ned.

"They were friends," Ned says. "Clapton was in awe of Hendrix."

After that song, I demand complete silence. Proper respect must be paid. No music shall follow—at least for twenty minutes.

Just past Santa Barbara, I bring up money again. "I wish you'd at least take two grand."

Ned, at the wheel, shoots glances between the road and the ocean, sparkling under the high noon sun. "I'm not in this for the money."

"I know that, still—"

"I told you—when you have a decent roof over your head, a respectable car in your garage, and some semblance of a savings account, maybe I'll take a cut."

I take a look around and laugh. "You're preaching about a respectable ride?" I'm sitting shotgun in a 1983 Ford Jamboree Fleetwood truck camper that just turned 400,000 miles. Ned bought it when I was still watching *Sesame Street*.

"All I'm saying is right now, I'm fine."

"So how much do you make?" Point-blank and way personal, but what the hell.

"I make enough," he says, adjusting his wide ass in his captain's chair.

"Over six figures?"

"Never mind." That's a yes. If I had low-balled him, he'd correct me as a matter of pride. I figure he's pulling in about $130K a year, maybe more. A tenured professor at Caltech—the California Institute of Technology; the academic tech equivalent of playing for the Yankees. Ned's a world-renowned expert in something called combinatorics, which makes him a combinatorist. Fuck if I know what that means.

In the world of mathematics, he's a heavyweight—literally and figuratively. BS: Georgia Tech; MS: Carnegie Mellon; PhD: MIT. Taught at MIT and was a high-level theoretical contractor until just after the soul trap project combusted. Settled in at Caltech, where I found him when I hit L.A. a decade ago.

I smack him on the arm. "I'd feel a lot better about this if you'd just take your cut—like a real partner. If you're worried about some kind of conflict of interest that'll put your job in jeopardy—"

Ned lets out a stabbing, sarcastic laugh. "I'm tenured. I could walk into my classroom in a strapless gown and they couldn't fire me. End of subject."

"Must be nice to not need money," I say.

"Everyone needs money, Kane. Lots of it. I just don't need yours."

What Ned does with his money is a mystery. Besides the camper, he drives a Subaru. I've been to his no-better-than-average condo in Pasadena a couple of times. Spartan, but tidy. Simple living. Probably sleeping on a mattress stuffed with cash.

"I'm not around for a week next month. Conference in Chicago."

"Attending or speaking?" I ask.

"Speaking."

"About what?"

"The Unifying Concept of Subvariance. I'm also on a panel discussing an Ax-Katz-type theorem for systems of congruence."

"Ax Katz? Good name for a Jewish serial killer."

"Go ahead and fucking joke. Mathematics is one of only two pure things in the universe.

"What's the other?"

"Dig *American Beauty* out of my tape case," he orders.

"Oh, please." I sigh, a big heavy one. "There's not enough room in here for me to do my little gay Dead dance." I like to piss Ned off by pretending to hate The Dead. "When are you gonna lose those goddamn stickers?" Ned's a genuine article. He has three hard-to-miss decals on the camper—a Steal Your Face on the back door, a Skull and Roses on the left side, and dancing bears on the right.

"I swear to Christ," he warns, "if you mention those decals one more time, I'll drive straight to Tijuana and have this fucker painted the colors of the Mystery Machine. Won't bother me. You can ride shotgun and take the abuse. Are we clear on this?"

I dig Ned's cassettes out of the glove compartment. "Box of Rain" kicks in and all is right.

"Let's eat," Ned says when the song ends.

"Yeah, I'm hungry."

"What are you in the mood for?"

"I could go for an ostrich burger—what's the name of that place by the ostrich farm?"

Ned shakes his head. "The Hitching Post. It's been full of tourists after that *Sideways* movie."

"What about the place with the split-pea soup?"

"Reminds me of *The Exorcist*," Ned says.

When it comes to his meals, Ned's a two-year-old who dropped his rattle. He knows what he wants, and if I don't let him have it, he'll bitch the whole day.

"I know a good place," he says.

We roll into Solvang, a little bit of Denmark in California. It's a god-awful tourist trap of a town with more windmills than a miniature golf course. Ned pulls into the parking lot of the Solvang Restaurant.

"Where's the restaurant?" I ask.

"Right there, inside the windmill."

Fuck. Did I mention I pretty much hate everything? That includes theme restaurants. We walk in. Jesus. Imagine if Hamlet opened a Denny's. There's a gift shop, postcards on the tables, and a counter near the kitchen. Place smells like pancakes and syrup. I suggest the counter, but Ned rushes over to a Hispanic girl in a Danish maiden's costume who leads us to a booth. I glance up at the low ceiling's wood beams painted with Danish calligraphy. The one above our booth reads: *Godt begyndt er halv fuldendt.*

"What does that mean?" I ask, pointing to the phrase.

"Fuck if I know," Ned answers, his nose deep in the menu. "I'm a numbers man, not a cunning linguist." He cracks himself up, then thumps the table in pure joy. "Yes! I've always wanted to try them," he says.

"What?"

Ned's chomping at the bit when the waitress shows up. "Abe's *aebleskiver*," he orders.

"Raspberry sauce?" the waitress asks.

"Oh, yes," says Ned, like he's about to shoot a load.

The waitress looks my way. "You don't happen to have an ostrich burger?"

She shakes her head. "Gotta go to the Hitching Post for that," she says.

"You don't say."

Ned shoots me the bird.

"I'll have the Viking burger," I say, studying the description. "Hold the Thousand Island dressing . . . *and mayo?*" It comes out like a stunned query instead of a special request.

"Anything else?" she asks.

"Yeah. What does that ceiling beam say?"

She looks up, shrugs. "I'll ask my manager," she says.

"What the fuck is aebleskiver?" I ask Ned.

"You'll see. Just wait."

Gotta whizz. On the way to the john, I spy a tour bus pulling up. At the urinal, twenty Japanese tourists pour in and crowd me. I flush and shove my way past them. Am I in Copenhagen, Tokyo, or hell?

I follow our waitress back. Burger's burned. Crinkle fries are cold. Ned, knife and fork in hand, is about to dig into what looks like six red billiard balls covered in snowflakes. "Behold—aebleskiver," he says, handing me his fork for the sacred first bite.

Down the hatch. Interesting. Then the sugar hits me and ruins it. A pancake meets a waffle, meets an apple turnover, rolled into a ball dunked in raspberry sauce and dusted with powdered sugar. Sweeter than the Olsen twins when they were on that sitcom.

"Well?" Ned asks.

"Like a bag of sugar. A loaded gun for diabetics."

"But it's goddamn good." Ned digs in and doesn't come up for air until the waitress returns. "How is everything?" she asks.

"Heavenly," Ned says. I give her a disappointed shrug. "Is this Hamburger Helper in here?" I ask taking the top off my bun.

She shrugs. "Oh, I asked my manager," she says pointing to the ceiling beam. "It means: 'Well begun is only semifinished.'"

"I love a restaurant with a message," Ned says, diving back into his dish until his plate's clean. I eat half my crap burger and call it quits. An expired Slim Jim would have been better.

Can't get out of the place quick enough, but Ned disappears on me. Ten minutes later, Ned rolls out carrying a shopping bag. He proudly displays his new aebleskiver pan, plus cans of dough and filling, and two jars of raspberry sauce.

"Look at the quality of this thing," Ned says, holding up the weighty pan. "I'll have you over next weekend and make a batch."

"Right." I have a better chance of Metallica's Danish drummer inviting me over. Ned's follow-through percentage is in the low single digits.

On the twenty-mile drive from Solvang to Lompoc, we finally talk shop. "Are you sure you didn't just pass out?" Ned asks.

"She said I was dead."

Ned's not buying it. "How would she know?"

"How do you suppose that clown demon trapped them in those fun-house mirrors?" asks Ned.

"I don't know."

Ned looks over like a mad parent. He's jacked up on sugar. "Well, take a guess."

"I don't have any idea. It's the first demon I've butted heads with."

"Yeah, but you read all that demonology stuff. What do you think?" Ned wants more, but I ain't got it.

"We're figuring things out as we go. Remember?"

"Well, what do you think would have happened to you or Eva if he had pulled you into that mirror?"

I shrug.

"Come on, wild guess."

"My best wild-ass guess is that she or I would have fallen dead right there and Teeraal would have trapped my soul—or hers—in the mirror with the others."

"You gonna go back there?" Ned asks.

"Fuck no," I say, end of story. "Stacks Fabin can keep his money. Dude needs an exorcist, not me."

"You're lucky." Ned says. "Imagine: you and a dead reporter alone in a fun house."

"Back to jail," I say.

"Death row," Ned adds.

We're quiet for a few miles. Then Ned gets edgy and asks, "How do we know we're not going to run into a demon today?"

"We don't."

"We need some kind of screening process," he says.

"Go invent one and build it in."

We pull up to a mission-style church in a valley with a view of the ocean a few miles away. I called ahead. Father Demetrius is waiting on the front steps of the church. Surprising. He's tall, maybe six-two, with white hair and wire-rimmed glasses. Gotta be pushing seventy. From the robust FM voice I spoke to, I pictured him in his forties.

"Spooky-looking place," Ned says as we exit the camper.

"But look at the setting," I say. "And feel that air. This is the real California."

Meet and greet. Then Father Demetrius leads us inside and gives us the grand tour. Old school Catholic regal, an odd blend of Gothic cathedral and California mission, equal parts marble and wood. The towering wood-planked roof, supported by marble columns, looks like the bottom of an ancient boat. As Father Demetrius points out all the supernatural hotspots and we take notes and pepper him with questions, our voices bounce through the rafters. The priest shows us everything—where the ghost opens and closes stained-glass windows, rings the bells in the tower, slams doors, and moves statues on the altar.

"Have you ever seen him?" Ned asks.

The priest shrugs and seems troubled. "I can't say for sure. One time, I thought I saw something out of the corner of my eye."

"What?"

Father Demetrius hesitates, then says. "I thought I saw a face."

"What did it look like?"

"Big black eyes," he says.

Ned looks at me and raises both eyebrows. I can read his mind: *Oh, shit.*

The priest leads us to a pew near the altar. We all sit in a row.

"Thanks for the tour, Father," I say. "The stained glass is sweet. It's a nice church."

"And it should be a peaceful church," the priest says, glancing at the mural of the Holy Trinity on the ceiling above the altar. "I hope you can help me."

"I think we can," Ned says.

A shaft of sunlight streaks through a stained-glass window and illuminates a gold chest about the size of a shoebox on a marble stand next to the altar. It sparkles in the light like a movie prop. "Unrelated to the task at hand," I say. "But what's that blinged-out gold chest by the altar?"

Father Demetrius smiles with pride. "That's a reliquary."

I shrug. "Sorry, I skipped a lot of Sunday school."

Ned chimes in. "Well, I'm an old altar boy from Saint Augustine parish in Brooklyn. A reliquary contains a holy relic, usually a bone from the body of a saint."

"Get out," I say.

"That's right, Ned," the priest says. "Our reliquary contains the finger bone of Saint Anthony of Padua."

Seems pretty damn funny—people kneeling and worshipping a finger. I laugh. "Relics? A little morbid, wouldn't you say?"

Father Demetrius looks insulted. He raises a finger in objection. "Relics are considered powerful spiritual objects, worthy of veneration and capable of great protection . . . even miracles."

"What's Saint Anthony's story?" I ask.

I look at Ned, but he shrugs. "Ask me about baseball cards, not holy cards."

Father Demetrius smiles. Likes Ned more than me. "Saint Anthony was a thirteenth-century Portuguese saint. Born into great wealth. He was known to be tormented by demons that he battled furiously."

I glance at Ned and wink. "I like him already."

"Also known as the patron saint of lost items," Father Demetrius adds. "There's a statue of him over there," he says pointing to the side of the church. A monk, with a ring of hair around a huge bald spot, wears a brown robe and sandals and holds a little boy dressed in white. "Who's the kid?" I ask.

"The Lord Jesus," Father Demetrius says. "He once appeared to Saint Anthony as a little boy."

Ned stands. "We should set up the equipment before it gets dark. There's not a lot of light in here. I'm going to the camper."

I stand. "I'll come, too."

Father Demetrius stops me. "One last thing, Kane."

Ned's already out the door. The priest seems hesitant to speak. "What is it?" I ask.

Finally, he says, "I need your word that you won't tell anyone of this investigation."

"Okay," I say, "but why?"

Even though we're alone, Father Demetrius feels compelled to whisper. "I'm undertaking this . . ." He searches for the right word: "Intervention on my own—without the official consent of the church."

"Why me? Why not an exorcist?" I've been wondering about this since he called. It's good to finally ask him.

"If I were to submit a report, a long investigation would commence. It could take years before a decision is made."

I get it. "Lots of red tape and bureaucracy, I'd imagine."

"Yes," the priest says. "And by submitting such a report, I may be looked upon differently . . . suspiciously." He looks around the church and smiles at it warmly. "I love this place," he says. "I'm nearing my retirement. I'd rather spend what time I have left here instead of in the office of a psychiatrist or neurologist."

"I understand," I say.

The priest pats my shoulder. "That's why I need your utmost discretion. I mean—how would it look if the press got wind of a Catholic priest calling in a ghost hunter?" He raises an apologetic hand. "No offense," he says.

"None taken." I stare him in the eye until I convince myself I'm dealing with an honest man. "All right," I say. "You have my word. I'll keep it on the down low." He seems relieved. "Now I have something to discuss," I say. "My fee."

"Yes."

"Ten thousand dollars if and when we clear the church."

"That much?" the priest asks, surprised.

I'm firm. "Yes."

"This will be coming out of my personal savings account," he says, "not church funds."

"That's okay," I assure him.

He thinks about it. I can tell it's a lot of money for him. "I can do that," he finally says. Father Demetrius shakes my hand. "Then we have a deal." He hands me a key to the church and tells me to return it before we leave. "I'll leave you to your work," he says, making the sign of the cross over my head.

Damn, that was easy. Just got a raise. Maybe I *can* make a dime in this racket.

Just then the hair on my arms stands up and the raised kneeler attached to the church pew directly behind us slams to the ground. Father Demetrius jumps out of his skin. The thud echoes through the church.

Game on.

Nine

It takes a couple of hours to set up the thermal cameras and digital recorders. Ned syncs all the equipment to a handheld device he carries. After I unpack and power-up the soul trap, we're ready to rock.

It all starts slowly. We scour the church with EMF detectors looking for fluctuations in electromagnetic fields, but all readings are normal. We take a break around ten, get some air, and listen to playbacks on our digital recorders. No EVPs. Absolutely no signs of paranormal activity.

I walk from the courtyard back toward the church, but Ned protests. "This is a bust. Come on, let's hit In-N-Out Burger and head home."

"Not yet," I say. "There's something there—I know it."

Back inside, we reset the equipment. "Try to goad it out," Ned suggests. Sometimes, when souls won't manifest, a little provocation does the trick. Ned gives me a thumbs-up that the digital recorders are on and takes a seat in a pew.

"Come on," I shout. My voice reverberates through the silent church. "You like to scare Father Demetrius. You like to scare people who duck in here for a quiet moment. Why don't you try to scare me?"

"Or me?" shouts Ned.

Dead silence.

I throw in a little anger. "Are you a priest? Were you one of those priests that touched altar boys? Too big of a coward to move on?"

Nada.

"Did you go to church here?" I shout. "Are you attached to this place? Tell me. Come on."

Nothing.

I'm tired and pissed off and hungry. Maybe Ned's right. A bust.

"Listen to me," I holler. "You made your presence known when you slammed that pew behind me. Do it again."

Zilch.

One last angry shout before burger time. "All right—if you're too big of a wimp to come out and play, I'm outta here. We were here to help your dumb ass."

I hear a door open from somewhere in the back of the church.

Ned springs to his feet. "Did you hear that?" I nod and we race toward the sound. Ned monitors his handheld. "I'm picking up a heat signature on thermal cam two." Bingo. By the time we reach the spot where the camera picked up the anomaly, it's gone, but we pinpoint the door that opened. It's a small supply closet filled with cleaning supplies.

"Found its hiding spot," Ned says.

Back to the center of the church. I shout, "All right. We know you're here. Make your presence known. You wanna play games— bring it on."

Row by row, the kneelers in the church pews slam down. The soul trap vibrates and hums. The digital recorder near the altar picks up something. We listen. The *boom, boom, boom* of the pews slamming and then—a shrill giggle.

"Fuck," Ned says. "Don't like the sound of that."

"A woman?" I ask.

Ned looks pale. "Or a demon."

"I don't know."

We're staring at each other, stumped. Then—*bong*—a church bell tolls and we jump like scared cats. "I think I shit my pants," Ned says.

"Come on." We dart to the back of the church and leap up the steps of a spiral staircase two at a time. This has to be an incredibly powerful ghost to move a heavy bell. The tower is cramped. Trap hums in my hand. I inspect the bells. They don't move. "The bells are programmed electronically," I point out to Ned.

Ned finds the control panel. "The ghost isn't moving the bells— it's manipulating the energy field around this panel."

The bells tolls again. Deafening. "We're gonna break our ear-drums up here," Ned shouts. "Thermal cam one at the back just registered a hit. It's on the move again."

Whatever was there jetted from the bell tower to the choir loft and back to the church. "Damn, it's fast."

We zip back down to the church floor, and the life-size statue of the Virgin Mary that stands near the front door shakes. I aim the trap and fire, but miss. "It's gone," Ned says.

Bing. Bang. Bong. The church bells toll again.

The soul lures us up and down the spiral staircase from the church to the bell tower four times. We're left winded and sweaty. "Crafty SOB," Ned says, wheezing.

Whether it's ghost or demon, it's too fast to trap. It won't stay put anywhere long enough for me to even put up a phantom fence. "How are we gonna pin this thing down?" I shout to Ned.

"Wait," Ned says, sensing something. "Listen . . ."

We stop in our tracks. Silent. Listen for any sign of movement. Silence builds. Our hearts race. *Whaaaa!* The church organ blares. The organ notes are random at first, but slowly the banging of keys begins to take familiar form. *Chopsticks.* I run toward the altar aim-ing the trap, but the song ends midnote and *bong,* the church bell tolls again.

"Fuck it," I say. "I'm not letting this thing run us in circles any-more."

Bong. Bong.

Ned and I stand our ground.

Bing. Bing.

I match the notes on the organ keyboard.

Bong. Bong. Bing. Bing. Bong. Bong. Bong.

I answer the bells—play the matching seven organ notes. Our little game continues until we've played "Old MacDonald." At least the soul (or demon) has a sense of humor. When the song ends, all is silent. I can't resist the urge to play the opening riff from "Light My Fire."

"Kane, whatever you're doing, just keep doing it. I've got a big, fat heat signature just to the right of you. Whatever the energy is, it's trying to manifest itself. This thing wants to make contact! Keep its attention."

I pause for a second, then play the chord run from Elvis Costello's "Pump It Up," then the riff from "A Whiter Shade of Pale."

Ned inches his way toward me and in a near whisper says, "Still got a hot spot. And it's getting larger. My EMF detector is spiking."

"Whatever it is, it's curious," I whisper back.

I whirl to my right and throw the trap's emitter switch. I lay a phantom fence from the far right wall that runs the entire way across the church. The soul tries to dart through it but gets zapped. I've blocked its path to the bell tower. Inch by inch the soul tries to break through the barrier like a caged animal. It's a sitting duck. The soul trap vibrates. Crosshairs on the targeting monitor flash. Target alert blares. Point . . . and fire. In a hollow building with a lofty ceiling, the sound rocks the world. Everything's intensified: the rip, the boom, the suction. Ned and I hit the deck like the world's ending, like Jesus is coming to lay waste with some badass weaponry.

Target acquired.

We decompress, pat ourselves on the back, and pack the gear.

"I want to go in tonight," I say. "I want to wrap this case up."

Ned disagrees. "I don't like it. You know I only like to send you in when we're locked down at your place."

"Too bad. I want face time with this one—now."

"I can monitor your vitals from here, but I don't completely trust the readings."

"Go get it set up," I say.

"Listen—let me give you some worldly advice. Quit being a stubborn ass and listen to your elders."

I sigh and give him a tired stare. "Just wire me up—I'm stoked to go now."

"It's your call, Kane," Ned says. "One of these days I'm gonna tell you I told you so . . . but, oh, that's right, you won't be able to hear me because *you'll be dead*," he screams like Sam Kinison.

Twenty minutes later I'm lying flat on my back in the camper bed above the cab, NuMag helmet on, chakras wired and ready, goggles covering my eyes. Ceiling's less than a foot from my face. Sometimes when I'm floating somewhere between here and there, lost in the blizzard, I reach up, touch the roof, and imagine it's the lid of my coffin. Positive thinking.

Electricity hits my nervous system and begins to circulate. The helmet vibrates. Sometimes it's jarring, but tonight it feels like a warm blanket on a cold night. My routine is ingrained and I execute the breathing and relaxation techniques flawlessly. Maybe it's fatigue, or maybe I'm just getting better at this, but my journey inside doesn't take long.

When all is purple and I hear the electric hum and distant ring, I open my eyes and glance around, but there's no one there. Can't be. I hear a whimper and turn. In the far corner, almost completely concealed in shadows, is a sight I've never seen before in the trap.

A kid.

A little boy sits hunched, his head resting between his knees. He sobs. Enhanced by the tinny echo that attaches itself to all voices in the trap, it's an eerie fucking sound.

I'm used to sending rotten eggs down the disposal. But a little boy? What's he doing haunting a church?

I approach cautiously. For all I know, he's a demon in disguise waiting to pounce. "Hey, kid, lighten up," I say gingerly. "Don't be afraid. I'm not gonna hurt you."

The kid looks up. He's young. His eyes are covered by a little black mask, the kind that Robin wears. He has closely cropped red hair and wears a red-and-green-plaid shirt, Levis with an inch of rolled-up cuffs, and vintage black-and-white Keds.

"Why don't you take that mask off?" I say.

He hesitates, removes the mask, and reveals his tear-filled, brown puppy-dog eyes.

"I'm in big trouble, Mister. My mommy's gonna be so mad at me," he says through sobs.

"Who's your mommy?" I ask.

His sobs intensify. "She told me never to leave the church. Never!" he stresses. "Not until she comes to get me. She made me promise."

"It's okay. You don't have to cry. I know this probably feels like a scary place, but I'm not going to hurt you."

"Promise?"

"Promise."

"Okay. The kid sits up a little straighter and crosses his legs, Indian style. I sit on the ground across from him. "Hey, this floor's cold," I say. "Let's go over and sit in those chairs. Okay?"

The kid eyes me for a long time. "Okay," he says and stands. I lead him to a chair near the table.

"This is better, huh?" I ask with a smile.

"Uh huh."

"So where's your mommy now?"

The kid wipes his nose on his sleeve. "She had to go away. But she said she'd be back."

I nod, lean in toward him. "What's your name, kid?"

"Oliver. But everybody calls me Ollie."

Karl's words echo in my mind. "Ollie ollie oxen free."

"Ollie, huh? Ollie what?"

"Ollie Lonzi."

"How old are you, Ollie?"

"Six . . . and a half. What's your name?"

"Kane."

"Kane what?"

"Kane Pryce."

The kid finally manages a half smile. "I had fun playing with you and your friend in the church, Kane."

I chuckle. "We had fun, too. You're fast, kid."

"I know. I'm like the Road Runner. *Meep, meep.*"

"How long have you been living in the church?" I ask.

"A long time . . . I think."

"How did you get here?"

"My mommy brought me here." At the mention of his mommy, tears well up in his eyes again.

I reach out and touch the black mask that he's clutching. "You a fan of Batman and Robin?"

"They're okay," Ollie says. "But this is my Lone Ranger mask."

"The Lone Ranger?"

"He's the best. That's my favorite show."

"What year is it, Ollie?"

"How could you not know that?" Ollie asks, laughing.

"I think all those bells ringing in the tower scrambled my brains." Ollie laughs. "I'm a little confused."

"I know all about calendars," he boasts. "My mom taught me. It's 1957, silly," he says.

Whoa. Gotta tread lightly. "You understand what you are, right, Ollie?"

He looks at me like he's waiting for the punch line.

"What do you mean?"

"The fact that people can't see you. That you never grow up."

The little boy looks stumped. "I wondered about that. Am I like the Invisible Man?"

"Do you know what a ghost is?" I ask.

His muscles clench and go rigid. His little smile vanishes. "I'm afraid of ghosts."

"Me, too," I say, realizing I'm not making things any better.

Christ, how the hell do I serve this one up? I stammer for a few seconds, then finally say, "Look . . . I'm just going to ask this . . . straight up. How did you die, Ollie?"

The kid stands and backs away. He starts bawling. "I'm not dead! What do you mean?"

Damage control. "I'm sorry" is all I can think to say.

Ollie melts down, races back to the corner, goes boneless, and curls up. "Go away! Leave me alone." He stands and stomps his feet. "I want to go back to the church!" His tantrum intensifies. "I want my mommy!" he sobs.

I approach slowly. "Calm down there, kiddo. Everything's okay." I reach out, touch him on the shoulder, and pat. Instantly, his head is buried in my chest. He clings to me. I don't know what to do. I pity the poor kid. It doesn't even cross my mind to pull the lever and send him on. Who knows what's waiting for him? Did I mention I pretty much hate everyone? That includes most kids. But even I can't do that to this kid. "Hey, Ollie," I finally say. He looks up at me. He's Opie Taylor, but a hell of a lot cuter than Ron Howard. "Ollie—I'm taking you back to the church."

The sobs subside and the crooked half smile returns. "You promise?"

"I promise."

"Yeahhhh!"

"But," I add, "you have to promise to behave yourself. Don't give Father Demetrius such a hard time. Promise?"

He nods and smiles wider.

"Promise."

We look at each other and I smile at him. "Good."

"Will you come back and play with me again, Kane?"

"Sure."

"Yeahhhh. When?"

"Soon."

"Good. I'm by myself and it sure gets lonely."

"I have to leave now."

"Why?"

"Because I have to take you back to the church."

"Okay."

"Don't be afraid. You'll be back in just a few minutes. Trust me."

"Okay."

My exit door appears. "I'll see you soon," I say as I open it, step through, and spiral back to Ned's camper.

When I come to, I'm drained dry and nauseous as hell. Ned has already removed the NuMag helmet and Ganzfeld goggles and stripped the electrodes from my body.

"Why didn't you release the ghost?" he demands to know.

I'm groggy and slurring like I'm drunk when I tell Ned about the kid—about my plan to release Ollie back in the church. I force myself off the elevated bed and struggle to walk a straight line to the camper door. Feels like I'm staggering off a roller coaster with a dozen loops. "Give me the trap," I order Ned.

"Take a few minutes and get your bearings back," he suggests.

"Nah."

Ned disconnects the trap from the Tesla PC and we walk, like a couple of old geezers on a beach stroll, back inside the church.

I hold the trap, check out the illuminated blue button under the targeting monitor. The one button I've never pressed before. "It's this one, right?" I ask Ned.

"Yep. You really want to do this?"

I nod. A promise is a promise. "You sure this button works?"

"I'm sure that it should work," Ned answers. "First time for everything."

I press the button and a blinding stream of white light bursts from the barrel. The force is so powerful the trap is nearly yanked from my grasp. Sounds like a locomotive trying to outrun a funnel cloud. There's an audible "Yippee!" The white light morphs into a dancing ball that crackles, dissolves, and vanishes.

"Bet you never thought you'd be releasing a soul back into the wild," Ned says, marveling at the sight.

When the roar subsides, we're left in complete silence.

"Well?" I ask.

"I think it worked," Ned says with a hint of uncertainty.

I glance up at the rafters and shout. "Ollie, are you okay?"

Silence. Then the bells answer. *Bing, bang, bong.* On my way out I have an idea and tell Ned to wait. I climb to the bell tower, take the stuffed bear with the shamrock on his belly out of my backpack, and place it in the corner behind a stack of boxes. "Ollie," I say aloud. "Got a friend for you." The bell next to me swings gently.

It's five in the morning when we finally lock the towering oak front door of the church. "We have homework to do," I tell Ned. "You drive. I'm beat."

Ned heads to the camper and I return the church key to the rectory. When I bend over to place it under the welcome mat, a porch light pops on and I jump. My nerves are toast. The door opens and Father Demetrius, in a bathrobe, is smiling at me. "Good morning."

I hand him the key.

"How goes the investigation?" he asks.

"There's definitely a presence in the church," I say. "But it's not malevolent or evil. Don't fear it. Just smile when you sense it. It's peaceful."

"Can you rid the church of it?"

"Yes, but it'll take me more time. I'll call you when I'm ready to come back and finish," I say, and Father Demetrius bids me good night.

I'm whipped. We hit a drive-thru on our way to the freeway, but I can't stay awake long enough to have a single bite.

Ten

I'm all gung ho to search for information about Oliver Lonzi as soon as I get home, but I get sick as a dog and spend two days in bed. Nausea. Fatigue. The runs. Muscle aches. Fever. I figure it's just the flu, but Ned keeps insisting it's because of my last trip into the trap. Tells me the unaligned protons in my brain are causing my hyperactive immune system to actually attack my body. Warns me to steer clear of any reentry until I rebound.

Despite constant efforts to get off my ass and venture out, I just can't. All I do is listen to "Layla" about seventy times, isolate the Clapton parts, and try to play them until my fingertips blister. I get hooked on a *Twilight Zone* marathon on Syfy. Watch eleven episodes in a row. Vegging out on my back is about all I can handle. My head aches, my vision's still blurry, and my eyes burn when I try to read. Can't manage any serious web research.

I'm antsy. I need answers, but I can't help myself.

I call Ned. He tells me he'll do some digging around.

Then I call Eva. She seems pleased to hear from me. I ask her for help. Can she learn anything about Ollie? She doesn't hesitate for a second. Tells me to give her a few days and she'll call.

I don't hold my breath. Most people let me down. Don't show up when they say they will. Don't come through with a favor when I really need one. Don't follow up when they say they will. I shouldn't bitch. Most people who know me would say the same about me. Don't know if it's me or them. All I know is that it leaves my glass perpetually half empty.

Two days later, Eva catches me by surprise. She calls back, like she said she would, and tells me she has some information. We set up a meeting at my place and I invite Ned over. While I'm waiting for them to arrive, I rack my memory, trying to remember the last time someone actually did a pain-in-the-ass thing for me they'd said they'd do. Draw nothing but blanks.

Eva strolls in with a smile and a folder full of papers. Not only that, she seems pleased that she was able to help. What the fuck—a glass half full?

Ned shows up a few minutes later with a pizza, but all I can handle is a handful of saltines.

"You look like shit," Ned says.

"Thanks. I feel like shit," I say.

"You sound like shit, too," Eva says.

Eva delivers. She hands Ned and me duplicate copies of her clippings. "I spent three hours in the archives." She starts her summary. She does this for a living all right. Clear and concise. A real pro. "December 11, 1957," she begins.

> Donna A. Lonzi, age 27, along with her son, Oliver F. Lonzi, were killed when the car, driven by Mrs. Lonzi, sped off the road and toppled over the cliffs near Honda Point, just outside of Lompoc, California.

Ned interrupts. "Honda Point? Wasn't there some kind of naval disaster there in the '30s?"

Eva shuffles through her papers and hands us another article. "Actually it was 1923," she says. "Seven U.S. naval destroyers ran aground in the rocks at Honda Point and were destroyed. Three ships grounded, but were able to maneuver free. Twenty-three sailors lost their lives. After that, Honda Point also became known as Destroyer Rock."

"How the hell do seven naval ships run aground on a beach? What kind of fuckup was in charge of that operation?" I ask.

"No idea," Ned says.

Eva's all business. "Donna, a onetime actress who appeared in small roles in several Hollywood pictures. Here are two photos of Donna and Oliver," she says, handing us a copy of a newspaper article.

I leaf through my folder until I reach the photos. "That's the kid, all right. Shit, you've delivered the goods, Eva."

She likes the compliment. I can tell she works in an environment where praise is rare by the way she says, "Thanks."

The picture of Donna Lonzi opens my eyes wide. She's flat-out gorgeous—my type. "Wow," I marvel.

"Donna was a dish," Ned says.

"Check out that polka-dot dress," I say. I have a personal weakness for women in the Dita Von Teese mold—clothes on or off. I remember once when I was a kid, my dad had a *Playboy* hidden under the sink. There was a pictorial and article about Betty Page—the dangerous yet playful-looking '50s brunette. One image, of a topless Betty wearing a Santa hat, hanging ornaments on a Christmas tree, winking like she means business, did one hell of a number on the mind of this ten-year-old. Been chasing that look ever since. Suppressed it pretty well until Dita went and came along. I'm no stalker, but I'll get out of bed at 2 AM and jog across Hollywood if I hear from someone that Dita just arrived at a club. I want to come back in my next life as her garter belt.

Donna's face reminds me of someone. Not Dita. Not Betty. Someone I know. Spent so much time wandering from club to club in a drunken fog, it's a hazy memory. I can't put my finger on it. Great. This is gonna drive me nuts.

Ned pipes up. "Looks like Liz Taylor in that movie, the one with Montgomery Clift . . ."

"*A Place in the Sun*," Eva says.

"Bullshit. She looks like Dita Von Teese."

"Dita Von who?" Ned asks.

"Christ," I mutter in disgust.

Eva speaks up. "What do you know, Ned? Looks like Kane prefers brunettes."

Ned laughs hard at that one. "Don't worry; he sees to it that blondes and redheads get proper attention, too." Ned winks my way. "And didn't I catch you once with a bald chick?"

"Shut the fuck up," I snap.

"I swear—I thought it was Sinead O'Connor for a minute."

Bite my tongue or retaliate? Duck and cover, Ned. Here comes the grenade. "This coming from a guy whose second wife wore a blond wig. A freakin', flat-chested Dolly Parton," I tell Eva.

Ned sits up on the sofa and waves his hands in protest. "Flat-chested? Excuse me, but she had quite a respectable rack—"

Eva reins us in. "Guys," she interrupts. "Back to business. Please."

I shoot Ned the finger and ask Eva, "See what I gotta deal with? Welcome to my world."

Eva takes a sip of chardonnay she brought and continues. "Apparently, Donna and Oliver were driving from their home in Nevada on their way to visit her parents and sister in Lompoc. Donna's husband, Nicholas Lonzi, age twenty-six, did not accompany his wife and child on the journey and remained behind in Las Vegas."

"Nicholas Lonzi? You mean Nick Lonzi?" Ned asks.

Eva nods. I shrug. "Rings a bell," I say. "Remind me—who is he?"

Ned goes into his professor voice. "Nick Lonzi. The Vegas guy. The commercial—where he's on top of the marble temple beckoning mindless viewers like us to Vegas."

I've seen the commercial. "Right," I say, nodding.

"The guy's a fucking folk legend," Ned says. "He was on *60 Minutes* about ten years ago. Been around since the birth of Vegas." Ned looks at Eva. "Didn't he invent the slot machine or something?"

Eva glances at her paperwork. "Not quite," she says. "He invented the electronic slot machine."

"That's right," Ned says, remembering. "Back in the days of Bugsy Siegel, slot machines were primitive, complicated machines. Lots of gears . . . lot of ways for them to go on the fritz. This kid Lonzi comes along with technological designs that took slot machines to the electronic and, eventually, the digital age."

Eva adds, "He sold his technology to Bally, which was the first company to mass-produce slots. Nick cashed out for north of five million."

"In the '50s," I marvel.

"Starts investing all over Vegas," she continues. "Made a fortune. Starts giving back big-time. Becomes a huge philanthropist."

"I remember that from *60 Minutes*," Ned says. "Practically paid for a hospital in Vegas out of his own pocket."

"Built tracks of quality, affordable housing," Eva adds. "Built new schools. He's largely responsible for Vegas's big population boom in the '90s."

"Guy does more for his fellow man than Bob Fucking Hope," Ned says.

"Except he doesn't want praise or attention," Eva says. "Doesn't like the limelight."

"Which casino does he own?" Ned asks. "Is it the MGM Grand?"

"The Phoenician," Eva says, correcting him.

Eva hands me a photo downloaded from Google Images. "Here's Lonzi at age thirty." Big, strong, good-looking. She hands me another. "And here's a recent pic." Big, strong, older, but still good-looking. Downright rugged. Looks kind of like the world's most interesting man (minus the beard) from that beer commercial. "Guy looks pretty good for his age."

Ned nods and wipes pizza sauce from his chin. "I know. He's pushing eighty and looks like he could still kick your ass in a bar fight."

"I want to talk to him," I say.

"Good luck," Eva says. "Known to be reclusive. Hates publicity. Only deals with a handful of people."

"Sounds like Howard Hughes."

"Yeah, but I don't think he wears Kleenex boxes for shoes," Ned says, laughing at another of his own jokes.

"You got an address?"

"Lives at the Phoenician, on the strip," Eva answers. "Penthouse suite. Owns the biggest stake in the operation and has his office there, too."

"I'm going to Vegas," I declare.

"Forget it," Eva says. "He'll never talk to you." Her emerald eyes light up. "But he might talk to me."

"Ah, the reporter hat," I say. "I don't have one of those."

"Everyone loves a story about one of the good guys."

"You seem pretty sure of yourself," I tease.

"Getting people who don't want to talk to talk is my job," she says, all smug. I love the cockiness. "And when I want something, I usually get it."

"Well, excuse me all to hell," I say smirking. I'm sinking deeper and deeper. "What do you say—road trip?"

Eva gives it some thought. "Sure. Why not? I can sell a Lonzi feel-good story to my bosses." She jots down her address in Los Feliz. "Gotta be back the day after tomorrow—latest. If I'm going, I need to do some work tonight. I'm gonna bounce. I'm an early riser. Let's get on the road by seven." She talks fast and moves faster. *Bing, bang*, she's out the door after issuing her orders.

A road trip with Eva Kells. Fuckin' A.

Ned and I channel surf a little, but I'm beat. I fight to stay awake, but nod off watching *Ramsay's Kitchen Nightmare*.

An hour later, I wake up and Ned's gone. There's only two pieces of pizza left out of a fucking large. Didn't see Eva have a single slice. She left more than half a bottle of Jekel chardonnay behind, which I polish off, despite my queasiness.

Asshole Ned, belly full of pizza, pinned a note to my chest. It reads: *Call me after you talk to Lonzi.*

Refreshed from my nap, I grab my Telly, plug in, mike up, and get back to work on Project Layla. It's coming together. I'm in no way a Clapton or Allman, but I'm hearing their parts clearly. I'm understanding where they were coming from. I'm starting to feel it in my bones. This could be dangerous.

Eleven

I'm up at 6:30 AM. I stayed up way too late, but I'm totally jazzed by my improved guitar playing. Don't need coffee. I drink a beer in the shower, pack my duffel bag, don a black vest over a gray long-sleeve T-shirt with a Steadman caricature of Hunter Thompson from *Fear and Loathing*, stop for an oil change and fill-up, and head to Eva's.

I keep expecting her to cancel on me via phone message or text, but all is silent on my way over. She lives in a nice apartment building that sits directly under a power line on Waverly Drive. I was hoping to get a look at her apartment, but she's waiting for me at the front door with her stylish little red rolling suitcase. She's wearing an untucked lime-green blouse over a short black skirt and floral-pattern sandals. Damn, she's bangin'. She jumps in and we head up the 2, then east on the 210 en route to the I15, straight to Las Vegas.

While I was playing guitar last night I imagined all the witty things I would say to her, the deep and meaningful conversations we would have over the course of the four-hour journey. Fifteen minutes into the ride, after telling me she was up until five working on an unrelated story and clearing her schedule, she's sound asleep. Fuck.

I turn off my tunes, keep my speed steady, and drive in silence, alone with my (often dirty) thoughts. She's curled up in such a way that her skirt is hiked up high, revealing her long and lean legs. I can't stop looking. I can probably steer the car with my hard-on.

When I pass Barstow, traffic flies. Eva wakes up just short of Primm, about an hour shy of Vegas. She seems refreshed. I try a little casual chitchat, but she wants to get right down to business. "Help me construct a little time line," she says. "It'll help."

She takes out a digital recorder and I freeze. "I don't know," I say, dismissively.

"Look, I'll be honest. We may be able to get a book deal out of this."

"Really?"

"Just work with me a little." She consults her notes, turns on the recorder. "So the project was based in Colorado Springs. An eight-person team. You don't know whether it was civilian, government, or military—or a combination of the three. Do you know when it began?"

"1984," I say. I can't believe how she somehow draws info out of me effortlessly. I'm saying this into a recorder. "Apparently it was based near Pikes Peak—an unmarked building somewhere around where Tesla once had an experimental energy lab."

"And what role did your father play?"

"Not entirely sure. Ned says he was a lead designer."

"And what role did Ned play?"

"He designed and implemented the GUI."

"What's a gooey?"

"GUI—graphical user interface."

"Right," she says. "Duh."

"Ned was on the project for eleven months. Was the first member off the project when his work was done."

"So your father relocated to Colorado? From where?"

"He was a research fellow at the Stevens Institute."

"Where is that?"

"New Jersey," I say. "He and my mother moved in the summer of '85."

"Your mother's name was . . . ?"

"Angie . . . Angeline."

"And what happened to her?"

This is getting way too personal, but I'm in too deep. The car feels warm—safe. "She left me and my father in '90."

"You were so young," Eva whispers.

"I was seven. Don't know why she left. There one day, drinking her wine coolers and watching game shows, and gone the next."

"And you never saw her again?"

"Nope." Eva sits up in her seat. I lose the angle on her high thighs. "I'm so sorry," she says. I stare straight at the road.

"Must have been hard?"

"We all have sad stories" is all I say. "Next subject."

"And your father disappeared in '93?"

"Jesus," I snap.

"All right . . . sorry."

"No," I say. "Go ahead. I only want to talk about this once."

"And that coincides with the end of the project?"

"Seems to. I don't know what happened."

"And how did you end up with the soul trap?"

That whole phase of my life was pretty hazy. A lot of beer. Even more weed. "A guy who said he was a friend of my father approached me at the food court in the mall. I was seventeen. He gave me a key to a storage unit. Just left. I was too stoned to even chase him down. I went to every public storage facility within a hundred miles. Took me about three months to finally find it. The unit was prepaid in my name for twenty years. The trap was there, along with a sheet of paper naming some of the eight team members."

"Did you know what it was?"

"No. It didn't work. It was banged up, like it'd been dropped. I got it open and a lot of the circuitry was corroded. I didn't know what the hell it was."

"What did you do?"

"Looked up the first name on the list—Ned. Did a little research. This is way back in 2000, mind you—before Google hit big. Fled Colorado. Tracked down Ned at Caltech. Been in L.A. ever since."

We stop at Primm, next to a hotel in the shape of a steamboat, for a bathroom break and a fill-up. I grab a coffee. When we're back in the car, Eva picks right up. I feel like screaming "Give it a rest!" in her face, but I play along. Like I said, I'm only going to tell her this once. She better take good notes.

"Did Ned know who you were when you showed up with the trap?"

"Yeah. He recognized the trap the second he saw it. He kind of took me under his wing."

Eva smiles, nods. "He seems like a good guy. A bit annoying."

"Tell me about it."

"He sure likes you, though."

"I guess."

"Then what?" Eva asks.

"Then he tells me what the trap is."

"And?"

"And I thought he was nuts at first. But then I believed him and set about trying to make it work."

"And you succeeded?"

I nod, and add, "After about five years and tons of trial and error, we finally rebuilt the fucker. Ned created all of the software to run it. He spent a fortune."

"When did you actually use it for the first time?" Eva asks.

I'm trying to remember the date. "It was 2006. We trapped a ghost in a house in Tarzana."

"Jesus, you must have felt like Neil Armstrong walking on the moon."

"The trap went on the fritz right after that. Took us almost a year to get it working again. We did two jobs in '07. The trap seemed to stabilize. Then we spent about a year building the IVeR."

"What's that?"

"That's for another time," I tell her. "So that's it. "About four jobs in '08, three more in '09, four last year, and one so far this year."

"Can you detail all these cases?"

"Not today," I say, pointing to the Vegas Strip outside my windshield. "We're here." In the blazing noon sun, it's like a hazy mirage in the desert. I look at Eva and grin like a kid at an amusement park. "Vegas, baby!" I shout as I punch the gas pedal.

Twelve

I'm sore after four hours in the car, but as soon as I enter the Phoenician and hear the slots and the chucking of the roulette wheels and then spy my first cocktail waitress, I perk right the hell up. Sure the house always wins. Sure everyone's a sucker. But screw it all—this is Vegas. And there's no better place on earth to blow your savings.

The lobby and casino are done up Greek style. Towering statues of gods surround the casino floor. The urge to park my ass at a blackjack table is a powerful one. *It's a workday,* I have to remind myself. And the money from the Camarillo gig has to last me at least three months. Can't piss it away. I'll let myself blow a couple hundred bucks—tops—after we talk to Lonzi. Moonlight Bunny Ranch is out of the question this trip, with Eva here and all. But maybe I can talk Eva into catching the stage show with me. Devillusion—demon dancers in hell, a magician dressed up like the devil, and a dozen man-eating lions and tigers. Only in Vegas.

Eva heads right to the front desk to query the hotel manager about Lonzi. I race off to play quarter slots long enough to score a free Bushmills. Double. Eva comes marching over. She's pissed. "This is not a fucking party," she snarls at me. "Get serious."

I chug the drink and smirk at her. Two shots down. I'm on my way. "If we get to talk to Lonzi, how do you think I should bring up Ollie?"

Eva looks at me like I'm a toddler and she's an impatient mother. "Just let me do my thing," she pleads. "If I get to talk to Lonzi, I'll know when and how to bring it up."

"Bullshit," I snap. "You're not cutting me out."

"I may have no choice," she stresses. "Just trust me. Lonzi's communications director is coming down to meet me."

"Can't I hang around?"

She rolls her blue sky eyes. "Come on," she protests. "This is my job."

I'm like a kid whose mother just said no to a new Transformer.

"Just back off for a few minutes, let me do my thing, and if I can land an interview, maybe I can work you in."

"But—" I protest, but she cuts me off.

"Quit acting like an asshole," she snaps. And, to my surprise, I snap to attention and obey. Why can't I surprise myself like this when I play guitar?

Eva marches away and I linger in the shadow of a giant slot machine, studying her as she waits by the front desk.

A guy that looks like Tom Cruise, circa late '80s, comes strolling in wearing a form-fitting suit and a big cheese-ass smile and gives her a weak hug and a kiss on both cheeks. They exchange business cards and small talk. Christ. Then comes Eva's request. Lots of facial expressions and power gestures. Then some chitchat with plenty of phony smiles and playful pats on the arms and shoulders. Jesus. Then a more serious discussion. Eva leans in, listens intently, nods. It all looks genuine. She's good.

When Eva turns to admire the stained-glass ceiling panels in the lobby rafters that Maverick points out, he stares right at her ass while her back is turned. I feel like choking this schmuck to death with his $200 paisley necktie.

Maverick walks away and Eva glides toward me. "I'm glad I don't have to do that for a living," I say. It pisses her off.

"Well, it might have worked," she boasts. "I just got us a preinterview. And you're included—if you can look the part."

"What part?" I want to know.

"Junior reporter, under my wing."

"So Maverick might grant us an audience?"

It's the way I say Maverick. There's a cynical bite to it. Eva zones in. "His name is Randall Cleary. You're not jealous of a workingman in a nice suit?"

"No, it's his business card. I've always wanted one of those."

"Well, if you can pass yourself off as junior monkey-boy reporter under my command, you might be joining me and Mr. Lonzi." She says it all teasingly, but it's got a razor edge. "What did you bring to wear?" Before I can answer she grabs my duffel bag and unzips it. Contents: a long-sleeve Phish tee, a pair of clean black boxer briefs, a fresh pair of socks, Eric Clapton's autobiography, my shaving kit, and a box of Black Widow condoms (I never leave home without 'em).

"You're kidding?" Eva asks. "You're not kidding."

I yank the duffel bag out of her hands. Pushy. Hot—but pushy. "Try asking before you snoop," I snap at her.

"As soon as we check in, we're going shopping," Eva states.

I wrestle with asking Eva if she wants to share a room to save a few bucks (who am I kidding?), but before I even make a decision, she cuts in front of me and checks into her own room. At least my room is on the same floor.

We throw our bags in our rooms and hit the Strip, walking a few blocks to the Forum Shops at Caesars Palace. An hour later, I've dropped 1,200 bucks (about 10 percent of my fucking savings) on a pair of True Religion jeans, a white button-down Theory shirt, and a navy Burberry blazer. Eva chose everything.

I don't know why I went along with it. Strike that. I know exactly why. I finally put my foot down when she wants me to drop another 170 bucks on Cole Haan shoes. My boots will do just fine.

"We need to bring Lonzi a gift," Eva says. "Go find something," she orders. "I'm going back to the hotel and follow up with Randall. I'll call you in a bit." Eva dashes off before I can even pick her brain about a gift. What the fuck do you buy a man who can buy anything?

I dial Ned.

Two rings, then, "What? Hurry up, I'm watching ice skating. Did you meet Nicky boy?"

"Not yet," I tell him. "I need to take him a gift. Any ideas?"

"Let me call you back."

I hang up and duck into the bar at The Palm for a shot and a beer. I'm licking my wounds over the credit card debt I just racked up when Ned calls back.

"Lonzi likes cigars," Ned says. "Blurb on him in *Cigar Aficionado*. Prefers Cohiba Churchills."

"Thanks."

There's a high-end cigar shop nearby. I buy a box of Lonzi's favorites. When the shopkeeper rings it up, I nearly stroke out. "With tax, that's $327.24," he says.

I hand him my plastic. Feels like I got bitch-slapped. Is Ashton Kutcher gonna leap out of a humidor? "For a box of cigars?"

"Premium brands," he says.

"Do I get a blowjob with that?"

"Not from me," he says, handing me a handsome green bag.

Counting the room, the clothes, and the cigars, I'm out two grand and I haven't even gambled away twenty bucks yet. Fuck. I could have gone to the Moonlight Bunny Ranch and banged Air Force Amy in every position in the Kama Sutra for that sum.

I mope my way back to the Phoenician. If I get on a good blackjack run, maybe I can win some of the money back. Before I can even sit down at a table, I get a text message from Eva: *Randall Cleary and I are working out in the health club. Come join us.* Christ.

I go to my room, take a shower, slick back my hair with lots of gel, and don my new pricey threads. I look at myself in the mirror. Fuck. If Ned could see me now. It's a *Twilight Zone* episode where I'm a Bloomingdale's mannequin come to life.

I enter the posh health club. There they are, side by side, dripping sweat all over their elliptical machines. When Eva sees me she gives me a big grin and a wink. She likes my look. She ought to—she created it. Cleary gives me the once-over. It's as if he has the superhero power of being able to read labels through clothes. He respects the threads. I guess I passed the test.

"Eva says you're just getting started," he says, dripping sweat. "Where'd you go to school?"

I freeze. "Villanova" comes out of nowhere. Have no idea why.

"No kidding. I have a cousin who went there. What's your fraternity?"

I freeze again. Look to Eva for help. Her eyes are telling me: *Come on, play the game.*

"I never pledged," I say.

"A lone wolf?" Cleary asks, huffing.

"You could say that."

"Randall went to Yale," Eva says. Fuck Randall Cleary. Ivy League schmuck. I do my best to ignore him. I can't take my eyes off Eva in her spandex. Neither can Cleary.

"Bottom line," Cleary says, inhaling fully, "why should I go to bat for you?"

I clam up. Eva seems to speed up her pace on the elliptical. "We're the *Los Angeles Times*," she says. "If Mr. Lonzi is looking for fund-raising support on the new children's hospital, we have a substantial celebrity readership." Her mojo is working. Cleary likes what he hears. "And frankly," Eva continues, "I think Mr. Lonzi deserves a lot more credit for the work he does. I aim to help on that end."

"He'll have no interest in that," Cleary assures us. "But he is looking for more financial support."

"You have a friend and neighbor in L.A.," Eva says with a warm smile.

"I'm going to recommend that he do the interview," Cleary says as he winds down on the elliptical. "Mr. Lonzi's not going to sit longer than fifteen minutes," Cleary tells us as he steps off the machine, takes a healthy swig of water, and hands me his business card. I put it in my wallet. Maybe I can use it to pick out the gristle between my teeth if I eat ribs later.

Eva's aglow. Another notch in her pen.

"The parameters of the interview are simple," Cleary explains. "No recorders and absolutely no personal questions. Mr. Lonzi is an intensely private man. I can't stress this enough."

"Understood," Eva says, toweling off her face.

"Come to Mr. Lonzi's office suite on the sixth floor in an hour. I'll be waiting for you."

Cleary takes off toward the locker room, but stops short of the door. He turns and waves Eva over. They talk for about a minute. Eva smiles a couple of times, pats his arm playfully. Christ. Cleary heads off to the locker room.

"What did he want?" I ask when Eva returns.

"He asked me out tonight," she says with a grin.

I must have just snarled unconsciously. She knows I'm way into her. She's enjoying this.

"Are you going?" I demand to know.

"Depends."

"On what?"

"On you. Thought we'd catch a show or just hang out," she says.

Rainbows and sunshine and Halle-fucking-lujah from on high. Put that in your pipe and smoke it, Randall Cleary. "Send Maverick your regrets," I say. "Let's go see the Beatle Cirque show."

On the way back to our rooms, Eva gets serious, "I want you in there with me, but here are my parameters: I do all the talking. Are we clear on that?"

Her tone is a little strong for my taste. I raise my eyebrows.

"Promise me. This is my job and this is a legitimate interview. I can't risk my reputation."

"Okay," I say.

"If I see an opening, I'll take it. If not, I won't. Understood?"

"Yeah."

"Don't just look like you're taking notes," she adds. "Actually take notes. You have to play the part. I'll bring you a notebook and a nice pen."

"Okay."

"Did you get a gift?"

"Cigars. His favorites."

"Bring them. We'll meet in the lobby in forty-five."

"Okay."

"By the way," Eva says, "you look great."

I feel a little giddy. "Thanks."

Eva heads back to her room to shower. I go to my room, grab the cigars, and head straight to the lobby and wait for her.

Eva meets me a short time later, looking fresh and buttoned up. Black skirt and matching jacket. White blouse. She hands me a notebook and a Montblanc pen. "Make it look real," she reminds me again.

We're directed to the elevators for the office tower. Lonzi's office suite is tucked in the corner of the tower's sixth floor. It's small, but ultraposh. The reception area is designer perfect. Everything smells expensive. Lots of beautiful things: modern furniture, oddly compelling, framed art prints, and a drop-dead-gorgeous receptionist who has to be the poster girl for the Elite modeling agency. She rises to greet us and just keeps rising. With bare legs a mile long and cripplingly steep heels, she's pushing six feet. I have to look up—just barely.

Rail thin, yet top-heavy—as close to a Barbie body as these eyes have seen. A vision of silicone perfection and ginger flawlessness. Brown eyes. Long brown hair. A bronze, angular face. Brown pinstripe jacket and matching skirt.

"May I help you?" she asks. I expect to hear the voice of a torch singer. What comes out is more like Betty Boop. High-pitched, vacuous. Total bummer.

"Eva Kells for Randall Cleary and Mr. Lonzi." She doesn't mention my name. Pisses me off, but I swallow it.

"Please have a seat," the receptionist tells us.

Eva and I sit on a retro white sofa. I can't take my eyes off Barbie. Eva notices. "Enjoying the view?" she whispers.

I smile and shrug. I stand and walk across the room to have a closer look at the three framed pieces of art. They're dark, mesmerizing. Eve tempted by the serpent, a spiral staircase reaching from earth to the heavens, a warrior with a white beard holding a sword as he rides on a white stallion. "Pretty sick art," I say to the receptionist. "Who's the painter?"

"They're museum-quality William Blake prints," she says, as if it's obvious.

Randall Cleary emerges from a hallway off the reception area. "Welcome," he says, all cheesy and cheery. "We're all ready."

He leads us down a hallway to Lonzi's private office. Nick Lonzi, seated behind a gorgeous, streamlined blond-wood desk with a black granite top, stands to greet us. He wears a perfectly tailored black blazer over a gray turtleneck. His shoulders are broad. His salt-and-pepper hair is layered and combed perfectly—U.S. senator style.

Randall Cleary introduces us and Lonzi smiles and shakes our hands. Powerful grip. No liver spots. Manicure. Cologne. Eva and I sit in side chairs positioned directly in front of Lonzi's desk. Cleary sits on a sofa behind us.

"Before we begin," Eva says, "my colleague and I wanted to present you with a little token of our deep gratitude." She looks my way.

I stand and offer the cigars to Lonzi. "It's a real honor to meet you, Mr. Lonzi. I hope you enjoy them."

Lonzi takes the cigars, nods, and smiles. "You've done your homework," he says, a voice so commanding it could voice-over movie trailers. "I thank you—both of you." Lonzi slaps his hands on his desktop. "Unfortunately, my time today is limited, so let's get to it."

I open the notebook Eva gave me and prepare to write.

Eva clears her throat. "Your philanthropic efforts in the Las Vegas area are legendary. What can you tell us about your current involvement with the newly proposed children's hospital?"

"I'm currently spearheading an effort to help raise $100 million of the $525 million cost of this state-of-the art facility. We're about halfway to our fund-raising goal. Groundbreaking is scheduled for the first of the year. The hospital is scheduled to open in 2013."

The man speaks in sound bites. This is gonna be tough. But my head is down and my pen is flying.

"There are reports that you've personally contributed upwards of $10 million of your own money toward this effort," Eva says admiringly.

I peek up. Lonzi leans back in his chair. "I don't care to comment on that," he says. "I'm strictly focused on the $100 million fund-raising goal."

"Which leads me to another question," Eva continues. "Despite the untiring work you've done on behalf of the city of Las Vegas, we never see your name associated with the many projects you've spearheaded. But unlike many of your contemporaries, it's never the Nicholas Lonzi Sunrise Medical Center or the Lonzi Sports Arena or Nicholas Lonzi's Phoenician Hotel and Casino. To my knowledge there isn't a street named after you or a statue in your honor. Why is that?" The question just rolls off Eva's tongue. She's ultrasmooth.

"I'm a simple man," Lonzi replies. "Down to earth. Always have been. It's my honor and privilege to serve this city. I don't do it to satisfy my ego or garner praise. The only reason I've agreed to this interview is to remind our friends in Los Angeles that we need their help to make the new children's hospital a reality."

Eva is making serious eye contact now. She's good. Lonzi eyes her up like he still has a full tank of gas in his engine. Eva smiles at him. "Of all of your many accomplishments, what are you most proud of?"

"When I came to this town at the young age of fifteen, there was nothing. A single hotel and casino—the Flamingo. Today, Las Vegas is a thriving metropolis. I suppose I'm most proud of the explosive growth of Las Vegas, especially in the last fifteen years. Las Vegas is no longer just a place to gamble or be entertained. It has become a place to live, to raise a family. I like to think I've had something to do with that."

"That's an undeniable fact," Eva says.

He just said "family." There's her in. Come on Eva—bring it up.

She doesn't. "By all estimates, you have a net worth of over a half-billion dollars. You've been an inventor, an entrepreneur, a visionary, a philanthropist. You've succeeded at it all. What drives you—just months shy of your eightieth birthday—to continue to work so hard?"

"Simple," Lonzi says. "I have more to do. Always." Lonzi pauses and reflects. I'm older than this city," he says. "But this city feels young . . . so I feel young."

Eva grins at Lonzi. "You do seem incredibly fit for your age. What's your secret?"

Lonzi sits taller. He's eating out of the palm of her hand. "I exercise every morning. Eat well. Take care of myself. Think positively. Do that consistently and there's no limit to the life you can live."

"One last question," Eva says. I brace. This better be it. "You're twice a widower. You once lost a son. How did you cope with such loss and continue to stay focused and move forward?"

Bingo.

Randall Cleary springs to his feet behind me. Lonzi stands and stares down Cleary. They're both taken aback at first, then pissed off. "That's all the time I have," Lonzi says. He makes for the office door.

"I'm sorry. It wasn't my intention to offend," Eva says.

Lonzi ignores her. He's almost out the door. We'll never get this close to him again. What about Ollie? I panic—take a wild half-court shot.

"Mr. Lonzi?" I stammer.

He turns around. "What?" he asks sharply.

"I need to talk to you. It's important."

Eva's in a panic. She's shaking her head, mouthing the word *no.*

"Interview over," Cleary snaps.

Eva's turning white. Her eyes are begging me to shut up.

"It's about your son, Oliver," I shout.

Lonzi freezes in place. "What? What did you say?" His voice drops a notch or two in volume and bass.

"Oliver," I repeat.

He's rattled. "What about Oliver?" He's seething. Afraid he might stroke out. I try to reassure him. "I just need to talk to you."

Lonzi storms out of his office. Cleary chases him down the hall. Eva shoots me a murderous look. "What the fuck are you thinking?" she hisses at me. I feel the venom in her words.

Cleary returns a minute later in a full-out rage. "Thanks for fucking sticking a knife in my back," he screams at Eva.

She's in deep and she knows it. Yet she tries to play it cool. "Kane was just—"

He cuts her off. "I told you, you stupid cunt—no personal questions."

I explode, take two steps forward, and punch Cleary on the jaw. It lands, but not cleanly. "Apologize or you'll get worse than that," I scream at him.

Cleary charges me, throws a wild punch that lands, but not hard. I crack him right back. Then we're on the floor rolling around. Two guys the size of WWE tag-team champs barge into the office and pull me off him. Cleary's lip is bleeding.

"Out," orders Cleary. "Both of you. Now. Or I'll call the police."

Before the words are out of his mouth, Eva's already down the hallway. She darts past Barbie the receptionist and out the door. I chase her down. When the elevator door closes, she explodes. "Jesus Christ. You're fucking crazy. Do you know that? Jesus Christ Almighty. What's wrong with you?"

She continues to wig out the whole way across the lobby, to the guest elevators and all the way to her room. I'm hot on her heels, silent, drowning in her anger. She frantically packs her suitcase. "I'm sorry," I finally manage to say.

"I have to get back," she says, breathing hard. "Gotta run damage control." I realize she's not so much talking to me as herself. "It's six o'clock. If they call right away and try to cause a shitstorm, my bosses will probably be gone. That's good. I can catch a plane back to Burbank. I can beat them to the office in the morning. I can be there when it all hits the fan."

"I said I'm sorry."

"If you cost me my job, I swear . . ." She stops short of issuing a threat. "I could get fired for this," she says, finally looking at me. "Are you happy?"

"What kind of question is that? Of course not."

She zips up her suitcase and grabs her purse. "I don't have time for this. I have to go save my ass. Right now. I'll talk to you later."

I try to calm her. "So I fucked up. Come on—don't be so dramatic. Let's just figure this out," I tell her.

But she's out the door. I follow her into the hallway and watch her race to the elevator, wheeling her red suitcase behind her. A few seconds later, she's gone. Just like everyone else in my life. She's gone.

I think about chasing her, but stop myself. She's not coming back. I return to my room, plop on the bed, and try to assess the damage. It ain't good—that's about all I can deduce. I try to calm myself by meditating, but it's useless. I feel like shit (as usual). I'm getting a headache. I'm drained and restless and pissed off at myself and pissed off at her for being pissed off at me. I need to blot this out. I need alcohol. I need music. I need a lap dance.

Thirteen

I decide to start a long evening of debauchery at the hotel bar near the lobby. I'm not about to venture out into the Vegas night without at least a couple shots of Jameson to light the way.

As I'm about to take a seat at the bar, the two huge security thugs who broke up the brawl between me and Randall Cleary approach. "Mr. Lonzi wants to see you," the bald one says.

Great. This is my chance to fix things, to get Eva off the hook. "Fantastic," I say. They march alongside me and lead me past the ballroom, through a service door, and down a long, bare white corridor behind a kitchen. Nick Lonzi paces at the other end of the hall.

"What's your angle, shitbird?" Lonzi asks.

"Angle?"

"You don't work at the L.A. *Times*. I already checked it out. So what were you doing in that interview?"

"I need to talk to you, Mr. Lonzi. It's important."

Lonzi laughs like he has it figured out. "You look like a self-centered little prick, so it can't be a charitable cause. Let me guess—a film script that needs financing. Or is it a bullshit web start-up that needs angel funding?"

"This is about Oliver."

He's rattled. "What about Oliver?" He gives me a menacing look. "Who are you?"

"Just let me explain—"

"What—are you planning some tell-all book. Go ahead fuck-bag—give it a try. I'll sick an army of lawyers on you so fast, your ass will petrify in a courtroom."

"I'm not writing a book."

Lonzi moves in close. "I want to know—who are you?"

"My name's Kane Pryce. I'm a paranormal investigator. I've been in contact with the spirit of your son."

Lonzi gets right in my face. "Look me in the eye, punk," he orders. His stare is vacant. A hollow chocolate bunny. "I am not fucking amused."

I wave my hands, trying to compose my words. "I know this sounds crazy. I'm trying to tell you that your son is haunting a church in Central California. I'd like to take you there to see for yourself. There's a chance you might be able to communicate with him."

Lonzi lets out a halfhearted chuckle. "All right boys, time to earn your pay."

The blond goon shoves me at the guard who's shaved bald. The bald one puts an armlock on me and applies pressure at the elbow. I bend at the waist as pain shoots up my arm and explodes in my shoulder. "Get off me!" I scream.

Lonzi grabs a handful of my hair and yanks my head back so our eyes meet. "Cross my path again and I'll end you," he whispers in my ear. He turns to his bodyguards. "Take this bum for a stroll and show him what a nice job we did with the concrete." His voice is powerful again.

Lonzi lets go of my hair and the security guard on top of me grabs a mittful and proceeds to run me fifteen feet down the hall, face-first into a cement block wall. Like a bolt of lightning struck me dead. I am gone.

———

I come to on my back outside on the pavement. A paramedic shines a light in my eye. I'm lost in a fog. I hear the sirens—see the flashing lights. I feel the vehicle's acceleration. Can't remember dick after my head met the wall. Must have dragged myself out a side door.

I'm sick. I think I threw up, but I'm not sure. Become more alert once I'm in the hospital. The fog is lifting. A nurse takes my blood pressure, and has a quick look at my pupils and the purple contusion on my forehead. The doctor enters. She's a sweet-looking Asian with her black silk hair in a ponytail. She examines me with a concerned look. She orders a CAT scan.

"No," I say. "I don't have health insurance and I can't get stuck with a pile of medical bills."

I look at her name tag—Doctor Chiu. She's insistent. "You've suffered a concussion," she says in English. "The tests are necessary to assess the severity of your injury."

No shit, Sherlock. So that's what tests are for? "Sorry, I can't afford them."

A cop in his forties—buzz cut and the beginnings of a beer gut—peels back the curtain and steps in. Introduces himself as Officer Stokes. Doctor Chiu gives me a nod. "I have to alert the police department when there's been an assault," she says. "Hospital policy."

"Tell me who assaulted you," the cop barks. "We need to establish if charges will be pressed." He takes out a notepad.

My words are jumbled at first, but as I slowly spell out what happened, I gather steam and get pissed off and energized. "Damn straight I want to press charges," I tell the cop when I'm done. "I want you to nail them all." Occurs to me then that the cop stopped taking notes the second I mentioned Lonzi.

I reach out and grab the sleeve of Doctor Chiu's white jacket. "Give me every test you can. Give me a pregnancy test for all I care. Send the bill to Nicholas Lonzi."

The cop waves the doctor out, but she stands her ground. Officer Stokes edges closer. "So let me understand this," he says. "You fell."

I chuckle. "Right."

The cop calmly says, "You drank too much at the lobby bar and fell when you got off your barstool and struck your head."

It's not a joke. "What is this?" I hiss. "What the fuck? Nicholas Lonzi . . ."

The cop nods. "I know who he is. His portrait's hanging upstairs in the lobby."

"Write his name down and report it," I demand. "If you can't write, I'll write it for you."

Officer Stokes grins. "I suppose I should cite you for public intoxication. There were witnesses—waitresses, a bartender, dealers." My pride stings worse than the contusion on my head. "But I think I can let you off tonight with a warning."

I laugh and tell him *fuck you* with my eyes. "Only in Vegas," I say.

"You have three seconds to accept my fair warning or I will arrest you. I will search you thoroughly. I can only imagine what I might find in your pockets—"

"Accepted," I say, before he counts to one.

Officer nods. "Good day, sir," he says with a smirk before ducking behind the curtain. The click of his boot heels trail off. Doctor Chiu looks at me with tears in her eyes. "I hate this town," she says. "I hate this hospital. I hate this country."

I hop off the gurney. "God bless America," I say.

She whips out her prescription pad. "Here, take this," she says handing me a prescription for Vicodin—with five refills! "Fill it here in the hospital pharmacy. They'll take care of you."

"Thanks," I say.

"Least I can do," she says. "I advise you again to see a neurologist when you get back to L.A. I recommend UCLA Medical Center. Any signs of memory loss, dizziness, nausea—get to an emergency room immediately."

The twenty-four-hour hospital pharmacy is a ghost town. Dr. Chiu drew a happy face on the prescription. When the pharmacist sees it, he fills it on the spot and doesn't charge a penny. Only in Vegas.

———

Cab it back to the Phoenician, arriving just before eleven. I march straight to the lobby bar and wash down two Vicodin with a double Jameson. I go to my room, collapse on the bed, and sleep twelve hours.

I'm on the road by noon, still woozy, but just clearheaded enough to drive. Still exhausted and in a Vicodin trance, I crank my tunes, drop the top, and let the hot desert air whip through the car as I burn down the I15. Don't stop for a piss break until I roll into Barstow on fumes. Fill up at a grimy truck stop and thumb through a revolving rack of CDs near the counter. Spot the unmistakable cover of *Layla and Other Assorted Love Songs*—the sultry sleepy-eyed blonde with half her face concealed by a bouquet of white roses. Feel like I'm looking at a friend and, on a whim, toss it in my backpack when the cashier turns his back. Feels good. Haven't shoplifted in years.

Down the street, I pass a roadhouse called the Slash X Ranch Cafe and pull in. It's a hole in the wall. Caps left by patrons adorn the rafters and two guitar-playing mannequins are perched on a ledge above the bar: a Mexican bandito and an old bearded cowboy that looks a hell of a lot like Skeeter Jackson.

Jung's synchronicity fucking with me again.

The bartender tells me he pours the coldest draft in Barstow. "I'll be the judge of that," I tell him, ordering a Bud and a cheeseburger.

The joint is nearly empty. One other patron, a woman, at the other end of the bar. I pop two Vicodins, wash them down with my beer, and order another, plus a shot of Wild Turkey. Then I have one of those moments where booze, drugs, injury, and depression collide all at once, leaving me trapped in twisted wreckage at a treacherous crossroads. I need the Jaws of Life—fast.

The woman gets off her stool and approaches. She's a drunk, nasty, old skank who smells like cheap bourbon and ass. "Wanna dance?"

The bar is silent. "Dance to what? There's no music," I say.

"Buy me a drink, give me five bucks, and I'll go play some," she says, pointing to the jukebox.

"Nah," I say.

"Come on, you're cute." She leans on me. I watch her hand rub my thigh.

I glance up. "Cute? I'm as ugly as John Merrick."

"Who?"

"The Elephant Man."

"Who's that?"

"An ugly guy with a beautiful soul. Died at 27."

"Whatever. Suit your fuckin' self." She wanders back to her barstool, finishes off her drink, and leaves.

Now I'm alone at the bar. I'm not even aware of exactly when I start to cry, but the tears flow and I can't stop. I bury my face in my hands and nominate myself for pussy of the month. Make that the year. This is ri-goddamn-diculous. Better be a concussion side effect. Get a grip, dude. At least none of the five other assholes chowing down in the dining room have a clear view of me while I bawl like a little bitch. A wave of anxiety pours over me and I drown in a sobering reality check. That prick Lonzi is no saint. He's hiding something. I know it. When I mentioned Ollie, it unsettled him something fierce. But if I go after him again, I'm in for big trouble. Guaran-fuckin'-teed.

What am I doing? What am I going to do?

The reality check gets personal—goes deep. I have nine grand to my name. With my worthless shopping spree in Vegas, I now have about eight grand of credit card debt. I'm lost. I'm scared. I'm not at all well, physically or emotionally. I'm alone. I spent last Christmas Eve at a titty bar in the valley getting lap-danced by a chubette in a Santa hat. I drink too much. Add Vicodin to the mix, and I'm vanishing down the drain.

I almost call Ned, then Eva. But they're there and I'm here and what's the fucking point? I'm disconnected from them both. Alone.

More often than not, I'm moody and cynical and mean.

I'm a selfish prick. At times, despicable. I've never done anything for anyone but myself.

The Vicodin kicks in and I'm floating upward, but I can't dig myself out of this pit of despair. I order my third beer and second shot of Turkey, look up at a dirty cap that says "Show me Yer Tits," glance over at Skeeter plucking away, and make a firm resolution: Someday—soon—I'll figure out what the fuck I'm going to do when I grow up.

When I stand and steady myself a half hour later, my body feels no pain. But my broken spirit aches. The drive home is a blur. Feels like I'm hang gliding all the way to Hollywood while I listen to "Layla" over and over again.

Fourteen

I spend two days on the sofa in a Vicodin stupor, too depressed and languid to venture out of my apartment. Eva calls a couple of times, leaves a message telling me to call her. So does Ned. I blow them off. There's a knock on my door. I ignore it.

I wander around my cramped little dump in a fog and nurse wounds of the body and soul with my prescription opiates, Jameson, Lean Pockets, Eric Clapton's autobiography, and Internet porn. I'm too lethargic to work on "Layla." These are not my brightest days.

I wake up from a nightmare on my second night back. Can't remember the dream. Something was stalking me and Ollie—bearing down on us. I clutched him and we started to fly but crashed to the earth.

Can't get back to sleep. Grab the Lonzi folder Eva gave me. Go right to the photo of Donna Lonzi. A woman from another time, another place. A knowing little smile. Great eyes. Perfect lipstick.

Who the hell does she remind me of? It's making me crazy.

Thumb through the articles and paperwork. Read the article from the sparse Las Vegas newspaper of the day about hers and Ollie's death again. Donna is survived by her husband, Nicholas

Lonzi, age 26, of Las Vegas, Nevada; her parents, Lucia and Peter Carbone of Lompoc, California; her sister, Rita Merrill; brother-in-law Sterling Merrill; and nephew, Daniel Merrill of Arcadia, California.

Another article, in the *Los Angeles Times*, mentions Donna's short foray into motion pictures. This spurs my curiosity enough for me to finally get off my ass and, after forty-eight hours of Vicodin darkness, turn the light switch in my brain back on. I type the name Donna Lonzi into Google. Lots of Donna Lonzis, but not my Donna Lonzi. Then I type Donna Carbone. Find someone on linkedin.com. Obviously not her. Then a link to IMDb. Found her. Entry is light.

> DATE OF BIRTH: June 28, 1930, Goleta, California.
> DATE OF DEATH: December 11, 1957, Lompoc, California.
> TRIVIA: Married to legendary Las Vegas baron, Nicholas Lonzi.
> FILMOGRAPHY: 1949: *The Crooked Way*; 1949: Red Light; 1950: *In a Lonely Place* (a Bogart film); 1955: *Sudden Danger.*

Never saw or heard of any of these movies. I look closer—she only had bit parts.

I'm intrigued. Skip my morning dose of Vicodin. Can only buy the Bogart movie on Amazon or Netflix. These must have been B-minus movies. A couple of them are up for auction on eBay, but that will take too long. I want to see them now. Google around on the web—find a place in Silver Lake called Video Journeys that claims to have a big film noir collection available for rental. Ready to take a drive.

Video Journeys takes up the entire second floor of a strip mall at the corner of Griffith Park Boulevard and Hyperion. About half a football field of movies: current, classic, cult, noir, obscure, and XXX. I nab *In a Lonely Place* and *Red Light*. No go on the other two.

The owner has a private stash of noir. He has *The Crooked Way*. Offers to dupe it for me for ten bucks. I buy it.

I buy a six-pack of Harp and a bag of Doritos at the liquor mart below Video Journeys and race back to my apartment. Dig into Donna's movies chronologically. First up: *The Crooked Way*. Pretty cheesy. A World War deuce vet suffers from amnesia. Returns from Germany to L.A. to try to reclaim his identity. Turns out he was a two-timing gangster with a list of enemies longer than Tommy Lee's schlong. They all come gunning for him. Great scene in a carnival. Mr. Amnesia walks up to a shooting gallery and—there she is! Donna. Living, breathing. I'm stunned, cemented in my chair. Donna saunters up to him and hands him a play rifle. "Three bull's-eyes win a prize," she says. Her voice is low, soft, and sexy. She smiles—a little smirk that evolves and grows into a warm, inviting grin. She lights up the scene. Wow.

And that's it. Five seconds later, while Mr. Amnesia aims his shot, a gangster pops up from behind a barrel in the gallery and takes a real shot at him. Donna screams and runs for cover. Chase scene through the carnival. I fast forward through the rest of it. That's it for Donna.

Red Light is a decent little revenge story. Raymond Burr plays Nick, a guy in prison for embezzlement who gets revenge against his former boss by having the boss's brother, a priest, bumped off. The priest—with his dying breath—tells his brother that the clue to his killer can be found in the Bible from the hotel room he got shot in. So begins a big cat and mouse between the conspirator, the murderer, and the business owner, all intent on getting that Bible.

A couple of scenes play out in a little diner. Donna plays a friendly waitress. I watch her three scenes over and over. There's that voice. A little hip sway as she carries a tray of food. There's that smile again—it just grows and grows. She should have been a star.

In a great scene in *In a Lonely Place*, Bogart plays Dix Steele (how's that for a name?), a washed-up screenwriter with a violent temper. Bogie goes ape-shit during a road-rage incident, drags a guy out of his convertible, and puts a serious ass-kicking on him.

Donna plays the guy's sweetheart. She leaps out of the car and screams for the police. Her black hair, pulled into a long ponytail, sways from side to side as she runs offscreen. That's it—short and sweet.

Though I watch Donna in these scenes over and over, it's not enough. I need to find *Sudden Danger*. There's a homemade DVD up for sale on eBay. I contact the owner via email. Ask him to call off the auction. The only bidders might be a handful of film noir buffs. Offer him forty bucks. He accepts. Pay with PayPal. It'll take about four days to get here.

Seeing Donna. Hearing her voice. It somehow inspires me to pick up my guitar and work on "Layla." I'm just about ready to start recording the guitar parts. I get right back into my playing, all the while watching Donna on my TV and computer screens.

There's a knock on my door. I turn off my amp, pause the scene of Donna in the shooting gallery on my TV. It's Eva.

She came back.

I let her in.

"What happened to your head?" she asks.

I tell her.

"What?" she says, shocked. "I don't believe it."

"What—you think I did this to myself?" I ask, annoyed.

"No," she says, touching my black-and-blue forehead. "I mean I just can't believe this guy who's supposed to be a philanthropist is a . . ." She's searching for the right words.

"An egomaniacal thug," I say.

"Right," she says. "He has the world fooled."

I get her a beer. I'm a little distant—cool. It's not an act. I apologized once. Not doing it again.

"What did the doctor say?" she asks.

"She told me to see a neurologist."

"And . . . have you?"

I shake my head.

"Why?" she demands to know.

"I don't know."

"You're going for a follow-up," she says sternly. "I'll go with you."

"We'll see." Go with me? What is this? She acts like she really cares. I think I have a dopey smile on my face.

"Did you read the *Times* yesterday?" she asks.

"No."

"The Lonzi story ran. Calendar section."

"How'd it turn out?"

"Made him out to be more saintly than Mother Teresa. But it worked."

"Yeah?"

"Michael Douglas read it—contacted us. I put him in touch with Lonzi. They're going to throw a big fund-raiser at The Beverly Hills Hotel in August."

"So you're off the hook?" I ask.

"All is well," she replies.

An uneasy silence crackles. "Look," she says. "I'm sorry if I was . . . abrupt . . . when I left."

"Abrupt . . . and angry," I add.

"I'm an emotional person."

"Nah . . . really?" I ask sarcastically. Then with a little smile meant to test the waters I say, "It was justified. I did fuck things up pretty royally."

Eva returns the smile. "God, when you mentioned his son . . ." She laughs and cringes at the same time.

"So we're cool?"

"We're cool."

Eva drinks her beer. Notices the frozen images of Donna Lonzi on my TV and computer. "What this?" she asks.

"It's Donna Lonzi. She had a few bit parts in movies."

"And you went out and found the films?"

I nod.

"Why?" she asks a little too sarcastically.

"Because I'm interested," I reply, a little too defensively. I press Play. The carnival shooting gallery scene plays. Eva snickers. "Not much of an actress," she says when the scene ends.

Not sure why, but that snicker and comment offend me. "I think she's pretty good," I say. "Definitely has presence."

"In the thirty seconds she's on screen?" Eva asks. "Sorry, not seeing it."

I turn off the TV.

"So now what?" Eva asks.

"Now, we dig a little deeper into Lonzi's past," I propose. "He's hiding something—I know it."

"And he's violent," Eva adds, looking at my bruise. "Definitely not Mother Teresa."

"I know that's how these old school Vegas guys make their point," I say. "Lonzi grew up under Bugsy Siegel's wing. Look how that guy settled disputes." I kick it around in my mind, remember that vacant look in Lonzi's eyes. "I'm telling you. Something's not right with him."

"All right," Eva says. "I'll see if I can find out anything else about him."

"Thanks," I say. Ollie pops into my mind. "I want to go back to the church in Lompoc—ask Ollie about his dad."

"Can I go along?" Eva asks eagerly.

"Sure. Be here at ten tomorrow," I tell her.

She asks me if I want to grab a drink and I turn her down. I must be crazy. I tell her I still have a few cobwebs. I'm not lying. She leaves.

Before I plug my guitar back in and get lost, I dial Ned.

"Where the fuck have you been?" he shouts at me.

"In a semiconscious state." I tell him what happened. It doesn't seem to register. He's furious. "Don't ever do that again," he orders. "No radio silence—ever!" He sounds like an angry dad enforcing a curfew.

"Come on," I say with a laugh. "It's no big deal."

"It is a big deal. I thought you were in trouble . . . or worse. Why would you do that?"

"I had a concussion. I didn't feel like talking," I answer, honestly.

"Sometimes, you can be such a selfish prick," he says. "You don't do that to people."

"Whatever," I snap. "Sorry." Silence. "We're going back to the church tomorrow," I continue. "Eva's going with us. You in?"

"I'm in."

"Ten A.M.?"

"Fine."

No jokes. No smart-ass remarks. No ball-busting. I forgot that he really cares. I screwed up . . . again . . . as usual.

I lay out the newspaper photos of Donna and Ollie Lonzi around my guitar stand, plug in my Fender, set up my microphones, launch Pro Tools on my Mac, prepare for a few complaints from my neighbors, and commence rerecording "Layla" track by track.

Fifteen

The next morning, I'm exhausted and my fingertips are blistered. Stayed up until four in the morning. Started editing and mixing a few half-decent guitar parts. I'm drained.

On the ride north, I'm a zombie. Still haven't shaken my melancholy. Barely engage in the conversation during the ride. Ned and Eva debate Arnold Schwarzenegger's stint as governor. Ned's a card-carrying member of the Terminator hater club. She digs what the governor did in office.

Eva looks hotter than sin in her cargo pants, Paul Frank monkey tee, and Vans. Another chance to charm her, but I'm too disconnected. Another world away. Ned's holding his own with her. They can both be a little strong—dare I say, a tad grating. Can't say I'm surprised they're getting along.

They're having a smart-sounding conversation about corruption in the LAPD. Should join in. I have an opinion or two about the cops, but just can't muster the energy. Instead, I check out, don my earbuds, and sink into Radiohead's *OK Computer*. Sad music for my sad, sorry ass. I'm coming off like an antisocial freak. Can't help it. Can't stop myself. I don't feel like hearing my voice—or theirs, for that matter.

Ned tries to bully us into brunch at the Solvang Restaurant, but I nix the idea and wink to Eva for support. "You're wearing sweatpants," I tease him. "You can't be seen in public like that. We'll grab some grub *after* our work is finished. I'll even buy . . . to make up for the radio silence." Ned smiles. "Sorry about that." He nods at me. No further words need be spoken.

Father Demetrius seems more relaxed than the last time we met. He pulls me aside and whispers, "You know, Kane, I took your advice and assumed a friendly posture with . . . whatever lurks here."

"And?"

"It seems to have worked," the priest says. "Do you know, the ghost actually helped me extinguish the candles on the altar yesterday? I thanked it for its help and it rang the bells."

On cue, a bell in the tower tolls three times.

"My word," the priest says, startled.

I chuckle, mumble to myself, "Attaboy, Ollie."

The priest hands me the church key. "I'm closing the church to the public today, so you'll be free to investigate."

As soon as Father Demetrius exits, the paranormal activity begins. Ollie is present.

Ollie and I seem to have a strong bond. There are brief seconds when I can hear him without a digital recorder and see him in shadowy form without a thermal cam. I can't explain why. Neither Ned or Eva can see or hear a thing. Maybe it's because of the time Ollie and I spent together in the trap. Or maybe because he's the only spirit that I ever released and didn't banish. Who knows? It might be as simple as I just kind of like the kid.

Ned ducks out to the camper to do some work. Eva takes a seat in the choir loft, observes, and writes. Me? I need to make

Ollie feel comfortable so I can ease him back into the trap. So I play.

We start in the bell tower. Lucky Bear stands guard just where I left him. It's an episode of *Name that Tune*. I call the song, Ollie plays it clumsily on the bells. Eva pops her head in and then shakes it in disbelief. The playlist, in order, is: "London Bridge," "Row, Row, Row Your Boat," and "Happy Birthday."

We play kickball next. It's more of a balloon than a firm ball— light and airy. Ollie might be able to more easily move it. Me first. I boot the ball from one end of the church to the other. He seems to struggle to move the ball even an inch at first, but in no time, he's gaining power and using his energy to send the ball sailing. He even boots one all the way up to the choir loft and sends Eva ducking for cover. "Hey, watch it," she shouts with a laugh. "You almost nailed me in the head!"

We have a blast on the church organ. By the time we're done, we have *The Lone Ranger* theme—the William Tell Overture—down pat. The one-note version, at least. "Hi oh, Silver . . . away!" I hear Ollie call out in a ghostly echo.

"Did you hear that?" I shout to Eva.

"I think I heard something," she yells back from the choir loft.

When I was the kid's age, I always bugged my dad to race. He always won. "Okay, Ollie, first one from the altar to the bells wins."

"Okay," I hear faintly.

"Ready, dude?" I ask. "On your mark . . . get set . . . go!" I sprint, but before I reach the first step on the spiral staircase to the bell tower, a bell tolls.

"I win!" I hear him shout.

I laugh and congratulate him. Damn. A six-year-old kid can really wear you out.

"Again," I hear him implore. But I propose something else. I speak loudly and clearly. My voice echoes off the roof. "Ollie? I'm stoked to talk to you again, like we did last time."

An unusual, eerie silence. Eva leans over the rail of the choir loft.

I raise my hands in reassurance. "I know you're worried about leaving and missing your mother, but my friend Eva will stay here while you and I talk. If your mom shows up, Eva will come and get us."

Silence.

"What do you say?"

An energy whooshes by me, the hair on my arms and neck stand up, and I hear his ghostly voice whisper, "Okey-dokey."

"Stand by the organ and be very still," I tell him. "Play me a song while I go get something." While I'm taking the trap out of the case and powering it up, Ollie plays "Heart and Soul."

The trap hums and vibrates in my hand and the target acquisition tone rings out instantly. Fire. The sound scares Eva shitless. She screams from the choir loft. "It's all right," I yell up at her.

I can hear her footsteps echoing from the loft down the staircase in a hurry. When she meets me in the center of the church, she's winded. "That's the most terrifying sound I've ever heard," she says.

"But it's a good sound. Means I got him," I tell her.

"Now what?

"Now, I go in."

"Here?"

"In the camper. Come on."

Ned is huddled over his keyboard in the camper, lost in code.

I kick the table leg to get his attention. "What have you been doing in here all day?"

Ned is way in the zone. Deep. When he gets like this, he doesn't even know you're around.

"I said, what have you been doing?"

He continues typing for another half minute before finally acknowledging us. "I've been baking brownies, what do you think? I decided to make some adjustments."

"What kind of adjustments?"

"Mostly media scripts in the Cornerstone program. Graphic and audio assets. You'll see . . ." He's giddy, full and proud of himself. "God, I haven't touched that portion of the code since 1985. If it works, you and your little friend will love it."

Now I'm intrigued. "What did you do?"

Ned just smiles.

Eva watches me get wired up for my journey. As always, she jots in her notebook. As I'm about to don my helmet and goggles, she touches my arm and I get butterflies, I'm ashamed to admit. "Good luck."

"Thanks, Eva." I look in her eyes. I want to apologize for being aloof and moody. Wanna tell her she's pretty damn cool. And hot. What do I do instead? Gawk and stammer, "Thanks for being here." Fuckin' weak, dude.

The electrical current catches me off-guard. Tickles. Begins flowing around and down me and in less than twenty minutes, I'm in.

Even before I open my eyes, I sense the radical changes. Echoey yet whimsical calliope music has replaced the electric drone and far-off clang. I open my eyes and shield my vision. Bright lights. What the fuck? Eyes focus slowly. Looks like the Disney Channel meets Nickelodeon in here. New look, but same layout. Pulsating, warm, and welcoming primary colors. Looks like Crayola did the paint job. Flashing images on the walls of characters from the '50s—Bugs Bunny, Yosemite Sam, Road Runner, Howdy Doody, the Lone Ranger. A re-skinned table and chairs right out of Toontown. Sweet! How the hell did Ned pull this off?

Ollie, wearing his Lone Ranger mask, smiles at me from a plush purple-and-blue Cheshire-cat chair.

I smile back. "Yo—ollie ollie oxen free."

Ollie stands. "Kane, Kane . . ." He's stuck, searching for a comeback. It's on the tip of his tongue—then, with a giggle, he sing-songs, "Kane, Kane, the big fat pain." His giggle turns into a laugh. "That was the best day ever."

"I had fun, too." I raise my hand. "High five." Ollie freezes. Right. 1957.

"Raise your hand," I order. I slap his palm with mine. "That's called a high five."

"Neat," says Ollie.

"Cool."

Ollie jumps in place and starts chattering away like he just chugged a six-pack of Red Bull. Without a pause, he fires off a shopping list of questions. "Did you see how close the ball came to Eva? Did you see how fast I ran to the bell tower? Did you like how I splashed the holy water? Were you scared when I made the statue move?"

"I—"

"Doesn't the statue of the pretty lady remind you of my mommy?"

"I've never met—"

"That was super swell playing the organ like that. Do you watch *The Lone Ranger*, too?"

He finally stops to catch his breath. "So you're finally gonna let me talk?" I milk a long pause. "Wow. Okay. I like *The Lone Ranger*."

"He's my hero," Ollie says. "He's way better than Superman."

"How come you like him so much?" I ask.

"Because he's a good guy."

"Yeah."

"And he fights the bad guys," Ollie adds.

"Good guys and bad guys," I say.

"I'm a good guy. You're a good guy, huh, Kane?"

The jury sure as hell said I'm not—more than once. "I try to be," I say.

"Did you ever fight a bad guy?" he asks.

"Oh, yeah. Just ran into one."

"Then that makes you a good guy. Just like I figured."

I gesture for Ollie to sit and pull up a blue caterpillar couch and plop down on it next to him. "Let's just take a breather . . . and talk."

"What do you want to talk about?"

"Tell me about your mommy."

He takes off his mask and his eyes light up. "She's the best mommy ever." The light extinguishes a second later. "I miss her a lot."

"She told you she'd come back for you?"

"She promised. She told me to never walk through the light door. Not until she came back."

"Do you know where your mommy is?"

"No. She said she had to go away for a while."

Time to step onto the thin ice. I reach over and pat the top of his head. A clumsy effort. No damn good at this. "Ollie, this is important. I want you to think hard."

He nods.

"Do you remember being in an accident?"

He squints. "Maybe."

"Tell me."

He gets all fidgety, like he's holding in a monster pee. He puts on his mask, seems to struggle to recall. "I think I remember scary sounds. . . . Mommy being scared . . . screechy sounds . . ." He's getting scared, agitated.

I take him by the hand. "I know this is tough, kid. You're doing great. I'm proud of you. Think hard."

Ollie squeezes my hand. "I remember . . . bad shadows . . . a nice man in a white suit taking me and Mommy to this church."

A white suit? A church. Was it an angel? Do angels actually exist? I'm so excited by the notion, I squeeze his hand, probably a little too hard.

He pulls his hand from mine. His fear turns to anger. "I remember losing my favorite thing in the whole wide world."

"What?"

"My Lone Ranger deputy badge. It fell in the sand. Mommy pulled me away before I could pick it up." His anger transforms to sadness in a single instant. He cries. "If only I had my badge, I could have fought those bad guys." He buries his head in his hands. A few quick, intense sobs, then he raises his head as if a lightbulb went off. "Can you get me back my badge, Kane?"

"I don't know, Ollie." His bottom lip quivers. "Maybe," I say.

A look of hope. "That'd be swell," he says through sniffles.

"Do you remember your dad?"

"A little. He's tall. He's gone a lot." Ollie's giving his memory a serious workout. "He and Mommy yell at each other—a lot. I don't like that."

The thin ice might just crack on this one. "Was he mean to you?"

Ollie stares at his feet and taps his sneakers together. "Sometimes." Tears well up in his eyes. "But he's gone now."

I pat his shoulder. "That's okay. My dad went away, too . . . and I never saw him again either."

He shoots me the saddest little smile. "Really?"

"Really."

"Me and my dad never had fun like I had with you today."

That's when he hits me with it.

"Maybe you can be my daddy."

I don't know what to say. So I don't say anything. That's my style. Weak. I've pestered the kid enough for one day. I change the subject. "Ollie, I'm going to send you back into the church."

"Okay."

"Did you see Lucky Bear?"

"Yeah," Ollie says. "I like him."

"Good."

Ollie stands and hugs me. "You'll be back, right?" He looks so desperate.

"I'll be back." I hope my nose doesn't grow. Don't know if I can do this again. Not built for it. But if this is the last time I see him, I want to leave him with a good memory. "Before I go, I have a surprise for you."

"What?"

"You'll see." My exit door appears. "Meet me in the church," I say before stepping through.

I hurl as soon as I come to. Good thing Ned is waiting by my side with a trash bag. "Sorry you have to see this, Eva," I add.

"You okay?" she asks.

"It happens a lot," I say. "It's a rough trip."

I salute Ned. "Nice job on the décor, bro."

"Liked it?" he asks.

"Hell, yeah. And so'd the kid."

Takes me a good ten minutes to stop puking and get to my feet. On our way back to the church, I tell Ned and Eva, "Something's not right with Nick Lonzi. I know it. We have to dig harder."

They both nod in agreement, but I can tell they don't believe me. They think I'm overreacting—that it's personal. It's not. I'm right.

For the second time, I release Ollie from the trap. Can feel his presence right next to me when I take a seat in a pew near the front of the church, set up my iPad, and launch one of the videos I just downloaded. Got the idea when I was searching around for Donna Lonzi's movies. Seasons one and two of *The Lone Ranger*. When I launch episode one, I'm the only one who hears, "Yippee!"

First three episodes are the origin of the Lone Ranger, and damn if I'm not hooked ten minutes in. Ollie and I watch, side by side, as Texas Ranger John Reid fashions a black mask from the vest of his dead brother and becomes the Lone Ranger, meets Tonto, rescues Silver from a buffalo, forges his silver bullets, and teams up with Sheriff "Two-Gun" Taylor to take on the Cavendish gang.

Sometime during episode four, I drift off. An hour or so later, I wake up to find Ned standing over me with an EMF detector.

"What are you doing?" I ask, groggy and still a little sick to my stomach.

He waves the detector right next to me and it spikes. Eva leans over the pew behind us and smiles. "He's sleeping right next to you," Ned says. "Freakin' amazing."

I wake up Ollie when I stand up and stretch. Kid must be a light sleeper—afraid to miss his mom. "Gotta go now, Ollie," I say to the air around me. "See you next time."

I drop off the key to Father Demetrius and tell him I'm making progress, but the ghost is still there. An idea pops into my head on the way back to the camper.

"Let's go eat," Ned says as soon as I step inside. "We'll get you that ostrich burger."

"I want to make a stop first," I say.

"Where?" asks Eva.

"Honda Point."

"Destroyer Rock?" she asks.

"Yep. It's only a mile away."

"What for?"

I glance over at Ned. "You thinking what I'm thinking?"

"Donna Lonzi," he says.

"Right."

"You think she's still there?" Eva asks.

"Worth a shot," I say. "You still got that metal detector in here?" I ask Ned.

"Yeah," Ned answers. "So?"

"I'll explain later." Ned'll laugh and bust my balls if I tell him I want to do something nice for that poor kid. Probably a long shot, but maybe I can find that Lone Ranger badge that means the world to him.

And maybe—just maybe—Donna Lonzi's there, waiting for a man like me.

Sixteen

Ned, Eva, and I reach the cliffs above the accident site just after dusk. The sunset is gorgeous, but there's no easy way down to the rocky shore below. No stairs, no paved path—just a crude foot trail down a hundred feet to the beach through thick brush and exposed roots clinging to the cliff walls. Even in the day, with hiking boots, this would be tricky. In my leather boots, it's probably impossible.

As Eva and I breathe in the salt air and watch the sun trickle into the sea and the sky dissolve from orange to blue in a matter of minutes, Ned bounces out of the camper carrying a handheld megaspotlight he claims is from his deer hunting days. Major wattage that lights up the cliffside path and the crashing waves below. "It's gonna take courage and agility to make it to the bottom of this cliff," Ned says, "neither of which I possess. You two youngins inch your way down. I'll stay up here and thank God I'm neither one of you."

Ned hands me his metal detector. It's bottom heavy and awkward. "How am I supposed to get down there with this thing and the trap?"

"What do you need it for anyway?" Ned demands to know.

"I'm looking for something. I'll explain later."

Ned, always up for a challenge, goes back inside the camper and reemerges a few minutes later with a bungee cord that he fashions into makeshift carrying straps for the detector and the trap. He positions the load across my back and straps it tight with more cord until the weight is evenly balanced. He shoves a little garden shovel in the back pocket of my jeans.

"I can't believe you have a fucking metal detector in the camper," I say.

"I have everything in there."

"Except an air freshener."

"You know how to use a metal detector?" he asks in that parental tone I hate.

I roll my eyes. "Do I look like a senior citizen on the beach?"

Ned snaps his fingers and demands attention. "It's so simple, that even a young, fragile mind like yours can grasp it. Turn it on. When you're over something metal, it'll beep. Think you can handle that, dipshit?"

I turn to Eva. "You up for it?"

"Lead the way," she says.

We inch our way down like a pair of three-toed sloths, one step at a time, balancing ourselves on some of the steep drops with our hands. "You cool, Eva?"

"Right behind you."

Ned, perched atop the cliff above us, inches the spotlight with precision so that our next few steps are always illuminated.

"Looking good, guys," Ned yells when we reach the halfway point.

On a steep descent, my boots slip out from under me, rocks cascade over the cliff, and I skid fifteen feet down the path on my knees, stopping just short of a nasty drop-off.

"You all right?" an anxious Eva asks from above me.

"I'm okay. Be careful there."

Ned shouts down, "Don't fuck up."

"You're a real pal, Ned," I shout back.

"And don't forget it," Ned retorts. "I'm a real friend—flesh and blood. Not like those virtual ones you make on Facebook."

I'm about to look up and flip him the bird when my feet slip out from under me again. Whoa. This time I slide down the path on my stomach, but regain my footing quickly. About twenty feet to go.

"Hey, Kane," Ned shouts, "if you die, can I have that cool pair of boots with the silver-skull buckles?"

Eva laughs, but not really. "Why won't he shut the hell up and let us concentrate?" she asks.

"Because he's Ned."

I hit the beach and reach up and pull Eva down into my arms. We're standing in a horseshoe curve with a narrow beach. A dozen or more jagged rocks jut out of the surf like fangs. Not a pedestrian beach—that's for damn sure. Ours are probably the only footprints this sand has ever seen.

"Thanks for guiding me down," Eva says.

"No problem," I say. "It wasn't that bad. I got to look up and stare at your ass a couple of times."

"Oh really?" she says with a smirk. "Better focus on the task at hand instead."

"Hard to do when you're around," I say nonchalantly as I unstrap the metal detector and soul trap from my back and turn it on. I look back at Eva, who is still smiling. The Nick Lonzi debacle is far behind us.

Eva takes a seat on a rock and holds the trap as I comb the narrow shoreline inch by inch. "What are you looking for?" she asks.

I'm evasive. "Nothing."

"Tell me."

"Something that belonged to Ollie."

As I scan the sand near a boulder in the surf covered with a cluster of mussels, I can't shake the feeling that something is watching us from the darkness. I'm getting pretty damn good at recognizing this feeling. I don't mention it to Eva. Don't want her to panic.

The metal detector beeps.

"Find something?" Eva shouts from the rocks.

"Yeah, give me a sec—" I take the shovel out of my pocket, dig, and feel something big. I yank it from the sand. It's heavy.

"What is it?" Eva calls.

Ned shines the light right on it. "An old Chevy hubcap. Probably from Donna Lonzi's car."

I inch my way back toward Eva and the metal detector beeps again. This time it's a Ben Franklin half-dollar.

"Any luck?" Eva yells.

"Nope." I'm about to call it quits and commence a search on eBay, but a series of beeps stops me cold when I'm five feet from the rock Eva is sitting on. I shovel clumps of sand into my palm and sift through it with my fingers. In the third clump, I unearth a five-pointed silver star. I brush away the sand and it sparkles in the spotlight. Fake gems at the star points. A mask. And the words *Lone Ranger Deputy*. "Bingo."

Eva leaps off the rock. "You found it?"

"Yep," I say, handing it to her. "A little rusty, but I can shine it up."

She seems touched. "And he had this with him the night of the accident?"

"Yep."

She gets misty. "That's so sad." I pocket the badge along with the shovel.

An arctic winds blows past us with a whoosh.

"What was that?" Eva asks, alarmed. The trap vibrates madly in Eva's hands. She panics and drops it, but I drop to my knees and catch it before it hits the sand.

"It's picking up a soul," I say, excited. "This must be Donna Lonzi."

The frigid wind gust cuts through us again. "I'm freezing. The hair is standing up on the back of my neck and on my arms," Eva says, now terrified. She grabs my hand and I can feel her pulse racing.

"That's the soul," I reassure her. "They draw the energy around them when they try to manifest. Creates cold spots and sends electromagnetic charges."

Eva gasps like a bucket of ice water got tossed on her. She tears up, "The spirit—just passed right through me."

I hear a voice, electrically charged, barely audible. Can't distinguish if it's male or female through the static. Sounds something like, "Respect. Or repent."

"Did you hear that?" I asks Eva.

"I didn't hear anything."

The trap's monitor kicks on and the targeting program auto-launches. I take deep breaths and fight the urge to aim the trap myself. I let the unseen force target the soul left and right, up and down, for well over a minute. Whatever it is, it doesn't like having a weapon pointed at it. It jets around, soaring up and out of range time and again. Damn. I can't find two fixed points where I can lay down a phantom fence to pen it in. After several minutes of maddening cat and mouse, the crosshairs on the monitor finally flash. I pull the trigger fast. The entire shore lights up like a fireworks display on Chinese New Year and the unmistakable sound of a trapped soul thunders and echoes off the rocky cliffs surrounding us.

"Got it!"

The spotlight goes haywire. "Sorry, I dropped it," Ned says. "Scared the shit out of me. Did you capture one?" he asks.

I shout up, "Yeah."

Ned howls with laughter, yells down, "Leave you two alone for a couple of minutes and look at the trouble you get into."

"Do you think it's Donna Lonzi?" Eva asks.

"I have a hunch," I say. "We're gonna find out—right now."

Eva restraps the trap and the metal detector to my back and we begin our ascent. The climb up is tricky, but a hell of a lot easier than the descent. When we're halfway up, Ned tosses down a rope that he tied off around a tree trunk near the cliff edge. We pull ourselves up slowly and cautiously. When we reach the top, I march straight to the camper. "I'm going in," I announce.

"You got a screw loose," Ned barks. "Two trips inside in one day! In case you hadn't noticed, it fries your nervous system. For all we know, it could kill you."

"Dude, just get me in there," I snap. "Save the lecture."

Eva seems spooked. "Maybe you should listen to Ned—"

No way. What did one of the caps above that bar in Barstow say? *Git-r-done.* "End of conversation," I say.

Ned reluctantly powers up the equipment and hurls the bungee cords out the camper door in anger. "Fine. I'm done arguing, you stubborn ass."

"That's a first," I say, jabbing him.

Ned gives me a pleading look. "It's your life, kid. If you wanna risk it, I can't stop you."

I ignore him, recline on the camper bed, wire myself up, and begin the entry routine. I balance my breath easily and I'm ready to project, but Ned drags his feet at the computer.

"What's taking so long?" I ask, yanking my helmet and goggles off in annoyance. "Be patient," Ned barks. "I had to readjust the media settings. It's back to interrogation central," he says.

"You can change the look that fast?"

"I can now. The way I set it up, I can change it while you're in there," he brags. "You ready?"

"Pumped and ready," I say, donning my helmet and goggles and repeating the breathing and meditation exercises.

I'm gone in record time.

Seventeen

My mood sinks. Damn. It's not Donna Lonzi. A middle-aged sailor—gray hair and bushy eyebrows, tall—sits calmly behind the metal table beneath the interrogation light. He wears a white Navy uniform and a cocked cap adorned with a gold eagle and leaves on the cap's bill. Three yellow stripes topped with a single gold star are stitched in the fabric just above the wrists of his jacket sleeves. Two gold pins—an eagle and an anchor—are affixed to the high collar of his uniform jacket.

Disappointing as it is—it makes perfect sense. Honda Point was the location of an epic naval disaster in the '20s. Read all about it after Eva and Ned mentioned it that night in my apartment.

I approach him, dejected and anxious to get this over with quickly. "What's your story, sailor?" I quip, flopping down on the chair across from him and slamming my boots down on the tabletop.

The sailor stands and shoves my feet off the table. He looks at me like I'm a kid he's getting ready to spank. Points a finger in my face. "Young man, you will show me respect and address me by my proper rank and title. Are we clear?" He speaks clearly, confidently, with a velvety Southern accent.

Did I mention I pretty much hate everyone? That includes authority figures in any manner of uniform. I'm a centimeter from asking him how Popeye is, but, for once, I shut the hell up. Some ghosts hang around simply because they're confused or don't completely realize they're dead. I'll play it nice and respectful . . . until I know a little more.

"Are we clear?" he repeats.

"Sir, yes, sir," I say with a hair of sarcasm. I salute him for good measure, then extend my hand. "I'm Kane Pryce."

He clears his throat. "I am Commodore Edward H. Watson, sir."

Wow. I know the name. The big cheese himself. "I know about you. You were the commander of the mission that ran aground at Honda Point."

The commodore nods. "And I have accepted full responsibility for that mishap."

He speaks the truth. Wikipedia says Watson and his crew were experimenting with radio navigation, but the old hands in command of some of the ships didn't trust this new technology and dissension erupted. Entire crews were fighting among themselves. By the time they began negotiating the treacherous waters near Honda Point, it was an all-out clusterfuck. Some were navigating by dead reckoning, others by radio. Seven ships ended up running aground on the rocks and shore where I trapped Watson's soul. Even though events spun way out his control, and a lot of people besides him were to blame, Watson took the heat. Every last bit of it.

"Why are you still on the beach?" I ask. "Didn't you die years after the disaster, in Brooklyn?"

Watson eyes me suspiciously. "I passed away in nineteen hundred and forty-two," he says with that accent. "But my conscience wouldn't allow me to leave this earthly realm until I returned here and freed the souls of some of the sailors who lost their lives in the mishap and remained bound to these shores."

"That was an honorable thing to do." I say.

"Sir, it was my duty."

"But you were court-martialed. I read about it. You took full responsibility and saw to it that none of your subordinates were blamed or punished, even though they damn well deserved it. You paid for your mistake."

"Not in my mind," Watson says. "I could not rest until the souls of these men moved on."

"Did they?"

Watson nods. "I am pleased to say that over time, they have all passed through their doors."

I'm impressed. Hailing from Los Angeles, I don't meet many men of honor. "And you've been here, on the seashore, since your death?"

"I have."

Might be a long shot, but I have to ask. "Do you remember a car crash on the site? A woman and her son?"

Watson nods without hesitation. "I do," he says with his charming Southern drawl. "That was a long time ago. What an ordeal it was." Watson seems surprised. "How do you know about that?" he asks.

"I've met the soul of the boy."

Watson uncrosses his legs and leans forward in his chair. He's curious—concerned. "Is he safe in the church?"

He knows where Ollie is. Watson's white uniform hits me like a high beam. The nice man in the white suit. "You took him to that church," I say. "Please—tell me what you know."

Watson breaks eye contact and glances down at his buffed shoes. "That was the night I encountered pure evil."

"What do you mean?"

"When the car crashed into the rocky surf," Watson says, simulating the arc of the car hurtling over the cliff with his outstretched hand, "demons from hell surrounded the spirits of the mother and the boy."

"Demons?"

"Don't make me repeat it." There's fear in the commodore's voice. "My men and I intervened, but the demons were too powerful. My men, however, kept these intruders at bay long enough for me to guide the mother and her son to the church."

"And you made it there safely."

Watson's voice goes from fearful to angry. "But the demons followed us and used trickery to lure the boy from the sanctuary of the church."

"But he's still there," I say, puzzled. "What happened?"

"When one of the demons seized her son, the mother made a deal with him. She offered to surrender herself to him fully if the demon agreed to spare her son. A deal was struck. Before leaving with him, the mother warned the boy to never leave the church . . . unless she came back for him."

"Then they took her?" I ask.

Watson's anger turns to sorrow. "She left willingly, quite courageously . . . and they dragged her back to hell with them."

"Oh, no." My mind races to Ollie waiting day and night for his mother. "That poor kid," I say, resting my head in my hands and rubbing my temples. I look at Watson. "She's gone?" I ask, already knowing the answer.

"I'm afraid so," Watson says with regret. "I couldn't stop them."

Jesus. She sacrificed herself to save her kid. What a woman. She's already stuck in my mind. Now she's gonna haunt me. I have to know more. "What do you remember about her?" I ask him.

Watson ponders for a few silent seconds, looks at me, and says, "Mostly I remember how selfless she was. She only thought about protecting her child. She gave her soul to save her son. And once he was safe in the church . . ." He pauses. His deep Southern voice cracks with emotion. "Here was this beautiful young woman who should have lived a long and happy life. Not only dead, but dragged to hell by demons who would surely torture her for eternity. She . . ." Watson doesn't want to continue, but I look straight at him and my eyes say *please*. "She was terrified," he says reluctantly. "Her screams echoed from the valley to the sea." Watson grimaces as if he's hearing it all again. "I've never been able to get that sound out of my mind. It still haunts me."

Yes, even a ghost can be haunted.

"Do you know the name of the demon she struck the deal with?" I ask.

"His name was Alastor." I know the name. I try to recall Alastor from my demonology book, but demons are like Catholic saints—too many of them for me to keep track of in my mind.

This commodore's a stand-up guy. He fought for Ollie, for Donna. I have a sudden, overwhelming urge to help him. "You risked your soul to help them. You came back to help free the souls of your lost men. Pretty righteous, Commodore. Isn't it time for you to move on?"

Watson bites his fist and shakes his head like a scared kid in line for his first roller-coaster ride. His powerful voice deflates to a near whisper. "I fear the judgment of my creator."

I lean toward him across the table. I want him to hear this clearly "Look, all I know about you is what I read on a couple of web-sites—"

"Web what?"

"Never mind." I struggle to find the right words and stammer my way to a coherent thought that finally comes. "What I mean is . . . you seemed to have a lived a good life, even in death." Sounds weird but makes sense to me. I stand. "I'd say your soul is worthy of judgment."

He runs his index finger along the crisp crease of his uniform pants. "I thank you for those kind words."

"Trust me," I say. "I've met a lot of people in the same boat you're in—no pun intended. You don't have anything to worry about."

The commodore rubs his chin in contemplation. He stands and paces the length of the table.

"Besides the Honda Point Disaster, do you have any other regrets that keep you bound to earth?" I ask.

Watson looks at the door behind him. He seems to know where it leads without me telling him. "No," he says. "I lived my life as best I could. I have no regrets, no other unfinished business."

"Then forgive yourself."

Watson shakes his head.

"You probably miss your family . . . your wife," I say.

He nods. "I do."

"Then consider joining them. I'm sure they miss you, too."

Watson sits again, looks up, and stares into the caged lightbulb above him. "Perhaps it is time for me to face my judgment."

The lever appears by my side. "I can make that happen."

Watson notices the lever.

He turns and glances over his shoulder at the door again. "Then I believe I'm ready to face what lies beyond."

He reflects quietly, then stands and throws his shoulders back. "You can only delay the inevitable so long," he says.

I smile at him. "Sir, do I have permission to free you?"

He stands at attention. After a long contemplative pause, he says, "Permission granted."

I pull the lever and the door inches open. No demons lurking, no panic, no terror. For the first time, I can look into the abyss beyond the door without pain. Complete blackness save for a pinhole of light somewhere far in the distance. The sound is nearly melodic, but not musical. Vibrational. A cool wind. Distant voices—laughing, happy. Uplifting. The sound of ascension? Watson walks to the open door, turns, and looks at me. "Thank you, sir," he says before stepping forward. "Let's hope I'm not walking the plank."

I laugh out loud. Five or six steps in, he vanishes into the blackness. Anchors aweigh, Commodore Watson.

The door closes steadily and thuds.

When I pass through my exit door my thoughts are on Donna Lonzi. The girl with the smile that grows. Life sure ain't fair.

Neither is death.

Eighteen

I spent a solid week trying to distract myself and move on. Borrowed a Martin Eric Clapton Signature Acoustic Guitar from my neighbor Pat, and managed to record the acoustic tracks for "Layla." The strings really beat up my fingertips. Developing some hard-earned calluses. When I returned the guitar, I recorded Pat playing the bass line. He got all psyched up and took me over to his friend Joanie's house in Eagle Rock. She's a session drummer. Has a kick-ass, Tama double-bass drum kit set up in her soundproof garage and has a keen ear. After listening closely to "Layla" three times in a row, she started drumming it perfectly and seemed to channel Jim Gordon. Gordon was the amazing studio drummer who played on "Layla" and who also complained of hearing voices in his head. He went on to cave in his mother's head with a hammer and is still doing time for murder in central California.

Fortunately that little disturbing bit of rock-and-roll trivia didn't spook Joanie. She was all into playing my drum tracks and just blew me away with her precision. We bought a case of beer, ordered pizzas, and spent about ten hours jamming and recording. I felt like I was in a band. It was a blast and, for a whole day, I barely thought about Donna or Ollie. Next day I nailed down the piano solo at the end and really started assembling the song in Pro Tools. Damn if it didn't start sounding good.

Now, the only remaining hurdles are to try to reproduce the dueling Clapton/Allman solos during the song's finale and then record and drop in the vocal track.

Apart from Project Layla, I went out boozing twice, recharged Crowley's Goblet at the ruins of Houdini's mansion, went to a movie, got drunk at Teddy's, a club in the Roosevelt, and banged the stockings off a MILF named Cheyenne, right in her Mercedes.

Despite the active schedule, I can't drive Donna and Ollie from my mind. And now that *Sudden Danger* has finally arrived, I'm becoming obsessed with them all over again. I dive into the film, watch Donna play another small role, this time as the secretary for the lawyer of a blind guy under suspicion for murdering his wealthy mother. It's a shitty movie, but Donna looks different—more beautiful than ever. The movie is dated 1955—a full five years after her last movie role and four years after the birth of Ollie. The film sets me off. I can't stop thinking about Donna trapped in hell and Ollie, scared and alone—abandoned—in that church, hopeful for a reunion that will never come.

This feeling is not going to go away.

The DVDs are no longer enough. I scan the Lonzi folder again. I email the names from Donna's obituary—Rita Merrill, Sterling Merrill, and Daniel Merrill—to Detective Cliff DuPree's personal email address. He runs the names. Half hour later, he pings me back. Email reads:

1. Rita Merrill, age 82. Address: Wellington Courts Retirement Community, Arcadia. 2. Sterling Merrill, Died: April 13, 2003, age 77. 3. Daniel Merrill, Died: October 18, 1970, age 21. Killed in action. Viet-Nam.

He wraps up with an underlined sentence:

Why do you need this info?

I don't reply.

Drive to Arcadia. Smoggy day. It's an upscale nursing home. Four stars. Light years better than where I live. A courtyard with a waterfall, a dining room with a restaurant feel, a gift shop, and a beauty salon. These geezers live a cut above.

I stop at Information and register. Tell the woman behind the desk I'm Rita Merrill's great-great-nephew Oliver. She makes a call. A nurse shows up—a rotund African American just shy of five feet tall. Kind face. Cornrows. Ginormous bosom and an ass so wide it looks like she's smuggling two basketballs in her nursing scrubs. Her name tag reads: *Jonelle*.

"I'm afraid I have bad news," she says. "Mrs. Merrill passed away."

"When?"

"About six weeks ago."

"How?"

"Alzheimer's. It was a long, hard road for her."

"That's too bad," I say, maybe a little too lightly.

The nurse eyes me up a little suspiciously. "Mrs. Merrill said she didn't have any relatives left alive," she says.

"Very distant relative—on her husband's side," I reply, channeling Eva's smooth certainty. "Was driving through L.A., so I thought I'd say hello."

She buys it. Jonelle gives me a sympathetic smile. "Her personal items are packed in storage. We'll keep them for a year."

"Then what?"

"Dispose of them."

"Toss them out?" I ask.

"No. Nothing that impersonal. We'll donate it to Goodwill," she says. "You're welcome to go through her things . . . being a relative and all."

"Sure."

We take an elevator to a basement, and Jonelle leads me past a rec room to a large storage area packed to the ceiling with boxes dripping Christmas decorations. In the corner, five cardboard boxes are neatly stacked next to a life-size Santa Claus.

"Here they are," Jonelle says.

I thank her and she leaves. Tear open the first box—the biggest one. Contains an 18-inch TV and a record player from the '60s, the kind with the speakers built right in. Second box is full of vinyl albums. I thumb through them. Some cool, vintage stuff.

I look around—eye an electrical outlet. Plug in the record player and drop the needle on side A of *Bobby Darin at the Copa*. A snappy version of "Swing Low, Sweet Chariot" kicks in. It's impossible not to tap my feet.

The third box is packed with personal stuff. Knickknacks—she collected angels. A jewelry box: a few bracelets, a string of pearls, a ladies' Timex. Her purse—no cash in it.

Fourth box—framed photos. A lot of them. Uncover a photo of Donna, Ollie, and Nick. A wedding picture of Rita and her husband. A photo of a young man in his army dress uniform. A plaque on the frame reads: "Daniel F. Merrill, 1949–1971." Then I pull out a solo glamour shot of Donna.

When I tear open the fifth and final box, I strike gold. Photo albums. About a dozen metal canisters containing 8-millimeter home movies. They're labeled. I snatch two of them: *Donna's Wedding* and *Ollie's Fifth Birthday*. Search the boxes for a projector. Nothing.

The first photo album I open is the holy grail. At least fifty black-and-white photos of Donna, Nick, and Ollie. I'm mesmerized.

More photos. A cross-country drive in the early '60s. Rita and her husband look to be in their early thirties. Danny looks to be ten or eleven. They drive from California to Pennsylvania to visit family. They take old Route 66. Plenty of stops. They're in the Hershey chocolate factory. Women in white uniforms inspecting freshly wrapped bars of chocolate.

A photo album devoted to Danny. Young Danny hugging a mutt. Looks like a Norman Rockwell painting. A newspaper clipping. Front page of the *Foothill Leader*. Headline: *Heroic Boy Saves Dog*. Danny's dog, Smokey, falls off a bridge into the L.A. River wash. Got swept away. Looks like a goner. Danny jumps in, gets swept away, too. Ends up rescuing the dog. Gets a medal of heroism from the mayor of Temple City. Asked why he risked his own life, Danny commented, "He's a good and loyal dog. I had to do something."

I flip the record over to side B. "I Have Dreamed" plays. Nice strings. Return to Rita's life—laid out in front of me on a concrete floor. Thumb through the photo albums again. Donna and Ollie are there one day and gone the next. Danny is there, through boyhood and adolescence—then he's gone, suddenly. I can feel his absence as the pages roll on. The passage of time for Rita and her husband is marked by gray hair, vacations, makes and models of cars, stooped shoulders. Rita and her husband moved on, but part of them died with their son. I see it. And then, somewhere in his '60s—maybe '70s—Rita's husband is gone. She's left alone.

Now everyone in these photos—save for Nick Lonzi—is dead. Donna, Ollie, and Danny died way too early. Rita lived too long—ended up alone.

Anxiety is swallowing me whole.

Who's making up the rules here? They don't add up.

These five boxes, constituting an entire life, make me really sad.

Jonelle waddles in. Good Lord—that bubble ass. She takes a seat near me. "Mind if I join you?" she asks.

"Don't mind."

She smiles. "I like to take my breaks down here. It's quiet." She's stops to listen to the music for a second. "Who is this?" she asks.

"Bobby Darin."

"Mrs. Merrill loved her music," Jonelle says. "She'd be pleased you're playing a record."

"Was she a nice woman?" I ask.

"Very nice," Jonelle says.

"That's good."

"Toward the end, she used to talk to her dead son in her room—like he was there."

"He probably was," I say, but don't elaborate.

Jonelle tears the plastic off a pack of Hostess mini chocolate donuts and pops one. Washes it down with a bottle of chocolate-flavored Ensure.

That's a lot of chocolate.

"Have one," she says, holding out the donuts.

I shake my head.

"Find anything good?" she asks.

"A few things." I point to the photo album and home movies I plan to take.

"Sure you don't want to take it all?" she asks.

"Nah," I reply. "Wouldn't feel right about it."

I start packing up the boxes. Getting choked up.

Jonelle seems to instinctively zone in on my sadness. "Go ahead and cry if you want to," she says. "It's okay. There's a lot of sadness in this building."

I stop packing and smile at her. I'm sure I'll never see this little fat lady again in my life, and that makes me even sadder. Somehow our lives crisscrossed in this basement. At this unlikely instant, I wish she was my mother, sister, shrink, best friend.

I'm fucking losing it.

"Sure you don't want one?" she asks, again holding out the pack of donuts.

"Okay," I say. I reach over and grab one and take a bite. The taste shoots me back in time. My dad used to buy these chocolate donuts—the big ones. I remember us eating them together.

Gotta get out of here.

Quickly pack the boxes, grab the photo album and film canisters, bid Jonelle a polite farewell, and head back upstairs.

On my way out, an old man asks me to push his wheelchair to the dining room. I pop a couple of wheelies and he howls with laughter like a little kid. It reminds me of Ollie's laugh. Fucks me up even worse.

I practically sprint out, past rows of geezers lining up in wheelchairs for their lunches. When I make it outside, I breathe deep. Fresh, smoggy air. I hear "My Generation" in my head. Townshend nailed it. Better off dead than old.

I drive to a place in Burbank that converts 8-millimeter films to DVD. They'll also digitize the photos from the album. I hand over everything. Pay an exorbitant rush fee. More credit card debt. Fuck it. They tell me to come back in two hours.

Kill the two hours in a bar called the Blue Room. And, yes, it's blue. Old-school bar, a notch or two above a dive. I'm comfortable there. I catch a nice buzz, collect my treasure, and race home.

I dump the digital photos on my hard drive and start a running slide show. I can't wait to touch some of them up in Photoshop. Add some color. I've only seen Donna in black and white. I feel like I just won't know her—really know her—until she's in Technicolor.

I pour myself a drink, settle on my sofa, and start the DVDs. After tiny, minute-long scenes, seeing Donna on film for long stretches is mesmerizing, even if the camera was in the hands of an amateur. She was a stunning bride. A lavish short-sleeve white wedding grown with embroidered daisies. Layers of skirts. Short wedding veil. Carrying a bouquet of daisies. Nick had movie-star swagger and clean-cut looks. He hams it up with Bugsy Siegel. Nick's on his way. He knew it even back then.

Ollie's fifth birthday is nothing but smiles. Lots of relatives. A mountain of presents. Hamburgers and hot dogs and glass bottles of Coke. Nick gives Ollie a pony ride on his back. Ollie unwraps his Lone Ranger deputy badge, pistol and holster, mask and hat. In full costume, he hams it up right in front of the camera lens. I can read his lips: "Hi-yo, Silver, away!"

Donna cuts the birthday cake, licks icing off her fingers, smiles that smile. My eyes nearly fall out of their sockets. She's wearing a sleeveless floral sundress and dark sunglasses. The skirt seems short for the time. Her legs are flawless. She was Dita before Dita. Still reminds me of someone I know.

The film ends abruptly with Donna bear-hugging Ollie and smothering his cheeks in kisses. Huge, wide smiles. Looks like they're about to eat the camera. I go grab Ollie's Lone Ranger badge and start the DVD over. Make it about halfway through. A knock on my door. It's Eva.

"Haven't heard from you," she says. "Thought I'd drop by."

She hands me a folder. She's pulled out all stops, scored all of Nick Lonzi's records.

"What's the scoop?"

"He's clean," Eva says. "A couple of business-related lawsuits here and there over the decades, but no dark secrets. No skeletons. No arrests. One crazy conspiracy website out there claims he's part of a brotherhood of satanists along with a bunch of other celebrities."

"Like who?" I ask.

She tries to remember. "Let's see . . . Sammy Davis Jr., Steve Allen, Rupert Murdoch, Jayne Mansfield, Katie Couric, Ozzy Osbourne." She can't keep a straight face. "I did find one interesting thing, though."

"What?"

She points out a couple of pages in the file. "I have a source. Met her when I did the exposé on celebrity medical records being leaked. She was able to get me a copy of Lonzi's medical records."

"How?"

"She never says how."

"And?"

"He's fit as a fiddle for a man his age. But, talk about hitting triple sevens on life's big slot machine. Lonzi was diagnosed with throat cancer in 1956 and he beat it."

"That wasn't easily treatable in the '50s." I say.

"It's not easily treatable today," says Eva.

"Some guys have all the luck."

Eva looks around—the slideshow running photo after photo of Donna and Ollie, my television with a frozen image of Donna smiling and Ollie blowing out the candles on his cake, the Lone Ranger badge, two empty bottles of Jameson, a hundred pages of guitar tabs spread all over the floor, a bottle of Vicodin on the counter by the fridge. She's more than worried—she's a little freaked out. Gives me a "are you secretly a stalker?" look. "Looks like you've been staying busy." She watches picture after picture roll by on the slideshow. "Where did you get this stuff?"

I don't feel like talking. "Long story."

"Quite the detective." She goes to my refrigerator and takes a beer without asking. She's debating whether to say something.

"What?" I ask.

"You're not becoming obsessed with all this?" she finally asks.

"No," I lie.

"You did everything you could." I shrug. "Some problems don't have a solution."

"I know."

"Looks like you need a little cheer. Come on—I'll take you out to dinner."

"Nah."

"Then we'll go to the Frolic Room. Load up the jukebox and drink till we're legless."

"I'm still not feeling too hot," I lie. "But thanks for stopping by."

She's miffed. Doesn't like the brush. She chugs her beer. Say something, dumbass. "I'll snap out of this soon," I tell her. "I wouldn't be much fun right now."

"I understand."

"I really like you, Eva. Just trying to be honest."

"You really like that kid, huh?"

I nod.

"I understand," she repeats. She gives me a hug and quick peck on the cheek. I watch her walk down the sidewalk from my window next to the fire escape. She's a good egg.

I work on "Layla," but I'm too distracted. Return to the photos. Colorize and clean up a few of them. There she is—olive skin, jet-black hair, red lipstick, carrying white daisies. She's calling out to me. Crying for help.

It's right then that it all seems to come together like pieces of a jigsaw puzzle. I shoot Ned and Eva an email and ask them to come over tomorrow. I figured it out. Finally. I know what I want to do when I grow up.

Nineteen

"Why can't I go to hell?"

Ned crumbles up a blank sheet of printer paper and tosses it at me. "You're talking crazy, Kane. It's impossible—just forget about it."

Eva's stretched out on my sofa paging her way through my book on demonology. She seems a little too nonchalant.

I throw the wad of paper back at Ned. "If I can project my spirit into the soul trap, why can't I find some way to project it past the trap? Way past. Past life and death—all the way to hell."

"There is a way," Ned says. "It's called dying. Now just let it go."

"Come on," I say. "Where's the positivity?"

Eva closes the book. "All right. I'm going to speak up. I don't care. It's a little weird—the movies, the DVDs, the photos. What is it with you? Why do you feel so compelled to help this woman?" she asks.

"Because I like her kid."

Ned loses his cool and lets me have it. "Listen to me, Kane. You're not going down this road."

He means business, and I'm touched he cares about me. But . . . "I choose the road I travel—not you. I have to try this."

"Why?" Ned snaps.

"She's in hell."

Eva speaks up. "Maybe she deserves to be. She was married to a rough customer. Maybe she was a bad person."

"She wasn't. I know it."

"How?" Eva asks.

"I just know," I snap at her.

And out of nowhere, Eva says, "Well, God knows she was a lousy actress."

My temper flares. "Enough, already!" I shout at her.

She knows she crossed the line. Follows up with some basic logic. "But even if you could get to hell, what makes you think you could save her and bring her soul back?" Eva's always good at asking the tough questions.

Ned tosses his tweed cap on the sofa and runs his hands through his stringy hair. He's sweating. "Forget it, Eva. When he gets like this, there's no point in trying to reason with him." I nod. "Stubborn ass," he grunts.

"Let's hear what Karl says," I say powering up the IVeR.

"Is the crystal charged?" Ned asks.

I nod. Eva whips out her notebook and pen. I tune the ectometer and listen. It takes longer than normal, but I finally hear a far-off voice imitating guitar distortion and a thumping, rhythmic drum beat. Then he sings the first few lines of "Tomorrow Never Knows."

"Karl?" Nothing but static and feedback. "Karl? Are you downstream? Can you hear me?"

Nada. Then loudly, "Hello, Kane. Is your mind off?"

Eva jumps backward, startled. "Who's Karl?" she asks.

"My pet nowhere man," I say.

Eva reapproaches, cautiously. "No way," she says.

"Way," Karl responds.

"The demon Alastor. Talk to me, dawg."

Through static and squeals, Karl replies, "A monarch of hell. Commands a legion of eighty demons, including Teeraal, Azazel,

Asmodeus, Gressil." His voice cuts out then pops back. "The demon of family feuds, of sins that pass from parent to child."

"What else?" I ask.

Crackling dead air, then Karl adds, "He will kill you." The transmission sputters to a halt.

Eva tosses her notebook aside in frustration. "That's it? Get him back."

"It doesn't work like that," I tell her. Then I let her handle Crowley's goblet and give her a detailed run through of the IVeR. I feel more than a twinge of doubt and anxiety as she takes page after page of notes.

Ned seems relived. "Well, I'm glad you heard it for yourself."

"Heard what?" I ask.

"He'll kill you."

"He didn't say that."

"The fuck he didn't," Ned shouts. "You heard him—right, Eva?"

Eva nods. "That's what he said."

"I don't think so," I say.

"Don't start, Kane," Ned warns.

"You know what we need, besides some decent takeout?" I ask, looking at Ned. "We need a plan."

Ned and Eva are resistant at first, but I draw them in. For the next hour, we brainstorm over pad thai, spring rolls, and Kirin until we piece together our little fucked-up plan.

"All right, let's recap this," Eva says.

Ned volunteers. "You can have the last spring roll if you exercise brevity," I tease.

Ned clears his throat for effect and stands at my kitchen counter like it's a podium. "Okay, let's see. Pretty simple actually. Only three steps. Three major steps: lots of little substeps laced in there, but fuck those for now. First. Kane lets Teeraal, the fun-house demon serving in the legion of Alastor, kill him—for the second time, mind you—and take his soul to hell. Second. Kane uses a holy relic to weaken the demon Alastor long enough to snatch Donna's soul. Third. The EMT across the hall, who by the way has no friggin' idea yet what we're about to ask him to do, resuscitates Kane's dead body, bringing Kane's and Donna's souls back into the soul trap and then Kane's soul back into his body."

Silence. Then we all look at each other and laugh. We're talking about me dying, yet somehow my mood elevates. My sense of humor, on hiatus since I got that concussion, returns.

"Jesus Christ, listen to us," Eva says. "Do you hear what we're saying?"

"I know," I chuckle. "Sounds like we're chatting on chili night at the Gateway Mental Institution."

Eva's smile quickly becomes a worried frown. "You're really going to do this?" she asks.

"Yeah."

Ned dips the last spring roll in soy sauce and downs it in one bite. "I'm gonna go knock on your neighbor's door," Ned says with his mouth full.

"Invite him over," I tell him.

Ned leaves. Eva says, "Let's talk."

We go out on the fire escape. A police chopper overhead shines a light on an apartment building behind the 7-Eleven across the street. Eva gets close and whispers, "Ollie has a really good friend."

I'm about to thank her, but she silences me. "But I'm not going to let you go ahead with this."

"Sorry, Eva," I say, looking up at the chopper, not her. "I'm decided."

"You can't do it," she pleads. "It's too dangerous. It's beyond a long shot."

"It's my life," I remind her.

"Look at me," she orders. I take my eyes off the chopper and look at her. "You're not doing this. And remember what I told you—when I want something, I usually get it."

"Can I ask you an honest question?"

She nods. "Sure."

"What do you care what I do?"

The chopper noise is annoyingly loud. She leads me back in my apartment. "I care because you're my friend."

"Your friend? One of many."

"What's that mean?"

"I've seen your Facebook profile," I say. "You got something like five hundred. You can afford to lose one."

She seems a little pissed. "There are social networking friends." She thinks about it. "And then there are other friends—the work kind. People to have lunch with or hit happy hour with. They come and go. Actually been going a lot lately. But you . . . you're the real kind."

"The real kind?" I ask.

She thinks about it before she answers. I like that. "The kind that might just be around at my funeral." She pauses, then adds, "At the age of a hundred and three. The kind that you carry with you for the long haul."

Wow. I've been waiting my whole life to hear something like that.

"So . . . real friend . . . you're not going to do this. Right?"

I'm about to argue, but I stop short. She's probably right. She's tenacious. She won't let it go. There's a reason she usually gets what she wants. I don't know what to say.

"Right?" she repeats.

I look in her eyes. "Right," I answer. "You're right." I get on a roll. "Time to put it behind me and move on."

"Thank God," she says, relieved. She smiles. The smirk of a winner. She packs her leather satchel. "I have to go," she says. "Deadline in the morning."

I walk her to the door. I give her a clumsy hug. She surprises me with a four-star squeeze. A kiss on the cheek, and my knees buckle. She looks at me and our lips almost meet for just a second before she pulls away and hurries off. Intense. Sweat on my forehead. Heart pounding.

Ned returns with my neighbor Pat, who takes a few steps inside my apartment and freezes. He marvels at the IVeR, the gurney, the rack of computer hardware, the dual big-screen monitors, and the miles of wire. "What the fuck do you guys do in here?"

"Pull up a chair, and I'll tell you," I say.

Ned notices that I'm rattled, that Eva's gone. "Everything okay?" he whispers. "Did you come to your senses and call this off?"

I look at him. "Hell no," I whisper back. "Our fucked-up plan commences in three . . . two . . . one."

I hand Pat a Kirin and we get to work.

Twenty

Fucked-up Plan—Part One.

I track down where Stacks Fabin's carnival is heading next. Then Ned and I drive up to Lompoc to conduct a little experiment and to borrow—not steal!—something. If it works, our plan stands a chance. If it fails, put a fork in us.

As soon as the church closes for the night, we get the key and enter.

"Hey, kemosabe—I'm back." I shout. Ten seconds of silence, then *bing, bong*—the bells toll. A cold breeze howls by and the hair on my arms stands up.

"Kane," I hear from somewhere near the ceiling.

"How about we get together for a powwow?" I yell.

Freezing air encircles me. I hear, "Okeydokey."

"Can you hear him?" I ask Ned.

"Nope."

"Thanks, Ollie," I shout. "Do me a favor and stand still by the organ for me, will ya?"

Ned points the handheld thermal cam at the organ. "Damn if he isn't there."

I power up the trap and suck Ollie inside.

In the camper, I stretch out and wire up. "I'll have the Lone Ranger badge in my hand," I tell Ned. "Make sure it doesn't fall out when I leave my body."

"Let's hope this works," Ned reminds me.

I don my helmet and goggles, wire up, and start the breathing exercises. The all-or-nothing stakes of tonight's mission nags me. I struggle to empty my mind and balance my breath. It takes me nearly an hour to leave my body.

Ned has reinstalled the Cartoonville settings. When I hear the calliope music, I open my eyes to find Jiminy Cricket staring at me. My right hand feels strange—numb and hot. It burns. I open my palm and there it is—an astral projection of Ollie's badge in my hand. Never tried this before. Never a reason to. Fuckin' A. It'll be possible to pass me the holy relic, or at least the astral essence of it if I can make it to hell. I can check that one off the "wonder if I can do that in the soul trap" list.

The badge cools off quick, and I palm it in my closed fist and approach Ollie, who darts out of the chair shaped like the Cheshire Cat and bear hugs me. I recoil, just a little. I like the kid, but I'm still not comfortable with the whole "Wanna be my daddy?" line of questioning.

"Hi, Ollie, Ollie Oxen Free."

"Hi, Kane, Kane, the big fat pain."

"I've got a surprise for you."

He hops in place like a bunny. "What is it?"

"Look what I found," I say, opening my hand to reveal the badge.

Ollie lets out a scream and raises his arms above his head in triumph. "Wowee!! You got it back! My Lone Ranger deputy badge."

"Got your bling back, buddy," I say.

"You're like the best daddy ever, Kane."

Like the dick I am, I brush that one off like bird shit on my sleeve. This is why I never go to an animal shelter or a pet shop. "Listen, Ollie, I have an important question to ask you," I say, taking a seat on the couch shaped like a caterpillar. "Do you think you can help me?"

Ollie dons his mask, pins his badge on his shirt, and stands right in front of me. "Sure I'll help ya."

"Do you know where they keep the key to that gold chest on the side of the altar?"

"Sure I do," he boasts. "It's locked in the back room in the hallway behind the altar, the saa—the saska—the sa-cris-ty. It's on a key ring hanging in the closet."

"Do you think you can open that door?" I ask.

Ollie shakes his head. "The door's locked," he says glumly. What am I asking? Even a seasoned ghost in command of its powers probably would have a hard time moving a key across a room and unlocking a door with it. Would require massive supernatural energy and extreme finesse. Forget about it.

"Does anyone ever open that room?"

Ollie nods. "Sometimes the priest and nun go in there."

"Do you like to play pretend?"

"I love pretend," he says, swaying his shoulders to the beat of "I'm Forever Blowing Bubbles" on the calliope. "I pretend I'm the Lone Ranger. I make believe I'm Willie Mays. Sometimes I pretend I'm a dinosaur." Ollie roars—low and guttural—comical as hell, like a kid puking after eating too much Halloween candy.

It cracks me up. "I have an idea."

"What?"

"Why don't we play a little trick on the next person who's in that room? You pretend to be a dinosaur and chase them away."

Ollie belly-laughs. "That'll be fun."

"I'm going to send you back to the church again, okay?" I say.

Ollie nods. "Okay."

"I brought my laptop. We can watch *The Lone Ranger*."

"Laptop?" Ollie asks, confused. "You mean the tiny television?"

"Right."

"Okay, Kane. When will you come again to visit?"

"After I leave tonight, I'm going on a journey." I pause, choosing my words carefully. "It might be a little dangerous. If—" I stop and restart. "When I come back, I'll visit you again."

"Dangerous?" Ollie asks anxiously. "Will you be okay?"

"Sure."

"You gonna fight bad guys?" Ollie asks.

"Yeah," I answer.

Ollie glances down, looking all gloomy. He thinks, then shoots me a little smile. "Well, if you're going after the bad guys, you better take my badge. It'll bring you luck."

Ollie unpins his badge and hands it to me. What a friggin' kid. Damn. Why can't he just be a brat? I pin the badge on my black Jim Morrison tee. This little pound puppy deserves a bone. "Thanks, Ollie," I say. The words get stuck. "You're a good kid." It's not a bone. I mean it and I could kick myself in the ass. The kid has gotten to me and now I'm good and fucked. That selfish prick Nick Lonzi probably never even realized what a gem he had. And if I ever have a kid—or if I've had one out there I don't know about—I hope he or she turns out like this. "I'll keep it with me, kiddo," I promise. "When I come back, I'll pin it back on your shirt."

Ollie gives me a sad little wave as I step through my exit door. "See you in the church," I say before I'm cannonballed back to Ned's camper.

My eyes open wide. I'm nauseous and drained drier than a Bernie Madoff investment account. Forehead throbs. Ned hands me a bottle of water and I chug. "Get my Vicodin," I demand. Ned hands me a couple pills and I wash them down.

"You all right?" Ned asks.

"No."

"This has to stop," he snaps. "Do you understand?" I ignore him and stare at the ceiling. "You have to slow down," he continues. "Too many trips inside. You're gonna kill yourself."

I stare at my water bottle.

"You look yellow," Ned says, handing me a pocket mirror. "If your liver is shutting down—"

I cut him off. "It worked," I say with as much of a smile as I can muster. "I had the badge inside the trap."

"Damn," Ned says to himself as he stares blankly ahead. He seems to short-circuit—both happy that it worked and sad that our plan is still alive. "This just might work."

Fucked-up Plan—Part Deux.

I release Ollie in the church and we watch three more episodes of *The Lone Ranger* before I pass out. Ned rustles me awake just after dawn when the church door swings open and an ancient-looking, bespectacled nun enters. She's old-school penguin style. Black habit. A silver crucifix on a sturdy chain dangles around her neck.

"Here comes trouble," Ned whispers. "Takes me back to second grade when Sister John the Baptist flogged my bare ass with a hand-crafted Roman-style flagellum."

"You must be Kane and Ned?" the old nun says. The wrinkles on her cheeks and forehead are as deep and dry as the canals of Mars.

"Yes," I reply.

"Father Demetrius told me you were in the church. I'm Sister Agnes."

"Nice to meet you." I say, shaking her frail hand.

Ned waves me over. "I'll keep watch outside. Keep any bystanders out. Good luck," he whispers before leaving.

"I'm so glad you're here," the nun says after Ned leaves. "I get quite unnerved when I'm in the church alone. I believe there's a presence here."

"I believe you're right, Sister."

She smiles—seems nice enough. "Don't mind me. I'm just going to go about my business. I'll be preparing the church for mass this morning, so don't let me disturb you." The nun hums to herself as she goes about her chores: stacking church bulletins, lighting candles on the altar, double-checking that all the kneelers are up in the pews. While I shadow her from a distance, hoping that she'll open the sacristy door, I feel Ollie's presence alongside me. When she approaches the hallway behind the altar and pulls a key ring out of her pocket, my heart starts to race. She's humming "Ave Maria" when she opens the sacristy door and enters.

"All right, Ollie," I whisper, just short of the corridor. "Let's hear that dinosaur roar. Make it loud, kiddo. Use every ounce of energy you have." I hear a giggle and feel the chill of a cold breeze blowing by. I inch forward, linger just beyond the hallway, and wait for the shit to hit the fan.

I hear Ollie's ethereal giggle and then the pop of a lightbulb blowing. Ollie's drawing electrical energy from around him. Good. A terrified Sister Agnes, alone in the dark, asks aloud, "Who's there? Is there someone there?" There's a chilling silence, then a growl and ghostly roar that must sound to Sister Agnes like a hound of hell about to pounce. She screams and hauls nun ass straight down the hallway and out the side door.

I race to the open sacristy. "You even scared me, Ollie," I say, opening the closet door and snatching the hanging key ring. "You patrol the church," I tell him. "If anyone comes in before I put this key back, T-Rex 'em, buddy."

Another giggle as Ollie whooshes away, a wake of frigid air and flashing lightbulbs trailing behind. I sprint to the altar and try a handful of keys until I open the ornamental gold reliquary. "Bingo," I say, adrenaline pumping.

There it is—a human finger bone, ancient and withered. Supposedly belonged to Saint Anthony of Padua. We'll see. I take a Ziploc out of my pocket, bag the bone, and return the key ring.

"All right, Ollie," I say. "We did it. Joke's over. Okay . . . I gotta go now. I'll see you next time."

I hear, "Bye."

"Remember to be good. No troublemaking," I say.

"Okay."

As far as praying goes, I gave up on it about the same time I gave up on Santa. I've seen enough to know there has to be something out there. Whatever it is, it likes to hide in silence, so why bother?

But as I walk past the statue of Saint Anthony on my way out, I stop and give it a nod. What do I have to lose? Here goes nothing.

I don't know if you can hear me, Saint Anthony, I say in my mind. Feels weird—like I'm talking to Sonny, an imaginary friend I had when I was a kid—but I press on. *If you can hear me—I'm just borrowing your finger, not stealing it. That's a promise.* The little boy in Saint Anthony's arms has a content and peaceful smile on his face. *They say you're the saint of lost items.* I think of Ollie in his Lone Ranger mask. *Well, the little boy in here . . . he's pretty lost. Maybe you can help him, and me.* I look into the eyes of the statue. *They say you battled demons. I have to go battle a few of my own, so help if you wouldn't mind having my back on this one.* I nod, pleased with my little offering. I march toward the door with purpose. "Now let's go give 'em the finger," I say loud enough that it echoes.

Twenty-one

Fucked-up Plan——Part Three.

Logistics.

The C&S Carnival is pitching its tents in Sunland for the weekend. It's a little town tucked up against the foothills north of Burbank, not far from the horse ranch where I trapped Skeeter Jackson. Ned and I scope out Sunland Park, watch the carneys set up, and check into a fleabag motel—the Mount Gleason Motor Lodge—a few blocks away. We set up our equipment in room 27—my request—and I text Pat and tell him the fucked-up plan is a go.

I unwrap Saint Anthony's finger bone carefully and hand it to Ned.

"So that's it?" he says, studying it.

"Listen to me," I say, demanding his full attention. "You can't put it in my hand until I'm dead," I tell him. "I mean it. Flatline dead."

"Why?"

"A demon will most likely sense it," I say. "Can't risk it. Understood?"

"Okay," Ned says, tucking the relic in his shirt pocket.

When Pat arrives, he asks for his two grand up front. I hand him an envelope of cash and he makes me promise again that if I die, he walks clean. Fine. If I croak, Ned will clear everything out of the room except for my body and let the maid find me tomorrow morning. It'll be one of a hundred inexplicable deaths in L.A. Tag me and bag me.

Pat sets up a card table next to the queen-size bed and unpacks a box with a mishmash of medical supplies that he says he went way out on a limb to get his mitts on. Item by item, Pat tells us what everything is and how and when it'll be used. Fifteen Atro-Pens, each with a 1-milligram dose of atropine, that Pat will stab into my chest muscles at five- to ten-minute intervals to maintain even the faintest heartbeat when I'm near cardiac arrest. A blood pressure and pulse monitor. A Codemaster 100 portable defibrillator and heart monitor to track my heartbeat and zap it back to a normal rhythm.

Pat sends Ned to the nearest 7-Eleven for ice—enough ice to fill the bathtub. When the tub is full, Pat covers it with a thermal tarp. To keep my body cold after I flatline.

We triple-check that everything in the room is ready. Pat insists we crank the air-conditioning right before we leave.

We pile into Ned's camper. Pat's stressing over the timing. "We have two minutes tops to get Kane back to that room," Pat emphasizes. "If his heart stops for longer than that, his brain will be toast."

Ned pisses all over that parade. "There's no way we can get you out of that fun house, out of the carnival, into the car and back to the room in a hundred twenty seconds."

"Fuck," Pat says. He's a nervous wreck.

"No way," says Ned. "We have to call this off."

"We're not calling anything off," I say.

Ned cruises the perimeter of the carnival. We catch the mother of all lucky breaks. The fun house is set up against the park fence right next to Foothill Boulevard. It's afternoon and the carnival just kicked off, so it's nearly deserted. Mostly early birds—toddlers and parents. Ned pulls the camper alongside the curb. We're no more than forty-five feet from the fun house. And there's a break in the fence that's close. It'll take a textbook performance but it's humanly possible to get me out of the carnival and flat on my back in the camper in less than a minute. Pat can hit me with chest compressions on the way back to the motel room and that should mitigate the risk of cardiac arrest or brain death. Two minutes is doable. A few prayers to the patron saints of green lights might help.

Fucked-up Plan—Part the Fourth.

Only one thing left for me to do—muster the nut sack to march into that fun house, lure out a demon, and piss him off so badly that he has no choice but to drag my soul to his master in hell.

It's go time. Pat scopes out the fun house, looking for potential trouble. I pull Ned over to the food stand. I need all the good karma I can get.

"You're hungry? Now?" Ned asks.

"Hang on, I wanna say hi to someone."

The popcorn smells good. A fat, bald guy with bad skin and a red cap that says, *Buy a Beer, the End is Near*, asks, "Can I help you?"

I lean over the sticky counter and peer inside the booth. "Is Candy working today?"

The vendor looks surprised. "Candy?"

Ned nudges me. "Who's Candy?" he whispers.

"A girl," I whisper back.

"Jesus, another one?" says Ned, rolling his eyes.

"Were you a friend?" the vendor asks, hesitating.

"We were supposed to go out once," I say. As if I have to explain myself to this stranger, I add, "I kind of accidentally stood her up."

Ned laughs. "Jesus."

The vendor scratches inside his ear and frowns. "I don't know how to say it—so I'll just say it. Candy passed away last week."

I get a little dizzy. "What? How?"

"She was closing, doing cleanup, washing the ketchup bottles.

Somehow knocked the blender into the sink while it was still plugged in."

"Electrocuted?"

"Ouch," Ned says.

"That's what the cops said," the vendor tells me.

I must look pale. "You all right, Kane?" Ned asks.

"Man, that sucks," I say, bummed. "Poor girl."

"Thanks for telling us," Ned says to the vendor. "Howzabout giving us two corn dogs and two beers?"

Ned pulls me over to a row of bleachers at a Little League field just past the food stand. The beer is flat, but still tastes good. The corn dog is so greasy, it feels like a wet sponge. "I can't let that be my last meal," I say.

"I'll eat yours," Ned says, chowing down. "We'll trade." He hands me his beer and we sit side by side staring at the fun house that awaits.

"Where's Eva?" he asks. "Don't you want her with us?"

I'm watching the foam on my beer dissipate. "She doesn't know we're here," I admit.

"What?"

"She didn't want me to do this."

"Well, neither did I," Ned says, raising his voice.

"She's really relentless. She was in my face about it." I can't sell it.

"So you lied?" Ned asks.

I nod. Take a sip of beer.

"Shit," Ned says, all disappointed.

"What?" I ask, annoyed.

"You've got a lot to learn about being a friend," he says.

Time to change the subject. "I need you to do me a couple of favors," I say. Ned nods and chews. I reach in my pocket and take out Ollie's badge. "When I go down, make sure this is in my hand."

"For what?" Ned asks, finishing off the first tumor-inducing meatsicle.

"For good luck."

"You really like that kid, huh?"

I try to think of something nasty or sarcastic to say, but I can't. When you'll be dead within the hour, the truth is about all that works. "Yeah," I answer.

"Now you know how I feel," Ned says, grabbing my shoulder and giving it a squeeze.

Tears bubble up. Can't lose my shit. Keep talking. No crying. "Leave the other hand empty . . . until it's time for the relic," I say. Moist eyes. Cracking voice. Hold it together. "If I die—"

Ned cuts me off and wields his corn dog like a laser pointer. "All right. Conversation over."

"I'm serious," I say. "If I die, cremate me."

Ned musters up a phony laugh that sounds like it's coming from a stranger. "And where would you like your ashes spread?"

Good question. Never gave it much thought. "I don't know," I say. I take a sip of my beer and noodle it. "How about Angelina Jolie's pool?"

"Fuck, no," Ned says. "Too many kids whizzing in there."

I laugh and swallow a gulp of stale beer and what's left of the tears I'm fighting. "I know—I'll fix your wagon," Ned says with glee. "I'll go to Disneyland and dump your ashes in *It's a Small World*. You can listen to that little tune for all eternity."

"Then I'll have to come back and haunt you." Ned smiles and polishes off the second corn dog. "Remember to play 'Spirit in the Sky' at my funeral," I add.

"Done."

"Though I don't know why that matters because you'll be the only one there."

Ned stands, looks down at me. "Enough about dying, Kane," he says. "You can't die." He looks over at the fun house. "Well, you can die for about five minutes, but you can't die die. Won't allow it. Can't happen." Ned offers me his hand and yanks me up. "You're all I've got," he says.

"Poor you," I say. Then I add in a hushed tone, "Thanks, Ned."

I stand. "Now I need you to do me a favor," Ned says.

"What?"

S
O
U
L

T
R
A
P
P
E
R

"I need to say something."

"Shoot."

Ned gets serious. "I need you to listen to what I have to say objectively. No storming off. Don't throw a punch. Okay?"

Suddenly this is not Ned speaking. He's sweating. What the fuck? I nod, reluctantly.

Ned clears his throat and rocks on the bleachers. "I'm the person who led you to the soul trap."

At first I think he's joking. I'm waiting for the punch line. It doesn't come. "Bullshit," I finally say. "It was a guy—a friend of my father's."

"It was a private detective I hired to find you. I'm the one who hid the soul trap and those papers in the storage bin."

My temper flares. "What is this? What are you saying? What else haven't you told me?"

Ned won't make eye contact. He looks directly forward when he speaks. "It was 1993. I'd been off the project for going on nine years. Living in Pasadena. Teaching at Caltech. All of a sudden one night your dad shows up at my doorstep."

I feel like the air is being sucked out of my lungs. "And you never told me?"

"He was in a panic. He's holding what he calls a duplicate of the soul trap. Tells me no one knows it even exists. Gives it to me. It was hosed. Tells me the project has gone haywire. That the people at the top lied to him. That his life is in danger. He gives me the trap, begs me to hide it. Pleads with me to keep an eye on you."

I feel dizzy. Everything gets a little blurry. "What happened?"

"He was in and out my door in less than five minutes. Never saw him again. Poked around, made some calls, called in some favors. I found out a couple of days later that the lab where the project was based blew up. Burned to the ground."

"What about the people who worked there?"

"Presumed dead."

"Do you think my father destroyed it?"

Ned shakes his head. His voice cracks. "I don't know. I really don't."

"Why did he come to you? Were you closer friends than you've led on?"

"No," Ned assures me. "You didn't have friends on that godforsaken project. It was an eight-person team. Your dad was the team leader. Orders come directly from him. Where he got his orders, none of us knew. We were told not to fraternize, to disclose nothing, to consider everything above top secret. We were told we were all being watched. There was an air of paranoia about everything. We were all distant from each other."

"You're not answering my question," I snap. "Why did he come to you?"

"I don't know. He used to keep a little picture of you in his top desk drawer. I saw him looking at it a couple times. I asked him about you once in a while. Maybe that's why he chose me."

"So why did you feed me that key?"

"I told him I'd keep an eye on you. I knew your life was fucked up. I wanted to bring you closer. And I figured if no one came after the trap between '93 and 2000, if all it was doing was collecting dust, it was probably safe to reach out."

"Why are you telling me this? Now?"

"Who knows what's going to happen today? I wanted you to know the truth. And when you vanished on me after that trip to Vegas, I got really spooked. That's why I got so pissed off when you didn't call. There are aspects of this—potentially deadly ones—neither one of us knows about. You should know that."

And just like that—in the span of five minutes—everything changes. The man who seemed like the court jester turns out to be the puppet master.

"You know something?" I say, deflated. "You've got a lot to learn about being a friend." Suck on that, Ned.

I can't gauge my feelings. I'm not happy. But I'm not enraged either. Mostly I just want to block it out until my work here is done. I'll let it all sink in later. I'll either be cool with it, or not.

I make my way to the funhouse alone. Ned lingers behind. "I'll catch up in a minute," he says. "Gotta hit the john."

Pat waits for me in front. "It's closed," he says, "until dusk."

"Keep an eye open out here," I say. "I'm going in."

Ned shows up. When the coast is clear, I sneak in and scan the inner sanctum with my portable EMF detector. No sign of Teeraal, but the mirrors register big hits. He's not here or he's hiding. I have to lure him out.

I can hear voices in my head—crying from the mirrors—*Help me, save me, get me out of here, pray for me.* It's like a jackhammer in my brain. Makes me dizzy. I'm on the verge of passing out. Hazy faces peer out at me from a blue-gray mist on the other side of the glass. No bodies. Just faces. Faces inside dimly lit orbs. Many faces—terrified, tortured, hopeless, like fish trapped in a filthy aquarium with a dead owner decomposing on the nearby sofa.

I stagger to the fun-house door and wave Ned over. "Hurry up," I order. "I'm fading. Find me something to smash these mirrors—quick. That should get Teeraal's attention."

A few minutes later I hear Ned say, "Pssst." He hands me a mallet from the strong-man attraction.

"Both of you—get in here. Let's do this," I order.

Ned and Pat climb up the stairs and join me inside. "No one gets in here," I shout to Pat. He stands guard, one eye on the door, one on me. "Time to take out some aggression." I wind up, but stop dead when a spirit voice cries my name from a mirror behind me. I turn. It's Candy.

She screams. "Kane. Kane. Help!"

"Candy?"

Her voice is warped, full of distortion. "Help me, Kane. He killed me."

"Teeraal?"

She's frantic, banging her face against the glass. "He trapped my soul," she cries in despair. "Get me out of here!" Dozens of voices cry out with Candy. Their agony drives me to my knees.

I think about Ned lying to me and get angry. The anger gives me strength and I manage to stand. Grip it and rip it. I wind up, and—*smash*! One by one, I drive the mallet through the mirrors until the floor is littered with shards of glass. Driving wind tunnels like mini-funnel clouds jet out of the empty mirror frames. Orbs of light follow the trail of steaming air upward and outward. The voices in my head rejoice. Freedom. Salvation.

"Thanks, cutie," I hear Candy yell with delight.

"Find your door, Candy," I scream into the hot airstream. "Walk through it—hurry!"

Ned's holding the thermal cam and sports a look of pure panic. "Shit, look!" he screams, pointing to a pile of broken glass on the floor. A red orb emerges from the shards and slowly takes semihuman form. Teeraal, in a filthy and scorched clown costume, rages before us. "Who dares meddle with my mirrors?" he snarls with undertones of a hissing serpent.

"I do, you murderous little bastard," I roar back at him.

Fucked-up Plan—Part Five.

What did Dee Dee Ramone's headstone say?: *Okay . . . I gotta go now.* This is it. I'm ready. It's time. The clown squats low, then leaps up like he's on a pogo stick, over and over. I stand tall, surprise myself by showing no fear. "I freed every soul you trapped," I bellow with defiance. "It was me, Bozo. What are you going to do about it?"

I inch toward him. He bounces up from a squat so forcefully his grimy gloves touch the fun-house roof. He lands only a foot from me. "I'll feed on your soul," he hisses.

I grab my junk. "Why don't you feed on this?" I stare directly into his eyes. His gaze burns my flesh, but he blinks first. "You're nothing," I say. "You're weak. You're the lapdog of Alastor."

Just like that, Teeraal locks his mitt around my throat. I grab his bony hand and tear it away. We're Indian wrestling, our arms locked. "Look at you," I shout, choking on every last ounce of exertion. "A clown. A fool. The suit fits you perfectly, Teeraal." He boils with rage, finds a well of strength a mile deeper than mine, strength not of this world. "You're nothing but Alastor's little bitch," I manage to say before he drives me to my knees and puts a death grip on my throat.

"You can tell Alastor yourself," hisses Teeraal.

The last thing I see is Ned out of the corner of my eye. It's killing him. He wants to step in, but knows he can't. Teeraal yanks my soul from my body like a magician yanking a tablecloth out from under a china setting. From above, I watch my body drop face-forward on the glass-strewn floor and watch Ned and Pat dart to my side. The red door with the crystal doorknob stands in thin air to my right. It beckons me, but Teeraal has me tethered to a chain. As he yanks me away, my door vanishes.

All goes dark below me. I hear Ned and Pat, but I'm heaved farther from their voices by the second.

"Still has a faint pulse," I hear Pat say.

"Clock is ticking," Ned says in a distant echo.

"God, he's deadweight," I barely hear Pat say, straining with effort.

"If anyone asks, just say he's drunk and we're taking him home," Ned responds, grunting with exertion.

Their voices trail off and are gone.

There lies my body. Here lies my soul, bound in chains, being dragged away by Teeraal. We're on the go. Moving fast. It's getting hotter. Deep in the blackness looms an orange glow that burns brighter with every step Teeraal takes.

The fish took the bait all right. But it sure feels like I'm the one on the hook.

The clown seems to sense that I'm not completely dead. He stops in his tracks and kicks me viciously with his oversize boots. "Let go of that life," he shouts. "Die already!" He grabs the chains and drags me again.

Distant memories pop like firecrackers. Scenes from my life. I'm reliving the low points. Feeling pain I've dished out—girls fucked over, foster parents I've never given a fair shot, junk I've stolen, hatred I've felt for damn near every person who crossed my path. Never an ounce of forgiveness. Barely a sympathetic bone in my body. Suspicious. Always pissed off.

I'm yanked through this abyss of shame for what feels like hours. Too much time has already passed. It's too late. I'm dead.

Then Ollie's badge appears in my hand and I feel a spark . . . and a flash of pain. My body is still alive—barely alive—in that motel room. Somehow I know this. So does Teeraal. He keeps looking back at me in disbelief and rage. A sliver of hope. Maybe time passes differently on this other side. Maybe time slows to a crawl so we can relive our sins more profoundly, with more intensity. Maybe that's part of the punishment. Maybe time doesn't even fucking exist.

The orange glow I'm dragged through now burns red and takes shape. I'm being wrenched across solid ground—fiercely jagged terrain. When my eyesight returns and my vision clears, I catch my first glimpse of hell.

S
O
U
L

T
R
A
P
P
E
R

Twenty-two

Fucked-up Plan—Part . . . Whatever.

As Teeraal hauls me by my feet across a rock floor in a subterranean tunnel, I see glimpses of hell through narrow cracks in the cave walls. I see faces—men, women, young, old—attached to bodies of fire.

I try to blot out terror by remembering song titles with the word *hell*. AC/DC: "Hell's Bells," "Highway to Hell"; Guns N' Roses: "Right Next Door to Hell"; Kiss: "Hotter than Hell"; Pat Benatar: "Hell Is for Children"; Elvis Costello: "This Is Hell"; The Who: "Heaven and Hell." Beyond that, I draw a blank.

The journey doesn't take long. The tunnel ends at the opening of a vast cavern. When Teeraal pulls me to my feet, my body erupts in flames. My limbs and torso retain their shape but what was once flesh and bone is now fire.

I look in all directions. Feel like I'm standing in the end zone of a Flintstones football stadium. Natural rock formations create a coliseum-style setting. Hundreds of demons in all forms—some humanoid, some beast, some a perverted hybrid of the two—mill about in these rock bleachers, watching scenes from the lives of a dozen or so souls rotating around the edge of the cavern floor like numbers on a roulette wheel. These scenes—snippets from lives lived by utter scumbags—appear with vivid clarity in midair, high above the arena floor like some kind of holographic Jumbotron in a Vegas magic show. Directly in the center of this floor is a throne surrounded by a crowd.

As I take it all in, the pain in my body is immense. But it's the sound that really throws me off. I expected a million voices crying out in misery. Instead, it's a maddening buzz—a low and steady murmur of collective bitching and moaning. A nausea-inducing cacophony of a million lame excuses: *I shouldn't be here. This isn't the deal I struck. If only I'd have known. It was his fault I'm here. It was her own fault I killed her*, etc., etc., etc. The buzz drones on, pouring out of every corridor until my head threatens to split in two.

As Teeraal drags me to the center of the floor, I make out the figure perched on the throne—Alastor, surrounded by minions and slaves. As I hoped, Teeraal has brought me to his master the way a cat drags a dead mouse to his owner. When we finally reach the throne, Teeraal wraps the chain around my neck and forces me to kneel before Alastor's hooved feet. "You refuse to die, but die you will," Alastor hisses in my ear. He yanks the chain so tight, my vision blurs. I can't utter a word.

Alastor stands. I've seen a slew of horror movies. Pored through countless pages of demonology books. Still, there's nothing like seeing evil from head to toe—the real deal—live and in person. What little life I have left in my body is draining away at the blurry sight of him. Somewhere around eight feet tall. Bloodred. Ram horns. Heavily muscled arms. Black wings. Eyes of a hungry lion. Cloven hooves that kick up dust. Flame-tipped staff in his enormous hands. The glowing murky gold aura that surrounds all demons.

Alastor looks at Teeraal. "Well?" His voice is comprised of many voices, many sounds—male and female, beastly growls and roars. Despite its fragmentation, it's hypnotic.

Teeraal beams with pride. "For you, Master. A fresh soul in

need of torture." The clown bows to Alastor, who looks down at me, unimpressed with his gift. He spits in my face. "Entomb him."

Teeraal is disappointed. He takes it out on me, slapping my face a half-dozen times before yanking the chain and dragging me toward one of the hundreds of corridors jutting off the arena floor. Within these corridors are tiny nooks cut into the rock walls. Most of the nooks are covered with boulders. A few are open and empty. The chain is too tight. I can't turn my neck to get a look inside. Just flashes as I'm whisked a half mile deep.

Teeraal stops and hurls me inside a nook. "You'll die in there," I hear him say as a giant rock slides into place and seals me in. My body returns. I'm naked. It's cramped. Only enough room to sit cross-legged. There's a mirror in front of me. A boulder slams shut and seals me in. Darkness envelops me. Little air. It's not hot—it's cold. Freezing cold. I hear thumping on the walls.

Can't move.

Claustrophobia times a million.

I'm holding Ollie's badge. Where's the luck?

I panic.

I can't breathe.

I can't see.

I can't end up here.

I want to go home.

I wish I'd been a better person.

I squirm.

It just gets colder.

I'm suffocating.

Then, there's light. Dim. From around the mirror. A three-way mirror, like in a clothing store fitting room. There's no hiding from my naked reflection. I look bad, beaten. The image swirls. I'm hideous. Sad eyes set in a disfigured face. I open my mouth. No teeth. A tongue tipped with flicking forks. What is this—my true reflection? I don't buy it. I'm no saint, but I'm not that bad. Not evil. Or am I? I begin to sink into shame and self-doubt. What if the universe is perfect and I'm right where I deserve to be? No amount of denial changes the reflection.

This is the real punishment—seeing myself as I truly am. I'm losing my grip on that last thread of life.

I stare at myself for what feels like days. Alone with the stench—beyond foul. The stink of an open sewer flooded with human waste and after-sex. I'll never get it out of my nose.

My repulsive reflection dissolves into a scene. I'm living a moment again. A naked girl on a bed. Me skulking out the door. She sits up. "Where are you going?"

"Out to get coffee and roses," I say.

She buys it. "Hurry back."

She has the look I like, but I can't get away fast enough. She's nice. Too nice. That's the problem. Spent two nights with her and she's so damn nice it hurts. Can't deal with it. She's gorgeous and gullible—an easy target. I talk her into some nasty shit.

I'm out the door, down the sidewalk, and in my car. I'm laughing. Drunk, as usual. No condom. Didn't pull out. Don't even remember her name. One of many that year.

I see a series of quick snapshots of the girl's life after I ditched her. Her leaving a women's clinic, alone. She's way too sweet for L.A. A babe in the woods. Treated like a doormat by a dozen or so guys after me. One of them date-rapes her. Mother dies. Dachshund gets flattened on Melrose. Gets hooked on painkillers. Loses her job. Alone. Walls closing in. She offs herself with a bottle of Soma tablets and a half gallon of Absolut.

Holy fuck.

And then it hits me like a bullet between the eyes. That's who Donna reminds me of. That's the person I've been racking my brain to remember. Jesus Christ.

Then I see a little girl staring at me in the mirror. She's mine. She's hers. I know it. The little girl that never was. I try to shut my eyes, but they won't close. The scene dissolves to a place I know. Botanical gardens up in the foothills. I'm sitting on a bench in a shaded wood. The girl—three, maybe four—sits next to me. There's a sign next to a wooded path. I ask her to read it to me. She can't read yet, but she pretends she can. She tells me it says: *Many Bambis live in this forest. No guns allowed.* I laugh—hard. She's cute. Her smile floods the cave with fresh air. I can breathe. The stench dissipates. I can smell the brush and grass and flowers. She holds my hand and we walk. "Let's walk to the waterfall, Daddy." I love her and she loves me. Then she vanishes and I'm alone. It all dissolves back to my ugly reflection and that nauseating stink.

I only knew her for a minute, but I think I loved her. And I sent her mother into a downward spiral that ended in suicide.

This is real torture.

The rock rolls away. I crawl out. I'm standing in the cramped corridor among other souls. We're all bound together at the ankles—an old-fashioned chain gang.

The one behind me shoves me in the back—hard. I turn around. Can't be. I know him.

"Someone down here has a real fuckin' sense of humor. I thought it was you." Can't believe it. I'm staring into the face of Giuseppe "Gus" Uttini. Mob hit man. Trapped him in the basement of the Comedy Store, which was, at one time, Ciro's, a nightclub frequented by the mob. Used to take his victims to the office downstairs and bump them off. One day he gets bumped off and gets so mad he takes up residence. Takes out his rage on all the comedians. The laughter drove him nuts. Hated Sam Kinison the most. He was not happy when I sent him packing.

"Hi, Gus. Small underworld."

"No good, rock-and-roll-lovin' cocksucker," he snarls at me. "Better watch your back."

"What are you gonna do, whack me? I'm already dead." Yet I'm not. I can still feel a microthread of life. I'm still in the game. Gus can't know that. I didn't come all this way to let him fuck it up.

The soul chained in front of me, a fossil of a woman, turns and nods my way. "Hey. Name's Cora Wertz." She's New York. Or Jersey. Sounds like she's smoked a million unfiltered Camels.

I ignore her.

"What? No name?" she snaps. "Not very neighborly, are ya?" I glance at her. "I'm Kane."

She smiles—a mouth full of pearly dentures lit bright by her flaming torso. "Well, seeing as we may be chained side by side for the next few millennia, just thought I'd say welcome."

Did I mention I pretty much hate everyone? That includes basement-dwelling hit men and old biddies. But I need information—fast. My time here is running out. I feel it.

"How'd you end up here?" I ask.

"Poisoned three husbands," Cora says. "Sold my soul to Alastor and was acquitted every time. Lived a hell of a fine life in Palm Beach. Rich as an Ay-rab."

"Was it worth it?"

Cora glances around and throws her flaming hands in the air. "Let's see," she says, turning her gaze to me. "I had a few good decades full of kicks in Florida. Now I have grill marks on my ass. You figure it out."

"Did you ever hear about someone being brought here unjustly? A woman named Donna Lonzi?"

"I'm here unjustly," Gus pipes up.

I turn around. "You murdered thirty-nine people. Told me so yourself," I remind Gus.

"I never killed anyone who didn't deserve it."

"Her name is Donna Lonzi," I repeat. "She was forced to cut a deal with Alastor."

Cora laughs, a hard laugh that turns into a wheezy cough. After her coughing jag ends, she doesn't even attempt to mask her sarcasm. "Deserve it? Give me a break. That's what we all say."

"Does anyone ever get out of here?" I ask.

"What? Escape?" Gus laughs. "From Alastor? Are you kidding? He's the Duke of the Seventh Ring, for chrissakes."

Cora shoots Gus a look of contempt. "Why don't you suck seven rings of smoke out of my ass?" she snaps. "He was asking me. Face it, Kane, this is a one-way ticket to the farewell barbecue. Grab a hot dog bun."

"What if you're innocent?" I protest. "Isn't there any kind of justice?"

"Justice? That's precious," she says, wheezing.

"I'm going to show Kane here some justice," Gus adds.

There's a commotion behind us. Everyone turns and cowers. "What's going on?" I ask.

"Boy, you've got a lot to learn, fella," Cora says with a guttural laugh. "As it's your first day, I'll explain. Get used to it. It's the same every day from now until forever. Tomb time, followed by hellfire, followed by the march, followed by punishment. Then back to the tomb where it starts all over again."

Alastor appears in the corridor behind us. I look past Gus. The souls down the line bow to Alastor. He burns a random one with a staff. The soul collapses. A slave next to Alastor scoops up flames from the fallen soul's body into a gold chalice and hands it to Alastor, who quaffs it. "What's the story with that staff?"

"That's not just fire," Cora says with an air of drama. "It's hellfire. When that stuff scorches you, it forces you to relive your very worst sins."

"And the chalice?" I ask.

"He drinks your sins," Gus says. "Gives him power."

Alastor torches another. He reaches for his chalice. A slave fills it but spills a few drops of the flaming liquid inside, panics, and drops the chalice. She collapses and cowers.

Alastor kicks her onto her back and stomps his hoof into her throat, pinning her. He burns her with his staff. She screams. "Stupid sow!" he roars and hurls the chalice at her face. She struggles to her feet. A blast of hellfire from his staff fills the corridor with glowing light. I get a clear look at the trembling woman.

It's Donna.

Her face is still beautiful, but her eyes are lifeless. Her flaming body is slouched. "Cora," I whisper. "That slave Alastor just punished. Do you know her?"

Cora cranes her chicken neck and squints until a look of recognition settles on her leathery face. "I always think I have it bad until

I see what Alastor and his minions do to that poor girl. I mean, Alastor doesn't even notice most of us. He's been torturing souls so long, he couldn't care less. But with her, he's relentless. He enjoys it. He and his boys violate her every way imaginable."

Alastor grabs Donna behind the neck and drags her back down the corridor, out of sight.

The clock is ticking. My life is slipping away. I was close, but not close enough. "Will she come back this way?" I ask.

"Alastor doesn't let her leave his side. She just sits by his throne with that vacant look. She gave up long before I got here."

There's a thunderous blast from a horn. The chain gang turns and marches down the corridor toward the arena. When we emerge from the tunnel, I see the rock bleachers packed solid with demons. I can't look away—all of them hideous-looking, cross-bred experiments gone wrong. Animal heads on human bodies, human heads on beasts. Dwarves, giants, some naked, some robed—all cheering.

From the corridors, tens of thousands of the condemned march in procession, onto the arena floor and past Alastor's throne. The immensity of it hits me. This is the lair of a single demon—high ranking though he is—and there are more souls pouring out than I could ever count. Multiply that by the thousands of demons sharing power.

That's a lot of damned souls.

As we march toward Alastor's throne, I catch sight of Donna and try to send her mental messages. *Look at me. Look at me. One look.* Nothing. She never looks up. The roar of the crowd is too loud for her to ever hear me. Gotta jolt her from her apathy—give her an ounce of hope.

Approaching Alastor's throne I hear the hiss of a hot brand scorching skin, a moan of agony, and then a shrill voice shouting, "Murder!" with such excitement it sounds like a sports announcer calling a game winning home run. Scenes from lives play out in the air above the frenzied mob. They stomp and cheer as they watch through a man's eyes when he takes an ax to his family. I'm numb. Yet my eyes won't budge.

Another branding hiss and a scream. The voice booms to the crowd, "Rape." More demonic cheers.

"What is this?" I scream at Cora.

She leans sideways and identifies the approaching storm. "Every day it's a different demon," Cora says. "Looks like today it's Andromalius and his iron."

Shit. I know that name, from my book. Andromalius. Punisher of the wicked.

Another hiss of burning flesh. Another scream. "Pedophilia!" thunders the booming voice. The demons go apeshit. I can't watch.

The pattern repeats as we move. *Adultery. Incest. Bestiality. Child abuse.* Donna won't look my way. It's over.

Cora's turn. The iron hisses. She screams. "Triple murder!" A standing "O" from the demons. They're practically doing the wave. While all eyes look up and watch a scene of Cora pouring poison into a glass of scotch, my eyes zero in on Donna. *Look at me, goddamnit!* Nothing.

Then I come face-to-face with Andromalius. Smells of week-old roadkill. Pure white skin. Black eyes. In one hand, a branding iron, in the other, a gray serpent slithering around his long fingers.

An idea. Worth a shot. Andromalius hoists the iron, but just before it sears my forehead, I throw up my flaming arm defensively and let the iron strike Ollie's Lone Ranger badge, cupped in my burning palm. The opening scene of *The Lone Ranger* plays to the crowd, then quickly fizzles out. Murmurs of confusion spread. Andromalius looks stumped, embarrassed. The crowd erupts in mild laughter. They think it's a joke. Andromalius acknowledges the laughter—saves face. I clutch the badge and cower. Andromalius proceeds to sic his snake on me to the wild cheers of the crowd.

I'm kicked forward and the branding continues behind me. I glance back over my shoulder. Donna is staring at me. She saw it. I hold the badge aloft. Yes! She recognizes it.

I wave her toward me. Alastor doesn't notice, but he will. Message has to be short and sweet.

"What—what is that in your hand? Who are you?" she asks in a half whisper.

"I'm a friend of Ollie's. I'm here to save you." I say it too loud and could kick myself. Both Cora's and Gus's ears perk up.

Donna's eyes fill with tears. "Ollie? Where is he? Tell me."

Cora turns her neck and the flappy skin under her throat hangs like a turkey's wattle. Goddamned nosy old bitch. "Hold it together," I tell Donna. "Just listen. Ollie's safe. There's no time to explain. Stay close to me. When I say 'Now,' run to me and grab on. It's your only chance."

We freeze in place. Donna's eyes widen. "He's looking for me," Donna cries. She darts back to the throne. Alastor slaps her and shoves her to the ground.

"What were you two whispering about?" Cora asks.

Enough of Cora. Every second counts. "Mind your fucking business," I snap.

And then two fat mitts wrap around my throat from behind. Gus is squeezing with all his might. "You're alive. I don't know how, but you're alive."

The last ounces of life are draining away in my body. Out of nowhere, Teeraal bounces in and two mighty oversized clown shoes slam Gus in the face. He flies backward. "This one is mine," Teeraal hisses.

"Bring those pieces of meat to me," Alastor orders Teeraal.

The clown unchains me first and drags me toward Alastor. It's now or never. But I haven't flatlined, and Ned won't pass me the relic until I'm dead. Really dead. Fuck. Gotta quit clinging and let go.

Just before he hands me over, Teeraal gets startled, lets go of me like I'm dripping acid. "This can't be," he says, dumbfounded. "He *still* has a drop of life in him!"

Alastor seems pleased. He clutches my throat and squeezes. "Then I will drain his soul dry."

This is the moment I die. Really die. In the far depths of my mind, as if she's in a galaxy far, far away, I hear Eva in an echo chamber yell in a panic, "Flatline! Put the relic in his hand, Ned."

Saint Anthony's finger bone appears in my palm and morphs into something long and cold: a dagger. Two feet long—gleaming silver handle, crossbar, and blade. I hold it up. Looks like I'm gripping an upside-down crucifix. Alastor's eyebrows arch. "What is that? Who are you?"

"Wouldn't you like to know?"

Alastor's puzzled, but not afraid. He stares me down, armed for combat. "Fight me?" he growls in what sounds like a dozen voices before galloping forward in a full-out charge.

He lashes out with his staff. The only sharp blade I've wielded is the occasional steak knife. I'm clueless. Alastor swipes his staff and burns me. The blast of hellfire drives me backward into a wall and inward to a memory I'm forced to relive and the crowd gets to share. I'm in a foster home in Colorado. I hate these people. I'm cleaning them out, emptying the emergency cash from their strongbox. I pocket their cheap jewelry, microwave their cat. Hit the ATM and steal more cash. Head to the bus station. Good-bye, Colorado.

Alastor's wings extend and he glides straight at me. Just as he's about to strike a second time, the blade in my hands comes to life. I block the attack and drive him back. The capacity crowd of demons erupts. The fight's on. Donna rushes toward me. "Come on, kill him!" I hear her scream.

The dagger has him rattled. "Saint Anthony sends his regards," I say.

Alastor twirls his staff like a baton, spins, and flies at me—staff aimed at my head—but the dagger, which controls me, effortlessly blocks the flashy attack. I'd like to take the credit, but I'm just the vessel, along for the ride.

"How does it feel to go up against real power?" I yell.

"There is no greater power than evil," Alastor's legion of voices declare.

In one fluid motion, not of my design, I lunge toward him. An upward thrust cuts the staff in two and drives the dagger under Alastor's chin. He drops to his knees and falls backward, convulsing, foaming at the mouth. There's a collective gasp; then the crowd is stunned silent. The souls around me cheer.

I feel a weight on my back. A hot voice whispers in my ear, "I'm here. I'm holding on."

I spin Donna around and wrap my arms around her. "Hang

tight—this is going to be a hell of a ride . . ."

I hear the far-off echo of defibrillator paddles energizing and then Pat, across the ocean of life and death, shouts, "Clear!"

Thump!

We're flying, racing, rocketing upward, outward. The heat breaks. A cool breeze. The stench lifts. Our flaming bodies become whole again. I clutch the finger bone in my left hand, Ollie's badge in my right.

I manage a chuckle—it might even classify as a giggle. I went to the badlands. I left the bad guy on his back. I have the girl. I'm racing upward out of Dodge. I am the Lone Ranger.

Twenty-three

Day one.

Feeling like I rule one minute. Feeling like I'm dead the next.

I'm wrenched back into my body. Somewhere between consciousness and the morgue slab. I'm gagging, hacking, covered in ice and shivering, yet sweating. Thirsty as hell. Ned's in a panic. "I don't think he's gonna make it," he tells Eva.

Eva's face is inches from mine. "Kane? Kane? Can you hear me, Kane?"

It takes a mighty effort to open my eyes. Can't catch my breath. Try to speak, but choke on the cotton in my mouth.

"He wants to say something," Eva tells Ned.

"Calm down. Breathe, baby," she whispers in my ear as she strokes my forehead. "Just breathe."

I focus on the water stains that decorate the ceiling tile. Heart racing. I fill my lungs. Air. In through the nose . . . out through the mouth. One breath at a time. Breathing is shallow. I'm scared shitless the next breath will be my last. I want no part of the place I escaped from.

I shift my panicked stare from the ceiling to Eva, Ned, and Pat staring down at me from the bedside. Words are trapped in my chest, then throat, but they come, slowly, one at a time. "I will never tell anyone to go to hell again."

Ned's a wreck. He's laughing and crying. "Oh, baby, he's back!" he shouts. He trips over the edge of the bed trying to reach the trap, attached to the Tesla PC. "And . . ." he says pausing to check the status, "Donna Lonzi is in the soul trap! We pulled it off. We fucking pulled it off!"

I smile—a tiny smile. Even my lips ache. "Sweet" is all I can choke out.

Eva leans down, gets inches from my face. "You lied to me," she says. At first, I think she's sort of joking about it, but she's not.

"Sorry." Can't muster any other words.

"You're a good liar," she says.

I try to say thank you, but can only mouth the words.

"It's not a compliment," she adds.

I struggle to say, "How?"

"Ned called me," she says. "From the carnival. Right before you went in. I just got here."

"I'm gonna have to get a refund on that urn I bought you," Ned says.

Takes me forever to ask, "How many hours was I gone?"

Pat looks at his stopwatch. "Eight minutes, eleven seconds since the fun house. You were clinically dead for two minutes, 27 seconds." Pat checks my pupils. "Thank Christ. No signs of brain damage."

"Put on *Dancing with the Stars*," I choke out.

Ned cracks up. "That's it. Brain's toast."

I laugh. The effort to joke ends me. My eyes close against my will. I'm sinking, but still half lucid.

"He passed out," Eva says, panicking. "We need to get him to a hospital—right now, Ned."

My strength on fumes, I force my eyes open. "Tell her," I groan to Ned.

Ned pulls Eva aside. "If he's going to recuperate, he has to do it here—where we're safe. There's nothing a doctor can do for him."

"What? Are you crazy?" she snaps.

"This is way beyond medicine, Eva. Too much to explain, but it has to do with the soul trap. This is more about his astral body than his physical body. His spirit has to heal his flesh. If that doesn't happen, he'll die."

I'm fading, but manage to remind Ned, groggily, "Call Choi."

"Already did," Ned says. "He'll be here in the morning."

"If I make it that long."

Pat's wigging out. "I'm done. I'm out," he says. "Enough."

Who can blame him? Go through all this shit for a lousy two grand? "We owe you," Ned tells Pat. All I can manage is a wink and nod. Pat can't get out of the motel room fast enough. He hurriedly packs his equipment and supplies, double-checks he has his cash, and bolts. No good-byes. I can tell—he thinks I'm a goner.

Ned goes outside for a smoke. Eva plops on the bed and sits next to me. "Please, don't ever lie to me again," she says.

I know I've hurt her. "Okay."

She leans close, whispers, "I thought I lost you."

I manage to say, "I thought you lost me, too."

"I don't ever want to lose you again."

Am I dreaming? "What?"

She rubs a hand through my sweat-drenched hair. "I can't get you out of my mind."

I try to sit up. Not a chance. The effort spurs a coughing jag. When it finally passes, I say, "But I thought you were seeing someone. I thought you wanted to keep this professional."

"Maybe not."

I want to beat my chest and pull her down on this grimy mattress and get busy, but nothing works. I'm shot. Nearly paralyzed. "I'm stoked that you're into me, but . . ." The room gets darker. The bed spirals down. "But can you hold that thought until my brain and body . . ." I'm sinking. " . . . Start . . . working . . . again?"

"Just rest," I hear her say before it all goes black.

Twenty-four

Day two.

When I open my eyes, Ned informs me that I just slept for 27 hours and he has a call into Guinness World Records. Master Soon Choi, my prana healing and martial arts instructor, stands above me, raking my aura with his long fingers and flicking the invisible diseased energy into a bowl of sea-salt water on the floor next to the bed.

Master Choi's only a few years older than me, but he oozes calm and has the demeanor of a friggin' Yoda. Even when his studio in Santa Monica was robbed and ransacked last year, he never lost his cool. Just accepted it and calmly went about rebuilding. Two months later, he's back in business.

Dude's also in sick shape. Competes in triathlons and has a fifth-degree black belt in jujitsu. Tried to work out with him a couple of times, but I couldn't keep up.

Choi learned prana healing from a Korean guru when he was still in his teens. A girl I dated turned me on to it three years ago. Studied with Choi on and off since. I'm a believer. Pretty simple to understand:

We all have an aura—a bioelectromagnetic field—surrounding us. It's like an energy body around our real body. Physical problems are the result of blockages or breaks in our aura. Fix the broken or damaged energy body and the physical body responds in kind.

"What's your verdict?" I ask Master Choi.

"Your aura is broken in several places. Unable to flow, your energy is damming up. Your chakras are damaged and weak." He continues to scan and sweep my aura.

"Am I going to die?"

"Possibly."

Choi wouldn't know how to sugarcoat a donut. "Thanks for the positivity."

He scolds me with a silent look. "I want you to know what you're facing. Your energy has endured great trauma."

"Yeah, I know. I was there."

"I will do my best."

"I know," I say.

"Close your eyes and meditate," he orders me. "Bring the healing light through your crown chakra."

I try to meditate, but drift off to sleep. An hour later, I wake up and Master Choi is gone. Ned's at the computer, in the zone. His fingers are blazing. He's coding.

"Where did he go?" I ask Ned.

Takes a few seconds for Ned to realize I'm speaking. "Said he'll be back tomorrow. You're supposed to meditate on the twin hearts or some such thing. You know what that means?"

"Yeah."

"How do you feel?"

"Like the Grim Reaper's at the door."

"Hang in. This'll take time."

"I'm thirsty."

Ned grabs a bottle of water out of a cooler and holds it to my lips. My hands won't work. "I'm going in," I say.

"Bullshit," Ned says, yanking the water bottle away.

"I've been to hell and back for this woman. I want to meet her."

"I will disown you," Ned shouts. "You'll kill yourself. Your white count is high, your blood pressure is low. Your nervous system is fried."

"I don't care." I don't have the energy to argue. "It's my life, not yours," I manage to choke out.

"Stubborn ass!" he yells. "You've got fifteen minutes. That's it."

My limbs are useless. Ned has to do everything for me. He gives me the silent treatment as he wires me up and puts my goggles on.

"Let me know how you like the new look," he finally says, right before sending the electrical current through my sensors.

"What is it this time?" I ask weakly.

"A surprise for Miss Donna."

Entering the soul trap is a lot easier than usual. Guess it helps when you're already at death's door. I hear an echoey version of Fats Domino's "Blueberry Hill." Open my eyes. Ned dressed the place up to look like a '50s diner. Feels like I'm in the real Johnny Rockets.

And there she stands, right in front of me, transformed from a black-and-white image on a screen into a woman in Techni-fucking-color. She sips a strawberry milk shake—an absolute knockout. Mamma mia, where do I even begin? Long, black hair pulled back in a ponytail. Bloodred lipstick. Big brown eyes. Black-and-white poodle skirt and a tight pink mohair sweater, under which lies one of those gravity-defying bullet bras.

"It's you," she whispers. "Where's Ollie? Is this heaven? Are you an angel?" Her voice has a dreaminess to it. She pronounces her words clearly and fully.

"I'm Kane Pryce," I say. "Sorry, we're not in heaven, and I'm sure no angel. But I'm here to help you and Ollie." Better add the disclaimer: "As soon as I'm strong enough to move."

"You look strong. You're moving," Donna says slowly as she looks me over. "Where is Ollie?" she demands to know.

I raise my arms and look down at my astral body. "This is me in spirit form. My body's not in very good shape. Don't know if I'm going to live or die."

"I can't believe you're still alive," she says. "How lucky you are."

"Ollie's still in the church in Lompoc, right where you left him."

This sets her off. She laughs and cries at the same time. "Oh my stars. Is he okay?"

I nod and give her a wave of reassurance. "He's fine. A great kid. You should be proud."

Donna closes her eyes, smiles at the thought of him—wipes tears from her eyes. "I miss him so much."

"He misses you, too. As soon as I'm strong enough, I'm going to take you to him."

Donna clutches my hands and looks at me pleadingly. Her tear-drenched chocolate eyes have suffered and witnessed suffering.

"Are you real?" she asks with a whimper. "Tell me this isn't a cruel trick."

"You're safe," I say. "They can't touch you here."

Donna wraps her arms around my neck and buries her head in my chest. "Thank you," she weeps. "Thank you for saving me."

I spend the next ten minutes filling Donna in on the soul trap and my time with Ollie. I'm about to ask her about her husband, Nick, when Ned yanks me back. It's a rough ride back to my bed in room 27 of the Mount Gleason Motor Lodge.

I'm on my back hacking, struggling to breathe.

"You okay, Kane? I had to pull you out. Your pulse was tanking."

"She's something," I say. I wonder if they're my last words.

Ned manages a smile despite my latest brush with death. "That's what you always say."

My breathing remains shallow, but gets steadier. "Nice job on the décor, bro."

Ned takes a bow. "Too bad I couldn't drum up a soda jerk."

"Or take the cholesterol out of the fries."

Ned waves off that notion. "Cholesterol's what makes a fry a fry. Speaking of which—the Golden Arches beckon."

Ned goes on a burger run. I'm left by myself in the dim room staring at the water-stained ceiling. Can't die alone. Can't die until Ned gets back with his Big Mac.

There, with Donna, I felt alive, felt good. Just a few lousy minutes ago. Here—alone—more than half-dead.

Better get comfortable with this. Gonna be living this yin and yang until one of two things happens: I get better or I don't.

Twenty-five

D ay three.

Yin.

Feel like I'm stuck in a bad dream. Eva visits, but I can't say much. She brings me my iPad. That'll help. She's trying to be cheerful, but can't hide the worried look. I must look pretty damn bad. I tell her a little about Donna. She doesn't seem very interested. I fake that I'm sleeping and eavesdrop on her and Ned stressing over my 104° temperature and my low blood pressure.

Eva kisses me good-bye and I sleep for real.

Master Choi shows up and goes to town on my aura. He scans my energy field with his cupped hands and chants over me. I meditate—draw a healing white light from the universe into the top of my head. "Keep doing that," Master Choi orders. "It's helping."

Ninety minutes later, he's done for the day. The hint of a smile. "I've healed one of the fractures in your aura," he informs me. "I've unblocked an immense amount of energy."

I'm in the trap for another short visit with Donna. Another easy trip. As soon as she sees me, she races over.

"Where's Ollie? Is he here? I'm begging you—bring him to me." She's clearly tired of waiting and who can blame her?

I do my best to calm her down. Tell her I'm still flat on my back and she'll have to be patient.

A little while later we sit in the corner booth and listen to the Shangri-Las, "Leader of the Pack." Knowing my time with her will be short, I ask about her husband straightaway.

She's hesitant to discuss it. But finally, with some urging, she opens up.

"It was an unhappy marriage from the start," she says.

"Sorry to hear that."

"It takes a lot of energy to live with someone you've grown to hate," she says.

"What went wrong?"

"He drank all the time. And when he drank, he got mean," Donna says, repulsed by the memory. "He smoked incessantly. Sometimes he'd go days without sleeping."

Doesn't sound like the Nick Lonzi I met. Looked fit, sober, and rested to me.

"It got worse when he became obsessed with the occult," Donna adds. "Nick craved wealth. He had doubts about his own abilities. He worshipped the devil. That's why he summoned that demon. To bring him wealth and success."

Bingo. I knew the son of a bitch was evil. And I have a hunch about the demon's identity. "Was it Belphegor?"

Donna looks surprised. "Yes. How did you know?"

"He's the demon who helps people make discoveries that will make them rich."

"For the price of their souls," Donna adds.

Elvis comes on the jukebox. "Hound Dog." "So Belphegor was behind his designs for the electronic slot machine?"

"Yes. Nick sold his soul and made his mark and his fortune."

"But he got sick," I say.

"Cancer," says Donna. "Started in his throat and spread."

"Wouldn't surprise me if Belphegor gave him the disease so he could collect his debt faster."

Donna seems to dismiss that notion. "Nick was poison. He was cancer. I read somewhere, once, and I believe it as fact—the body is a mirror of the soul."

"But he lived."

"Thanks to Alastor."

"What?"

"He summoned Alastor to cure him."

Now I'm confused. Too many demons in the picture here. "But he had already sold his soul to Belphegor."

"This time around he traded Ollie's soul for a cure. For a long, abundant life."

What did Karl say? The demon of sins that pass from parent to child. "And you died in the process?"

"Yes," says Donna.

No-good son of a bitch.

"It was meant to be, though," she says. "I couldn't have lived without Ollie."

I reach over and clutch her hand. "The Great Pretender" by the Platters plays. "I know about the accident," I say.

I watch Donna's thoughts race back to that night. She seems to relive the entire accident it in her mind before she speaks of it. "By then, I'd left him for good, and was trying to get back to my family in Lompoc, but Alastor and his legion came for Ollie while I was driving. They surrounded the car. I couldn't see. It was dark. I lost control." Donna buries her head in her hands and weeps. "We were flying and then our souls were torn from our bodies."

"I'm so sorry. You were so young."

"27," she says. Another member of the club. Jung's synchronicity fucking with me again.

I think twice about it, but finally tell her that Nick is alive and well and that I met him. She's not at all surprised. A deal is a deal.

"I told Eva," I say, more to myself than to Donna, "that he was no good. That a darkness surrounded him. She didn't believe me."

"Who's Eva?"

"A girl I know."

Donna bites her tongue a little, then finally asks, "Is she your girlfriend?"

I chew on that one. Yes wouldn't be true. Not yet. Neither would no. Something is definitely brewing between us. A maybe would work, but it makes me sound lame. "Eva's a friend," I reply. I remember Eva's words. "A real friend. She helped me reach you."

"Oh." I read her body language. She seems a little relieved. "Well, thank her for me."

"I will."

Donna shakes her head. "I just wish I could look Nick in the eye, just one last time," she says.

"I plan to do more than just look him in the eye."

"Let it go," Donna warns. "You've seen who protects him. Your life—your soul—is worth more than that." She's probably right, but I argue a bit, hoping it impresses her.

She's a stunner, sitting across from me, tapping her finger to "Good Golly Miss Molly" on the jukebox. "The commodore told me what you did. How you sacrificed your soul to save Ollie's."

Donna shakes her head. "It was an easy decision," she says.

"It was a brave one," I say.

Then, without warning, my exit door appears. I don't want to leave, but Ned is forcing the issue. I'm sucked through the door and yanked back to the room.

Yin.

Ned is pissed. "When you see that door, use it. Trust me. There's always a good reason why I'm opening it for you."

"All right."

"Don't make me drag you out. A lot of things could go wrong."

"All right, I said." I'm still harboring a mini-grudge at Ned for not telling me the truth about the trap.

"You were in there way too long," Ned says. "No more journeys inside until your nervous system rights itself."

I'm weak and struggling for breath, but pissed off enough about Nick that I have to let off steam. "Nick Lonzi is responsible for their deaths. Bastard sold Ollie's soul to Alastor."

"Damn," Ned says. "Sacrificing your only son. Freakin' biblical shit."

I want to move, but still can't. Can't sit up. Better than yesterday, though. Arms move, but hands can't grasp. No strength. With every ounce of energy I have, I manage to prop myself up for a couple seconds. Then I collapse on my back.

"Look at that," Ned says, grinning. "That's what a politician would dub 'progress.'"

"I'm going back in tomorrow," I tell him.

He sighs, completely fed up with me. "I know you are," he says. "Stubborn ass."

Day four.

Yin.

Eva brings breakfast, but I still can't eat. I tell her Donna sent her thanks and she asks, "For what?"

"For helping," I remind her.

She doesn't seem too enthusiastic.

Eva manages to get a glass of orange juice down my hatch. It perks me right up. She also brings a portable DVD player and we watch *Shutter Island*. She curls up alongside me and I manage to get my limp noodle of an arm around her. She rests her head on my chest. It's nice. I'm out halfway through the movie. When I wake up, she's gone—back at work.

Master Choi shows up in the afternoon and sets up the bucket of saltwater next to the bed. For two hours, he meditates over me and rakes my aura, never once touching my body. Ned rolls his eyes a couple times as Choi flings negative, diseased energy into the bucket. Ned's not a believer. That's why he'll be dead before his time. Stubborn ass.

Yang.

"Not today?" Donna asks when I arrive.

"Not yet," I say. "Sorry. I know this is really hard for you."

I'm determined to stay a little longer in the trap. Despite the disappointment of another day without Ollie, she seems happy to see me. I tell her about my time with Ollie, and, for the first time, I catch that smile—the one from the movies—the one that starts small and grows into a wide grin. God, what a face. What a sweater. Sweet baby Jesus!

The conversation just flows.

"The little dude loves the Lone Ranger," I tell her.

Donna smiles warmly and lets out a sophisticated little giggle. "I know," she says. "Ollie started wearing his mask all day and night. He even slept in it."

"You wanna hear what kind of son you have?" I ask.

Donna leans toward me on her elbows and rests her chin on her hands. "Yes. Tell me."

"He gave me his Lone Ranger deputy badge for good luck when I came to find you."

That makes her proud. "That's Ollie. He's so sweet."

"I know," I say. "I can't get enough of him."

She smiles that smile again.

I wonder if I should bring it up? What the hell. "You know, I saw all of your movies." I say.

Donna raises her eyebrows. "That must have taken about ten minutes."

"You were good," I say. "You lit up every scene you were in."

She blushes. "My, that's a nice thing to say."

"It's true. You were great in the shooting gallery scene in *The*

Crooked Way. And the way you jumped out of that convertible in *In a Lonely Place. . . ."*

"I auditioned for the part of Mildred Atkinson."

"The murder victim? You would have been great."

"The director said I didn't scream convincingly enough."

"I noticed there was a five-year gap between your last two movies."

"Nick never wanted me to act. And then Ollie came along. But when Ollie went off to school, and I quit caring what Nick thought, I started auditioning again."

"You would have been a star." I mean every word.

"You're very kind," she says, smiling at me warmly.

My exit door appears. I trust Ned has a reason for me to leave. I hug Donna good-bye and feel what she has packed under that sweater. And with that, I'm hurtled back to room 27.

Day five.

Yin.

I'm sitting up in bed feeding myself a cup of yogurt. My color is back. My headache has gone from perpetual migraine to hangover.

Ned eats his seventh meal in a row from McDonald's. This time it's two Egg McMuffins and hash browns. I tell him my brush with death has left me with a heightened sense of awareness and that I can hear his arteries closing. I think he buys it.

When Master Choi finishes for the day, he tells me that my aura is repaired and that he will work next on my chakras. My homework for the night: meditate on charging my aura with a dose of chi—life force. I promise to try.

Ned tries to talk me out of going back in. "You need to take a break," he warns.

"I have to go," I argue. "Donna's seen the other side. She has knowledge I need—we need. She plans to tell me a lot of important things today."

"No Ollie?"

"Not yet," I say.

"Damn."

Soon.

Twenty minutes later: "Elvis is my dreamboat," Donna says. "I saw *Love Me Tender* eight times." Donna and I sit hand in hand, hanging out by the jukebox, listening to Elvis's greatest hits. Something is definitely happening between us.

My feet tap to "Jailhouse Rock." "I'll give Elvis his props," I say. "But he was just the tip of the iceberg."

"Then all I need's the tip," she says.

I give her a hot look. She rewinds her words, thinks, gets it. "Oh my," she says, blushing.

There's so much music I want to share. "But after Elvis came Dylan, the Beatles, the Stones, the Who, Springsteen, the Sex Pistols, another Elvis—Costello—the Clash, U2, Nirvana, the Chili Peppers, Green Day, Rage, Radiohead, Nickelback . . . I'm going to tell you about them all." I glance at the jukebox and make a mental note for Ned.

"Wait a minute," Donna says, her sophisticated giggle getting naughty. "Did you say sex pistol?"

My door, and . . . *whoosh*—

Yin.

Getting fucking sick of room 27.

"She's smokin'," I say, before I even open my eyes.

"How smokin'?" Eva asks, catching me by surprise.

"Oh, hey, Eva," I say, acting groggier than I am.

"Ned said you were holding down food. I brought you a panini from Pinot Bistro."

"Thanks," I say. Chicken pesto. Smells good.

Eva has a nose for news. She knows something's different. She starts grilling me about Donna. There's that pushiness again—like when she got me to buy those bullshit expensive clothes and cigars for Lonzi. She's not going to win this battle. I clam up. Donna's off-limits. I take a few bites of the sandwich and act like it's making me sick even though it's fucking delectable.

"My head is pounding and I need sleep," I tell her. "Can we talk later?"

She's hurt. I'm a dick. She leaves without an argument.

"Get me back in there," I order Ned, when she's gone.

"No way," he snaps. "Not until tomorrow. For your own good. Meditate like your guru told you."

"Can you pump my iTunes library into the trap's jukebox?" I ask.

"Sure. That's doable. Stuff in the jukebox now is my own MP3s."

I'm stoked. Assembling playlists in my mind.

After Ned downloads my library, he snatches the panini from the to-go container.

"Freeze," I shout. "Unhand the panini and step away."

"You said you were sick."

"I'm fucking starving," I say. "Hand it over."

Ned hands me the grilled-to-perfection sandwich and I scarf it, along with the fries and side salad. Finally a full stomach.

"You look a lot better. I think I'll go home tonight," Ned says.

"I'll be all right," I tell him. "Go."

Ned helps me to the shitter (God bless him). Good news—my legs are moving; bad news—they can't quite support my weight. Ned gets me back in bed and takes off.

I lay there and try to meditate on lassoing that healing current of energy from somewhere out there in infinite space, but all I can see is Donna's one-of-a-kind smile. And that sweater.

Doesn't help a bit that all I can hear through the walls around me are muffled moans of people shtooping.

Day six.

Yang.

Shake things up a bit. Start the day inside the trap. Donna has a field day with my iTunes library. We listen—mostly to new stuff—and talk for a couple of hours. She's way into what she's hearing.

"All right," I say. "Top ten artists, based on what we listened to this morning."

"Ten," she says. "The Prodigy. I love the *boom, boom, boom* in 'Thunder.'"

"You and me both."

She's thinking hard. "Nine. I think I'll say Art Brut. Funny, but it has a great beat."

"You're gonna love punk. Wait until you hear the Clash, the Ramones, and UK Subs."

"Eight," she says, tracking a figure eight on the countertop, "would have to be Lady Gaga."

"You should see what she wears," I tell her. "Or doesn't wear, actually."

"It makes me want to dance," she says, swaying her shoulders.

"That's what it's made for."

"Seven. Hmm . . . I did like 'White Lies.' The singer's voice is very mysterious. That song 'To Lose My Life' was really touching."

"I like that one, too."

"Six. Probably DeVotchKa. Such a blend of styles."

"They sound like they're from Russia, but they're from Colorado."

"Five. I'd say Bob Dylan."

"I thought you'd like him."

"He paints with words," she says.

"You dig folk music," I say with a tinge of surprise. "Folk rock was just around the corner from 1957."

"Four. I loved the Black Eyed Peas."

"They're just flat-out fun."

"Three. I suppose I'll say 'The Girl from Ipanema.' Loved it. So sultry."

"Great to listen to poolside with a tropical drink," I say. "Number two?"

"'Layla.' Derek and the . . . ?"

Fuckin' A, she picked it. My heart melts like a warm Hershey bar.

"Derek and the Dominos," I say, bouncing off the ceiling. " 'Layla' is a classic song. A classic album. You know, most of those songs are about one girl that Eric Clapton was in love with. A woman he couldn't be with."

Donna's eyes widen. "He must have really been in love. Was her name really Layla?"

"No. The name Layla comes from an ancient Arabic love poem—*Layla and the Majnun.*"

"What's the poem about?"

"A princess who was married off by her father to someone she didn't love. Her broken-hearted true love was driven mad when he couldn't have her. That's what *majnun* means—madman."

"Very romantic," Donna says.

"And your number one?" I ask, knowing exactly what's about to come.

"The Beatles," she says.

"Of course." I played her an assortment of Beatles tunes first and they knocked her blind.

"John, Ringo . . . ," she says, recalling.

"George and Paul," I add. "It was George's wife that Eric Clapton wrote all those songs for on 'Layla.'"

"His wife? Oh, dear," says Donna. "Sounds messy."

"Love usually is."

"Can we listen to the Beatles some more?" she asks.

"Sure."

My door appears. "I'll be back soon," I say.

Just before I step through the door, Donna says, "But, Kane, Elvis is still better than any of them."

I laugh my way back to godforsaken room 27.

Yin.

I'm able to disconnect my own sensors. My fingers are working precisely. "No Eva today?" I ask Ned.

"Here and gone already," he answers.

"Really?" I'm relieved and Ned knows this.

"I told her you were likely to stay in for a couple of hours. She didn't want to wait."

"Hmmm."

Ned looks pissed. "You know, she really seems to care about you."

"Yeah."

"And she's *alive!*" he punches the word Kinison style.

I don't reply.

Twenty-six

Yin.

Master Choi arrives and surprises me. Suggests we go to up into the Angeles Mountains for our session. I feel like I just got out of prison. We drive about an hour, up the 2 Freeway in his Saab convertible, through rugged mountain terrain, to Mount Wilson and pull off near the observatory. We walk a short distance to a deserted clearing. I'm still weak. The walk drains me. The view is stunning. It's a crisp day, the kind of day in L.A. just after a rain when the smog dissipates and the view is clear. From our perch we can see past the entire Los Angeles basin to the ocean. It's a healing day.

I stretch out on a blanket and Choi touches up my aura. I meditate deeply. The fresh air is like a cleansing tonic. I can feel a flow of vibrational energy circling my body in a steady current. The top of my head buzzes. My crown chakra is open. The power descends down the center of my body and reenergizes my forehead, throat, heart, solar plexus, spleen, navel, and sex chakras.

I breathe deep and strong.

Feels like a full body orgasm.

Master Choi seems pleased. "My work is done."

"I owe you my life," I tell him.

"Then live a good one," he says.

We walk back to his car. On the drive back to the motel, I offer him cash. He refuses, with class. Bids me farewell in the motel parking lot and tells me to follow up with him in a week.

I'm back.

I'm whole.

I open the door to the motel and feel like I just got stabbed. Ned is seated in front of the monitor and Tesla PC. Eva is lying on the bed, wearing the NuMag helmet. She's removing the Ganzfeld goggles and soundproof ear buds. She looks pale, faint. She's practically incoherent.

"What the fuck?" I shout.

Eva tears the helmet off, leans over the side of the bed, and pukes. Ned darts out of his seat and catches the last of her vomit in the motel trash can.

"Oh my God . . . Oh my God," Eva cries.

Ned rolls Eva on her back. "You're okay," he assures her. He applies a cold cloth to her forehead. "Take it easy—you're back."

I snap. "You fucking sent her in?" I shout in his face.

"Shhh . . . ," he says sternly.

"Don't hush me."

"Take it easy. Think of her. You remember what it was like for you the first time."

"Outside. Now," I grunt at him.

Ned leans down and whispers to Eva. "We'll be right back. You just rest. You're okay." His little show of care and concern makes me sick.

We march about a block north to the parking lot of an abandoned gas station where Ned has been parking the camper. I get angrier with every step I take. All of Choi's work is shot to shit. I'm ready to fry Ned's fat ass, beat him with his aebleskiver pan.

Inside the camper, I grab Ned by the collar shove him against the wall. "Where the fuck do you get off sending her in there?"

Ned raises his fists defensively. "Take it easy."

"You had no right," I shout. "That's my place!"

"Your place?" Ned snaps back. "Your place that I helped create."

"We're supposed to be a team. You should have asked me."

Ned's not backing down. He's getting angrier. "She wanted to go in, so I sent her in. What's the big fucking deal? I mean, make up your mind. Is she a part of this or not?"

I go for the jugular. "What? Did you think you might get in her pants? All your bullshit talk about Watergate and Arnold Schwarzenegger. You think you're impressing her?"

"Watch it." He's so pissed he might take a swing.

"You fucked me over once by not telling me the truth about leading me to the trap . . . about my father. Now you fucked me again. I don't even know you."

"Well, I'm the only person who knows you," he says jabbing a finger in my chest. "Don't forget it."

"Maybe I need to make some changes," I threaten, all cocky.

"Be my fucking guest. But first, let's finish what we started. Let's get paid, and then you can do whatever the fuck you want."

I storm out of the camper. Eva's next on my chopping block. Ned huffs and puffs, hot on my heels. I throw open the motel room door, but Eva's gone. A note reads: *Feeling sick. Going home. See you tomorrow.*

"She's lucky," I mumble.

"No, asshole—you're lucky. Wake the fuck up and realize it."

"What?" I yell. "Lucky to have friends like you? Like her? I trusted you both and you fucked up. I'm better off alone."

Ned turns to leave.

"Sit your fat ass down," I hiss. He stops. "Get me back in there. Now!"

Yang.

Donna seems relieved that it's me.

"I'm sorry," I tell her. "I didn't know Eva was coming here. I would have warned you."

"It's okay," Donna says.

"No, it's not okay," I assure her. "Pisses me off."

"She was nice enough."

"What did she want?"

"To talk," Donna says. "We just talked."

"About what?"

"About things. . . . About you."

"Jesus."

"She really likes you. I think she's in love with you."

"Please," I say, waving it off. "I hope she didn't bother you. You've been through enough."

"She didn't bother me," Donna says. "She was only here a few minutes." She pauses, searching for the words. "She's . . . a little pushy."

"I know."

"A little . . ." Donna lets it hang.

"Intense . . . aggressive . . ."

Donna smiles that smile and nods. "Yes. Well put."

"I'm sorry."

"Nonsense." Donna leads me to the jukebox. A minute later we're listening to the Go-Go's "We Got the Beat."

"If I were alive, I'd be eighty," Donna tells me.

I laugh. "Cradle-robber."

"Would you still have me?"

"Of course."

"We'd turn some heads."

"I could polish your dentures, carry around your oxygen tank."

Donna smacks me in the arm and gives me that sophisticated giggle. "Eighty's not that old. Age is a state of mind."

We give the music a break, catch our breath, and just sit silently for a long, calm spell. It's a comfortable silence. Then we start talking . . . this time for hours, about a lot of things, none of them too important.

I've never been with anyone so easy to be around. I have only a few vague memories of my parents. One of those memories is of a night when I crawled into bed with them during a thunderstorm. I felt so safe and protected. That's how I feel when I'm with Donna. It's effortless.

We get to talking about what we'd been through together. It's not pleasant, but it's like we have to. We've been to hell and back.

"Getting hit with that hellfire," I say. "Being in that tomb . . . I can't shake it."

"You're not supposed to shake it," Donna says. "That's what makes it real punishment."

"I can't imagine you had any great sins haunting you. You're too nice. You didn't earn your way to hell. You were forced there."

"We all have our dark secrets," Donna replies.

"Care to elaborate?" I ask. I realize instantly it's way too personal. But to my surprise, she answers.

"I wasn't very kind to my parents."

"Kids can be like that," I say.

"It wasn't when I was a kid. I was a grown woman. My parents didn't approve of Nick. I said a lot of terrible things to them I wish I could take back. I hurt them."

Donna's face is full of regret. Then she snaps herself out of it. She gives me a quizzical look I haven't seen yet. "How about you?" she asks.

I'm not about to tell her I'm a no-good, drunken, womanizing prick, so I dance around it. "I've hurt people. A lot of people," I say. "I hurt one person pretty badly."

"A girl?"

"Yeah." I could say I didn't mean to, that I didn't know what I was doing, but that'd be lame.

Donna doesn't pry. Classy. Eva would have me spilling my guts. "We can't change the past," Donna says.

"You're right," I say. "We can't right some of our wrongs. All we can do is try not to make the same mistakes again." I make a mental note to listen to myself for once.

A short time later, I'm telling her things I never shared with anyone. My voice cracks. "It was tough," I say, wiping away tears. "My mother just left us. Just like that. I was seven. And then, when I was ten, my dad was gone, too."

"Did he die?"

"I wish I knew," I say. "He just disappeared."

"What happened to you?"

I enter virgin territory. I've never spoken about this to anyone— not even the counselors who tried to pry it out of me when it happened. The words don't come easily. "I came home from school—let myself in. Watched TV. Dinnertime—no Dad. Rockies game came on. Their first season. They sucked, but we watched them anyway. Made the popcorn, like we did. No Dad. Bedtime—no Dad. I had my own room, but I liked to sleep in a little tent in the corner of his room. I hated being alone. I liked hearing him snore."

Donna listens patiently. "Good Lord," she whispers. "What did you do?"

"I didn't sleep that night. Got up. Went to school. Sleepwalked through the day. Came home. Ate something. Waited. Another ball game on the tube. No Dad. Don't think I slept that night either."

Donna takes my hand. "I'm sorry," she says with tears in her eyes.

Now the tears are running down my cheeks and the words are stuck in my Adam's apple. Somewhere deep, though, it feels good to finally put words to the memories. "Fourth day, I fell asleep at school. Woke up screaming from a nightmare in Social Studies class. Mrs. Krinock takes me to the principal's office. Principal can't track down my dad. The jig is up. I crack and admit I'm alone. Next thing I know I'm living with total strangers."

Donna glances away, says, "At least you weren't alone anymore."

"Yes, I was," I say. "I learned real fast you don't need to be by yourself to be alone."

"I'm so sorry," she says, stroking my hair.

"They never said good-bye."

"Don't hate them," Donna advises. "Don't carry around that kind of anger. Who knows what happened? What they were facing? Look at me and Ollie . . ." Her words are like medicine. She knows.

I hug her and she embraces me tightly. I look in her eyes and drown like a kitten in a sack. Our lips meet the second my door appears. Ned and his fucking timing. She pulls back. I know I have to leave. Can't risk damaging my physical or astral body again. Scarlett (O'Hara, not Johansson) nailed it: "Tomorrow is another day."

"You have to go home," Donna says, walking me to the door.

"I am home." I tell her, before stepping back to Ned and room 27.

Twenty-seven

Day seven.

Yin.

I go for a walk around the block. I feel okay. Not great. Not even good. Just okay. But good enough to go. A weeklong journey from the brink of death to the land of the living.

I've survived room 27. I've survived two daggers in the back. Time to go.

The tension has eased, just a little. When I get back to the room, Ned's packing up, but I stop him short of disconnecting the equipment. I want to go in one more time before we leave.

"This makes no sense," Ned says. "Seems like the more time you spend inside the trap, the stronger you're getting."

I nod. "It's the company I'm keeping."

"This is not how it's supposed to work."

There's a knock. Eva. Ned ducks out. On his way out the door, he glances at Eva and whispers to me, "Remember, she's alive."

Eva. A good egg. Came to visit every day. Hot. Smart. She's into me. Sassy. Pushy. A couple of weeks ago, I thought about her non-stop. Now I barely notice when she's in the room.

"How do you feel?" I ask.

"Like I have the flu—but I don't. Now I know why you always look so wiped out."

"It's a rough ride."

"Well put."

My temper flares. "You should have asked me if you could go in the trap," I say. I stop way short of tearing her a new asshole, like I did to Ned.

"Fair enough," she replies. "But I can give you five reasons why it was a good thing. Five: I now have a full understanding of the experience. It'll allow me to write about it more clearly. Four—"

"Stop," I say, cutting her off. "Isn't it really as simple as when you want something, you usually get it?"

She smiles. Her smile is so different from Donna's. "Well put."

"What did you think of her?" I ask.

Eva smirks, all smart-ass. She shrugs her shoulders.

"What?" I snap.

"Nothing," she says with a grin.

"What? Say it."

"Well . . . ," and then the floodgates open. "She's a little phony. Don't you think?"

"Phony?" If she had a pair of balls, she'd be spitting teeth.

"I mean that voice—all soft and low. The way she bats her eyes. That cheesy smile . . ." She laughs.

I pretend like I'm going to sneeze and bite my palm. Just shut up. Don't return fire.

"She likes you," Eva says.

I don't answer.

"Not at all uncommon. Many women fall for men who rescue them."

Try to calm my breathing. Remind myself to be a better man—to treat her well. She's not a bad person. Go light.

"But she can't have you. You're taken. You know. When I want something . . . ," she says with an ornery laugh and tilt of her head.

I let out a sigh that becomes a little chuckle. She looks at me quizzically. This is not comfortable.

"Gotta say, you're looking good, Kane," she purrs. She rubs her body against mine. "You look like you might be ready for some physical activity."

"I don't know about that," I say.

She grabs my hand. I pull away, avoid eye contact.

"Kind of convenient—we're already in a shady motel."

I let out a totally phony chuckle. "Life is fucking weird."

She looks none too pleased.

Water's bubbling. "That's your response?"

I shrug. I'm not going to be a dick.

"Are you kidding me?"

I shake my head. I'm not going to be an asshole.

"Do you remember the things I told you when you came back?"

I was half out of it, but I remember one of the things she said: "You couldn't get me out of your mind."

"Well . . . ?"

"Well, what?"

Water's steaming. "What do you think? About me?" Her anger dissolves into an unexpected vulnerability. "I'm trying to tell you. I want us to be together."

What can I say? You're hot for me and I'm hot for a ghost? Instead, I stammer. I babble and make no sense. She gets the point. Finally I piece some coherent words together. "I just think it's best . . . if we just—"

"Just what?"

The words won't come.

"Say it," she snaps.

"If we keep things professional." There, I said it.

Water's boiling. Can't tell if she's hurt, jealous, or furious. Might be all three at once. She's not used to rejection.

"You can't be falling for a ghost," she says with a sarcastic snicker.

"Don't be crazy."

"You are. I can tell."

Did I mention that one of my golden rules is never argue with a woman?

Just run the other way. Vanish. Do not expend emotional energy. But when cornered in a motel room with no way out, give it a shot. "Eva, just listen to me—"

Water is boiling over. "I can't believe this."

"Eva—"

"Fine. If that's what you want. Fine."

She reaches for the doorknob. I block her. "Listen, I couldn't have done any of this without you—"

She shoves my arm aside. "I have to go." She's out the door, in her car, and burning rubber.

Yin. Yin. Triple yin with a yin chaser.

Ned's silent when he returns. He knows what happened. "Let's make this quick," he says, prepping the equipment. "We need to pack up and scram."

"Okay."

Right before he sends the current through my sensors, he says, "Tell the dead one I said hi."

Yang.

Donna and I sit in a booth side by side holding hands. An MP3 of my work-in-progress on "Layla" plays on the jukebox. It isn't done yet—no vocals, no finale solos—but I play what I have anyway.

"It's beautiful," she says. "You're playing the guitar?" she marvels.

"Yep," I say, proudly.

"You're so talented," she says.

"That's really nice of you to say," I tell her. "Thanks."

An hour later, we're talking about a different world from the one she left. "I think it's wonderful a woman ran for president. What did you say her name was?"

"Hillary."

"And a black man is president?" she says with disbelief.

"An African American lives in the White House, which, ironically, was built by slaves."

Donna gives this news serious thought. "That's good," she says.

I spin to the other side of the booth and face Donna. "I hate to change the subject, but it's time to bounce. Time to get you back to Ollie."

Her beautiful face beams. "I can't wait," she says, clapping her hands.

I lean over and touch her cheek. "I just wanted to thank you. Something about my time with you. It healed me."

Donna's smile melts me. "And you healed me, Kane. My spirit was broken. You saw."

"Your spirit was broken and my body was lifeless. We make quite the couple."

She strokes my hand. "I agree. Quite the couple."

I look deep into her eyes. I'm about to swing for the fences. "You know, I saw a picture of you once. In a newspaper clipping."

"And?"

"And . . . my eyes got dizzy. It wasn't enough. I went out and scoured Hollywood for your movies."

"And?"

"They weren't enough. So I tracked down some of your old home movies."

"From where?" Donna wants to know.

"Your sister, Rita."

She pulls back, looks up. "Rita. My God, she'd be . . ."

"Eighty-three," I say.

Donna's mind wanders far off. Memories flood her. "I can't imagine that. Eighty-three. How is she?"

I lie. Don't want to upset her with the truth. "She gave me some pictures of you. Some home movies."

"And?"

"They weren't enough. So I had to come and get you."

She pauses, then says, "Before you go, I have to say something."

"Not about Elvis, I hope."

"Kane, you're a fine man."

I don't handle compliments well. I try to joke it off. "You haven't seen me when I drink whiskey." Then I realize: It's not a joke.

"I mean it," she says. Her brown eyes fill with tears. I wrap my arms around her and squeeze. She squeezes me back hard.

"The way Ollie talked about you," I add. "The kid he turned out to be. The acorn never falls far from the tree."

She looks up at me and smiles.

"You were worth it, Donna."

A few teardrops land on that pink sweater. "I . . . I think I'm falling for you," she whispers hot in my ear.

"I think I already fell."

We kiss. I shake. She trembles. We tumble into the booth and I'm on top of her. We roll onto the floor, lips locked. I yank up her sweater. The strap of her bullet bra falls off her shoulder. "Oh, Kane," she moans. "Is it even possible for us to . . . in here?"

"Let's find out," I whisper.

And we do.

Yin.

Room 27.

"Well, that's one more thing on the 'wonder if I can do that in the soul trap' list that I can check off," I tell Ned when I come to.

"Christ, I can't even get laid in the real world and you're banging away out in the ether. Details. I want details."

I smile. "Other than saying it was the finest few hours of my life—that's all this gentleman is going to say."

"A gentleman, huh? Damn, she must be good. By the way, you were only in there for five minutes," Ned adds with a hearty laugh.

Ned and I check out of the Mount Gleason Motor Lodge. Miserable place.

We hit the freeway and head north to Lompoc. Dial Eva. No answer. Leave her a message and invite her to join us. After everything we've been through together, I'd like her to be there for the reunion.

Twenty-eight

It's foggy in Lompoc. While Ned preps the equipment in the camper, I track down Father Demetrius in the rectory. The priest is thrilled when I tell him that my work is almost done.

"What form of payment are you expecting?" he asks.

"Nothing wrong with cash. That's what you get in those collection baskets, right?"

He doesn't laugh.

"How would you like to pay me?" I ask, trying again.

Father Demetrius whispers, even though we're alone in the building. "The money shouldn't come directly from me."

"What then?"

"I'd like to transfer the money from my account into my brother's bank account. Would a personal check from him to you suffice?"

I think for a minute. My damn conscience is nagging me. I've been thinking of doing this one pro bono. He's a priest, they're not rich, it's a church, and after all, I kind of owe Saint Anthony. But this is also my work. Hard work. Hazardous work. And it's a business. Decision made: no freebies. "A personal check from your brother is fine," I tell him.

He gives me the key to the church and walks me out.

When Ned and I enter, Ollie lets the church bells toll. I stall for a while, waiting for Eva, but she's a no-show. Ollie's anxious. It's time.

I hand Ned the soul trap. "You feel comfortable pulling the trigger?" I ask him.

"Just this once."

"All right. I'll tell him what's up."

Ned nods. I close my eyes, feel for Ollie.

"Hey, Ollie . . ." I call. I feel an icy breeze blow by. A cold spot forms right next to me—waist high.

I hear, "Hi, Kane."

"I have a big surprise for you, kemosabe. I brought someone to see you."

The cold spot swirls around me. It's hard to make out his response. "The Lone Ranger?" I hear through crackling static.

"Even better. I'm going inside to meet you. Ned will come back in the church in a minute to bring you to me. Okay?"

An echoey "Okeydokey."

"Make sure you stand real still for my pal, Ned," I remind him.

Another distant "Okeydokey."

"See you soon."

I race out to the camper and Ned wires me up. "Well, you pulled this off," Ned says. "So go enjoy it. You know the drill."

I interrupt my breathing exercises and say to Ned, "Give me some time alone with Donna . . . before you trap him."

"Yeah, I figured that."

I'm so pumped I can't steady my breathing. Can't empty my mind of the million thoughts racing through my brain. It takes all my concentration to make the journey.

Buddy Holly plays on the jukebox: "That'll Be the Day."

"You're back," Donna says with delight. "Where's Ollie?" Panic spreads across her face. "Oh no, is he gone?"

I grab her and hug her tight. "Don't worry. He'll be right here."

She frantically searches for the closest reflective surface. "Oh, my stars. How do I look?" she asks, glancing into the glass window of the jukebox.

"Gorgeous."

She turns and smiles.

"And happy," I add.

Then it hits me like a bolt of lightning. This is it. This is the end. I have to say good-bye.

Or do I?

As if she's reading my mind, Donna says, "I wish we could be together."

"Maybe we can," I say.

"How?"

This notion hadn't occurred to me until this very second. I have a choice. "Maybe I can join you?"

Donna looks confused, processes this statement thoughtfully, then understands what I mean. "No, you can't."

"I could."

She breaks out of our embrace and backs away from me. "I won't allow it. I'd never forgive you . . . or myself."

"Why?" I snap.

"Because you have life."

"So?"

"So?" she asks, heatedly. "It's a precious gift, Kane."

"You're the gift," I say, pulling her back toward me.

Again she pulls away. "No," she insists. "You belong with the living. We belong with the dead. That's the way it has to be."

"It's my decision."

Donna looks at the door on the far wall of the diner. That door. "We have no idea what lies beyond that," she says, pointing to it. "No guarantee we can even stay together. For all we know, the slate gets wiped clean. You can't risk it."

"But it's my life," I point out again.

A red fingernail gets pointed in my direction. "I died when I was your age," she says through tears. "It wasn't enough time. It's never enough time. Don't throw it away." She pleads, "Promise me."

I hear something. Ned is aiming. Won't be long.

"Forget it," I say.

"Promise me," she cries.

"Okay, I promise." I don't want her to be angry or sad when Ollie arrives. But this isn't over. I can't let go of the notion that I have a choice.

One thing's for certain. It's not going to end today. Not like this. No way. I'll drag this out until I'm damn well and ready. Gotta find a way to keep her here. "Listen, I have something else to ask you before Ollie gets here."

"What?"

"Remember when you told me you wish you could look Nick in the eye one more time?"

"Wishful thinking," Donna says.

"Not really. I can make that happen. Before I send you and Ollie away . . . before we say good-bye, would you like a moment with your ex?"

After a long, contemplative pause, she says, "Yes, I believe I would."

"It means you and Ollie have to stay here a little longer. We'll have to go to Las Vegas."

"We can wait," she says.

I've never heard a ghost being sucked into the trap before. Sick sound. Must be what it sounds like to be an ant inside a vacuum-cleaner bag.

Ollie arrives and focuses his gaze on me. "I sure missed you, Kane. What's the surprise?" He glances around. His playroom is gone. He takes in the diner setting, a little discombobulated. "Hey, what's goin' on around here?"

"Someone wants to say hello," I tell him.

And then Donna says from the shadows, "Ollie?" And he turns and sees his mother. He nearly melts into the floor.

"Mommy?" Ollie and Donna rush into each other's arms. They weep and laugh. "Oh, Mommy, you came back. Just like you said."

Donna kneels and bear-hugs Ollie. "Mommy's here," she whispers. He clings to her.

Ollie turns to me. "You found her?" he asks.

I nod. "Sure did, kemosabe."

Ollie grabs Donna's face, looks into her eyes angrily, then pleadingly. "Don't ever leave me again, Mommy."

"Never."

"Promise?"

"Promise. With all my heart," she swears.

I'll never forget their faces. Ever. It was worth going through hell.

For the first time since the soul trap fell into my hands, I feel like it doesn't have to be a curse. It can do some good.

I want to approach them, but don't.

"And then Kane came to play with me and keep me company," I hear Ollie tell her.

"He's quite a guy, isn't he?" she asks, glancing my way.

Ollie whispers to her. "I really want him to be my daddy. Can Kane be my daddy? Please. Please."

I feel like a third wheel. They need time without me hanging around.

"I have to go now," I tell them.

Donna stands and approaches, but I raise a hand and she stops. "No, Kane. Please stay," she insists.

"Yeah, don't leave," Ollie chirps.

"I'll see you soon," I say. "I promise."

My door appears. Donna looks at me, mouths the words, *Thank you*.

"Vegas, baby," I say to her as I step through my door.

Catapulted back to the camper and feel sapped. "Go tell Father Demetrius the church is clear," I tell Ned. "Tell him net 30 on the payment."

Ned scratches his head. "What gives? You didn't release them?"

"Not yet," I say stretching on the camper bed. "Goin' on a road trip first."

"What? Where?"

"Viva Las Vegas," I sing.

"Aw, fuck no," Ned sighs. "You're not gonna leave well enough alone, are you?"

"Not in this life or the next," I say.

Twenty-nine

How can I knock two 300-pound guys unconscious before they know what hit them? That's the question I wrestle with in bed when I wake up at the crack of ten. With no apparent answer and as hungry as Rosie O'Donnell, I call Detective Cliff DuPree and tell him I'll treat him to breakfast at the 101 Coffee Shop on Franklin, a diner a few blocks from my place. He tells me he ate at six, but like a healthy hobbit, he'll meet me for second breakfast.

I get there first and pick a corner booth up against a stone wall at the far end. I'm through two cups of java by the time he gets there.

"You picking up a check?" he marvels. "This must be important." The waitress, a little brunette with a butterfly tattoo on her neck, pours him a cup of coffee before his ass even hits the seat. She digs him. Into tight button-down, short-sleeve shirts and biceps, I guess.

"Two big guys—offensive-lineman big—come at you. How would you take them out?"

DuPree takes a swig of coffee. "Shoot them in the chest. Cave in their skulls with a baseball bat."

"No. How do you do it without inflicting serious damage? Let's say the person they're coming after can't afford to be arrested for attempted murder or assault with a deadly weapon."

DuPree shoots me a smirk. "What are you up to?"

Our waitress is back, gives DuPree the eye. I dodge the question. I'm all set to order a ham-and-Swiss omelet, and then DuPree goes and orders the Cajun catfish and eggs with sourdough toast and that sounds too good to pass up.

When the waitress closes her pad and leaves, DuPree asks. "Do they have to be unconscious?"

I noodle it through. "No. Not really."

"Hit 'em with a taser. Then cuff 'em."

I noodle some more.

"Make sure they're cuffed to something sturdy. Don't want them dragging a chair around. They could hit you with it."

I nod.

"Might want to nail them with pepper spray first before you whip out the taser."

"How might one—with a long arrest record—acquire a taser?" I ask.

The waitress brings our toast first. She didn't have to, but she wants to flirt with DuPree some more.

"It's easy. Can get them a lot of places. Place out in San Bernardino—called the Arms Farm. Not far off the ten. Guy named Gustavo owns the place. Crazy fucker. Don't mention my name or you will make my shitlist."

"Thanks," I say.

"I'll ask a second time. What are you up to?"

"I'll buy you breakfast again next week and tell you."

The waitress rubs her tits all over DuPree's shoulders when she puts our plates on the table. A half-dozen splashes of Tabasco all over my plate and this just became a meal to remember.

DuPree points a fork full of catfish at me. "Remember what I told you—you're too smart to end up in prison." He reaches over and jabs me. "Or are you? Sometimes you really make me wonder."

I shrug. "That waitress so wants to fuck you."

"Nah."

"Yeah."

"She just wants a big tip."

"Exactly."

He laughs. "You think so?"

"Trust me. I know a thing or two."

DuPree laughs.

"Well?" I ask.

"Well, what?"

"You gonna make her day?"

He laughs again. "My wife'll get a kick out of this."

"Wife? You're married?"

He nods and takes a bite of catfish.

"Never pictured it. Where's your wedding ring?" I ask.

"A smart cop never wears one."

Makes sense. "Never take your work home," I say.

"Or your home to work," he says.

We scarf our breakfasts and I say so long to DuPree and walk back to my place. I search for the Arms Farm on my iPad and Map-Quest directions. San Berdoo's not too far off the beaten track on the way to Vegas.

I get a surprise when I walk into the Arms Farm. I pictured Gustavo as a suave Latin-American arms dealer. Instead, he's a Mexican immigrant in his fifties, wheelchair-bound, cerebral palsy. Feel bad for the guy. His speech is so affected, I have to work through everything he says one word at a time. I drop 459 bucks on Michigan Pepper Spray (Gustavo rates it four stars), two pairs of Winchester handcuffs, a roll of duct tape, and the Streetwise Small Fry Mini Stun Gun, delivering a million volts of stun power in a device the size of a cigarette pack. Gustavo gives me what should be a quick lesson on how to use everything. The Small Fry kicks ass. A bright blue current pulsates between the prongs, and the nasty electric-sounding buzz is pretty menacing. I'm in and out in twenty minutes, down the 10 and up the 15 to Vegas.

I crank my tunes and punch the gas. Perfect day. A hot desert breeze blows through my convertible. The soul trap rests on the front seat next to me. I think a lot about Donna and Ollie inside. Wish they were riding shotgun with me on a road trip somewhere cool—Disneyland, Legoland. What the fuck is happening to me?

Then I think about Nick Lonzi and my temper gets as hot as the desert outside. Angrier I get, the faster I drive. Feel like I'm wardancing behind the wheel. Pump myself up. Feel like flattening an animal on the road and painting my face red with its blood.

Roll into Vegas at dusk itching for a fight. Pack my backpack with the trap and my Arms Farm arsenal and march straight into the Phoenician for my showdown. Don't even come close to making it past security at the elevators to the residence suites or office tower. Everybody needs to be badged in. And they're serious about it.

It's getting late. Lonzi's probably left his office for the day. Need to figure something out. Gotta find a way to get into that office tower. I have an idea. Dig through my wallet. Still have the business card from that putz, Randall Cleary. Okay. What would Eva do? I'll call him. Lonzi's all about fund-raising. I'll tell Cleary I'm reaching out on behalf of a celebrity who wants to offer help raising money for the new hospital. Which celebrity? Gotta be a player. Gotta have a track record with charities. Who? Angelina Jolie. Hell, I'll throw Brad Pitt in for good measure. Perfect.

I dial Cleary's number and extension. Get a message—Randall Cleary is no longer a part of the Lonzi Enterprises team. All inquiries should be directed to—I hang up.

Maybe Cleary's on to bigger and better things. Maybe he can make a call to Lonzi on my behalf. It's worth a shot. I check out Cleary on LinkedIn. Looks like he started a company of his own—Cleary and Associates Public Relations. There's an address—Paradise Road. Close.

I drive over. It's a condo building. Fucker's working out of his house.

Knock on his door. He opens it.

"Is this Cleary and Associates?" I ask.

Cleary does a double take, then recognizes me. "What the fuck do you want?"

"Hear me out. I'm here to talk business," I say.

"Business?" Cleary says. "You fucking cost me my job."

"What do you mean?"

"Lonzi fired me the day after that interview. You totally fucked me over."

"Sorry," I say. And I mean it.

"Well, thanks," Cleary says, all sarcastic. "That really gives me the closure I've been looking for."

"Can I come in?" I ask, politely.

"Oh, by all means," he says. Smart-ass.

I step in. His crib is pristine—a Crate & Barrel fuck pad. The antithesis of my shithole on Yucca. The guy has a stainless-steel egg poacher on his kitchen counter for chrissake.

Cleary's not alone. The Barbie-doll receptionist from Lonzi's office struts out of his bedroom in a white T-shirt and criminally short denim cutoffs. She grabs her purse and keys, kisses Cleary, and says, "Gonna run some errands." Totally ignores me as she walks by.

"So is that one of the associates?" I zing.

"What do you want?"

"I need to see Mr. Lonzi. Is there any way you can help me?"

"No," he snaps. I'm about to take one last shot—toss out the name Angelina Jolie—but Cleary goes off. "Fuck Nick Lonzi." I give him a sympathetic look. He erupts. "I was being groomed for general manager—of the whole damn operation. I paid my dues. He made promises. He owed me. And what's that old mummy do? He shitcans me."

He's bitching up such a storm, I can't help but join in. I tell Cleary about my run-in with Nick Lonzi and his bodyguards. He believes me. Lonzi boasted about it when he fired Cleary. Word spread.

Suddenly we're allies. Go figure.

"You picked the wrong bull to fuck with," Cleary tells me.

"So there's nothing you can do to help me get a meeting?" I ask.

Cleary shakes his head. "Lonzi isn't even there. In New York. I think he's back late tonight or tomorrow."

"How do you know?"

"Loose lips . . . and all that."

"Well, I'm not leaving until I see him," I say. "I'll find some way."

Cleary gets a beer for himself and doesn't offer me one. Prick. He's mulling something over. "What do you want to see Lonzi about?" he finally asks.

You want the truth? You can't handle the truth. "I plan to sue his ass for assault and battery. I want to give him a chance to make right before my lawyer serves him."

It's a good solid lie. It works. "I might be able to help you."

Relief. "Shit, that's great," I say.

Cleary drains his beer. "If I help you, what's in it for me?"

Prick. "What do you want?" I ask.

"Dollars and cents."

"How many?"

"Make me an offer."

"Five hundred bucks."

"I was thinking five thousand bucks." Shit.

"Eight hundred," I counter.

"Come on, I have to buy letterhead for Cleary and Associates. Four thousand, and that's my final offer."

I mull it over. Shit. I'm down to $7K or less in my account. I have bills to pay—a stack of them. This will damn near clean me out. I think of Donna. Ollie. "Done."

Cleary returns a minute later with a badge. Barbie's badge. "This will get you up to Lonzi's office. The rest is up to you."

"Won't she miss it?"

"We're leaving for Cabo in the morning. Long weekend. She won't miss it . . . until next week. Then she'll get a new one. After you destroy this one. Deal?"

I reach for the badge. He yanks it away. "Payment up front."

"Come on."

"Sorry. Business . . . and all that."

I spend the next half hour in front of Cleary's computer and on the phone wire-transferring the money. Prick.

"Get inside the hotel tomorrow morning. Lay low. Real low. Your photo might be on a database. They use facial recognition software from Homeland Security."

"Shit," I mutter.

"When I say lay low, I mean hide. Find a rock and crawl under it. I'll make some calls. I'll text you when I know Lonzi is in his office. Go there fast. And look like you belong in an office tower. Lose the rock-star look. You'll stand out."

Fuck you, I say with my eyes. I'm too broke to go shopping. I'll wear what I want. But I nod politely. "Thanks. Good point."

I give Cleary my cell number. He gives me the badge.

"Have a good time in Cabo," I say.

"Thanks. I will. After all, you're paying for it," he says. Prick.

I hit the Strip. I don't have any cash, but I have plastic. I can do a lot of things with my night. Gamble. Drink. Strip club. Good meal. Score a ticket to the Beatles Cirque show. Instead, I book a room facing the fountains at the Bellagio, order room service, crack a bottle of Veuve Clicquot Brut, open the curtains wide just before showtime, and then do something I probably shouldn't do. Release Donna and Ollie from the trap.

I want to show them the Las Vegas Strip in all its trillion-watt glory. I want them to see the Bellagio fountains.

Their energy swirls around me. "Surprise," I say aloud next to the window. "This probably isn't the Las Vegas you remember."

I hear a distant "Wow!" from Ollie, but can't hear Donna's voice. I turn on my digital recorder, but can only make out a static-charged garble.

Wonder what they're saying to each other gazing out at the twinkling buffet of lights and the ballet-dancing waters. Even twenty-two stories up, on the other side of thick glass, you can feel the *boom* when the fountains blast sky-high to "Singin' in the Rain."

The vibe in the room changes. Thrill and excitement becomes something else. Air grows cold and the lamp on the end table starts to shake. A far-off scream—can't tell if it's Donna or Ollie. Room lights flicker. Music that accompanies the fountain show cuts in and out on the TV. They're trying to tell me something. What?

S
O
U
L

T
R
A
P
P
E
R

Digital recorder picks up their voices, but it's too garbled to make out. Panic time. Grab a pen and paper for them out of the desk drawer, but they can only summon the energy to jiggle the pen. Rack my brain. Then I remember a scene from a movie. Race to the bathroom, close the door, and blast the hot water in the shower until the mirror over the sink fogs up.

"Tell me, Donna—on the mirror."

A line forms on the foggy glass, then another—letters, then words:

there are demons

"Where," I shout.

A little further down the mirror, a single word forms:

everywhere

"What do you mean?" I ask, sweating through my shirt. "Where are the demons?"

I hear a squeak of a finger on the glass and Donna's response covers practically the entire mirror:

around people
in the air
on the street
in doorways
in windows
Ollie is scared.

"All right, I'll get you back inside. Stand still by the window," I say. I hear another squeak. The mirror says:

Nick?

"Tomorrow," I say.

I turn off the shower and head back into the room. I'm drenched.

The trap identifies Ollie first, then Donna. I pull the trigger in succession. The sound rattles the window. Front desk will be flooded with calls asking if a bomb went off. Check the controls. They're safe inside.

Demons? All around? Must have to be dead to see them. No wonder they call it Sin City.

I need to think. No gambling or boozing tonight. I shut the curtains, dump the Champagne down the drain, lock the door, and barricade it with the dresser. Not that that'll keep evil out, but it helps me rest a little easier.

Like a prizefighter the night before a bout, I'm in bed early, sober and edgy. I run scenarios in my mind. Chances are this'll go wrong. I figure there's a 90 percent chance I'll get arrested. Probably multiple charges—trespassing, breaking and entering, assault with a deadly weapon. Shit, maybe even attempted murder. I'll go to prison—for years. Fuck my life up but good.

I can leave now. Walk away from this. No shame in that. Go my way and let Nick Lonzi go his.

I stare at the soul trap lying on the bed next to me. I weigh it all. Close my eyes and paint a black-and-gray picture of my life behind bars. Inmates all around me. Utterly alone. It's fitting.

She needs closure. So do I.

Decision made. No regrets. I tuck the soul trap under my arm and drift off to the booming and spraying sounds of the fountains.

Next morning I don my Fear and Loathing shirt and breeze into the Phoenician. Lay low around the sports book, but get paranoid when a few people look my way. Duck into the first men's room I find and spend an hour in a stall listening to a dozen guys taking noisy dumps around me. Good morning.

My iPhone vibrates. Cleary's text message reads: *In his office.*

I make my way to the office tower, avoiding eye contact as I badge through, and jump on an elevator free and clear. Get off on the sixth floor and march down the hall like a badass. If this were a Tarantino film, it'd be eight seconds of slow motion.

Throw the door open and burst into Lonzi's outer office dripping adrenaline. By the time Lonzi's two bodyguards recognize me, I've already gone apeshit on them. Like my heart rate, everything's in warp speed. Pepper spray in the goons' eyes. Small Fry taser shots right in their barrel chests. Cuff them both to the legs of the marble receptionist's desk that's not going anywhere, and duct-tape their mouths shut. They're down and out in less than a minute.

A statuesque temp receptionist emerges from the hallway to Lonzi's office and surprises me. She looks at the carnage, takes a deep breath. Fuck. I leap toward her and manage to get my hand over her mouth and muffle the mother of all screams just as she lets it fly. She flies backward and I land on top of her.

"Shut up. Don't make a sound," I order.

I pull back my hand an inch or two. "Don't kill me," she pleads.

I'm drenched in sweat, stinking of adrenaline. "Unless you want me to fry the silicone in those D cups, you better jiggle on over to that closet and don't make a peep." I tape her mouth shut and her hands behind her back. She bolts toward the closet like her stiletto heels are Nike track shoes. I shove her inside, barricade the closet with a chair, and march down the hallway.

I turn the knob, open the heavy wood door, and enter Lonzi's office gingerly. He has his back turned to me, bitching someone out on the phone. He doesn't hear a thing. I clear my throat. He turns, recognizes me, and slams the receiver down.

"You again?" he grunts.

"Me again."

He gives me a murderous look and points at me like his finger is a dagger. "This is my fucking place of business, you little shit. Do I show up where you work and slap the dick out of your mouth?"

"This time, Nick, I brought a few friends." I pull the soul trap out of my backpack and point it at him. He thinks it's a gun. Ducks for cover behind his desk like a pussy. I walk behind the desk where he cowers. "Remember this?" I ask, flicking Ollie's badge at him. It bounces off his forehead.

"What's that?" he asks.

"It's your dead son's good-luck charm."

"Where did you get that?" He rises and seems to grow his balls back. He sizes me up and realizes I'm not going to shoot him.

"I found it on the spot where you had them killed," I say.

He flinches, presses a code on his desk phone. "Get your ass out of here. I've already called security."

"You should have called an ambulance." I charge, tackle him dead-on into the wall, and pummel his face with compact punches. Geezer can still scrap. For every punch I land, he blocks three. Knees me in the balls while I'm straddling him and manages to get back on his feet. But I'm 27, amped up, and pissed off, and he's 79 and caught off-guard, and all the evil in hell can't change that. I hit him with a wild right hook and back it up with an elbow to the nose. Blood spurts from his nostrils like the Bellagio fountains. Then I'm back on top of him, landing clean head shots.

"Get off me," he whimpers, but I can't stop. I stand over him and plant my boot in his ribs and kidneys.

"Coward!" I growl. "You sold out your own son, you son of a bitch!" I scream between kicks.

Lonzi's about an inch from unconsciousness. "I don't know what you're talking about," he groans in a manner that confirms he knows full well.

"I've got something that'll remind you," I say, grabbing the soul trap, firing it up, and releasing Donna and Ollie.

Eerie sounds of static-charged voices and unnatural movement fills the room. Nick screams like a five-year-old waking up from a nightmare. I can hear Donna and Ollie, just barely, but can't see them. Nick's expression—mouth and eyes open wide—says it all. He sees and hears them. "It's them . . . Donna . . . Oliver," Nick cries.

The hair stands up on my neck. The cold breeze of Ollie blows by me. I hear Ollie—all echoes—say, "Who's the old guy?" He doesn't recognize his father.

SOUL TRAPPER

"He's nobody, Ollie. Just an old, confused man."

"My badge!" I hear Ollie say. I pick the badge up off the floor and pocket it. "Got it, Ollie."

"Yeah."

"I'll meet you back inside. Hold still for me, buddy."

I strain to hear his response: "Okeydokey."

The trap auto-targets Ollie and I pull the trigger. The sound sends Nick scurrying for cover. Ollie's safe.

I enjoy watching Nick cower in the corner. He's on his knees, gazing up, transfixed, speaking into thin air pleadingly, like a child visionary seeing the Virgin Mary when no one else can. Nick buries his head in his hands and weeps.

I hear Donna's voice. "Don't cover your face, Nick. Look at me."

He continues to cower.

"I said, stand up and look at me," Donna orders. Her voice grows clearer.

Nick obeys. Stands like a child full of shame, then tries the charm. Pathetic to watch this walking Viagra commercial grovel. "Donna. Donna, baby. You're my girl."

Did I mention I pretty much hate everyone? That includes geezers who still think they have a way with the ladies.

"Look me in the eye, Nick," Donna orders.

Nick stares ahead blankly. There's silence, then a crackling, buzzing *whap*! Nick's head snaps to the right. *Whap*—to the left. Ouch. That had to sting.

A whirling dervish of negative energy pours out from one of the Blake prints on the office wall. I look closer. It's a painting of Alastor. And it's coming to life.

"Donna," I shout around the room. "Stand very still. I have to get you back inside."

The trap goes haywire. Can't target Donna. Gotta aim at her myself. Fire. The deafening rip, thunderous *clap-boom*, and megasuction are music to my ears. They're both safe.

Alastor emerges from the Blake print. There's a gaping wound under his chin from my dagger. On the opposite wall another print morphs to life. Another demon—Belphegor—a cloaked, hunched bald guy with a long, black beard and spiked horns—appears and stands alongside Alastor.

Nick sees them and screams like a hallucinating schizophrenic off his meds.

Alastor's voice booms in the room like he's speaking on a mic. "I promised you a long life and you've had one. Now that Kane Pryce has taken the life you gave me, you must pay—with your own. It's time."

Nick cracks in two. "No!" he begs like a coward.

Belphegor speaks. "And I've come to collect my slots jackpot," he says in a shrill voice.

Nick barrels out of his private office screaming. He trips over his bound bodyguards in the reception area, but just keeps running—out the door and down the hall.

Before the demons give chase, they stop and glare at me. My eyes lock with Alastor's and I feel my soul burn. I clutch the trap with a death grip, remembering Charlton Heston's speech to the NRA: "From my cold, dead hands." (He has those now, by the way.) "Today is Lonzi's day of reckoning," Alastor says. "Because you have interfered, your day will come."

I try to be all sarcastic. "When should I expect you? I'll bake something."

Alastor rubs his long fingers over his wound. "That would ruin the surprise."

I smirk like I'm not scared, but truth be known, I'm shitting my pants. Now I have to grow eyes in the back of my head. From the sound of Nick Lonzi screaming all the way down the hallway, being in Alastor's crosshairs isn't a pleasant experience.

The demons dematerialize before my eyes. Their dark energy beelines in Lonzi's direction. I follow. Nick screams, then silence. He's in the elevator, going down.

I'm on the next elevator down. I hear a commotion in the casino before the doors even open. It's still morning. Casino crowd is light, but the few panic-stricken gamblers flee in all directions. The demons stalking Lonzi—glowing in their hellish auras—are visible to everyone.

"Oh my God, what's that?" I hear a woman at the slots ask her husband when I run by.

Hubby seems surprisingly at ease. "Don't worry, honey," he laughs. "They're just performers from Devillusion."

Security hits the casino floor like the National Guard, trying to calm and corner Lonzi before the gamblers get spooked enough to quit spending coin.

"Just calm down, Mr. Lonzi," a security guard says soothingly.

Another guard comes up from behind Nick. "We're not going to hurt you, Mr. Lonzi. We're here to help."

I'm only a few feet away from the security guards when they're about to bear down on Nick and the demons. They all freeze, too scared shitless to approach.

Alastor and Belphegor finally get their mitts on Nick. Alastor strikes with his staff and cuts Nick's right arm off at the elbow. It lands halfway across the casino. Blood spurts from the stump. He screams for only a second, then goes into shock. He's losing blood fast, should be flat on his back. But somehow he's still on his feet—running, one last, mad dash across the casino floor. Pure adrenaline.

Alastor and Belphegor enjoy the chase. Both security—and the demons—finally corner Nick at the progressive slots pit. As the demons claw and the guards reach for their tasers, Nick tries to escape by leaping up and trying to scramble over the top of the grand-prize Escalade hanging over a bank of slot machines. He slips, grabs the bumper with his remaining arm, and dangles like a side of beef in a butcher shop.

Alastor and Belphegor close in. They growl like starving animals. As Nick hangs from the bumper, painting the yellow Hummer red, Alastor and Belphegor zone in on the cables and chains suspending the vehicle from the ceiling. They reach up, pull, and jerk at the air like they're yanking a rope in an invisible tug-of-war. The Caddy shakes. They're exerting an unseen force that's stretching the suspension cables, weakening the chains that hold the Escalade aloft. Nick writhes in this dark force. He screams. Surrenders. The cables twang. The chains snap. Ka-fucking-*boom*! Splat and a half.

The sound of Nick Lonzi's soul being ripped from his body, devoured, and dragged off by Alastor and Belphegor is something I'll hear every night when the lights go out. And one eye will always stay open.

The demons vanish. Chaos erupts. A few minutes later, a crisis team shows up and swings into action. The casino is roped off in a matter of minutes. Hotel doors are locked down. Takes less than an hour to scrape Nick off the floor. Police don't know what to make of it. Neither does the mayor or the governor of Nevada when they show up to plot the cover-up. I'm hauled to a security office and grilled. I play dumb, like I'm a tourist in for the day. Deny any involvement. Lonzi's bodyguards try to make a beef against me, but their reputations and arrests records are worse than mine. Detectives can't even find the temp secretary. She bolted the scene as soon as someone let her out of that closet.

The whole thing is a giant clusterfuck. The police have a royal mess on their hands and they know it. When detectives grill me a second time, a few people from the hotel and the governor's office are in the room with us. They don't know what to do with me. I'm complicating things. So this time, I tell them the truth. Tell them everything. Sound like a complete fucking nut—but a really eloquent one. Fifty-fifty chance I can wriggle my way out of this mess. I spell it out for them—websites, blogs, tweets, conspiracy theories. Demons loose in a casino is bad for business. I promise to use all technological means to let the world know what happened. I tell them I have a big mouth and a lot of time on my hands.

The room empties and they're all off to confer. Twenty minutes later, after signing a statement that I didn't see anything occur in the casino, I walk clean.

I hang around in the shadows until the casino reopens. When I finally leave, there's no trace that an accident even occurred, that a

Vegas legend died. They comp all of the witnesses and go with the story that it's all just a publicity stunt to promote Devillusion.

I see a CNN news flash on the television in the casino bar. Nicholas Lonzi—noted philanthropist, inventor, and entrepreneur—passed away peacefully after a brief illness at the age of seventy-nine. Tributes start pouring in. There's a sound bite of Wayne Newton, tears in his eyes.

What happens in Vegas really does stay in Vegas.

Thirty

I bid farewell to the Phoenician and stop at Ed Roman's Guitars just off the Strip to blow off steam before my drive home. It's known as the biggest guitar shop in the world. As big as an airplane hangar. Packed to the rafters with every model guitar on God's green earth. If you're cool about it and know how to play, you can wander around and plug in nearly any make or model in any one of the hundred amps lying around. I wander around aimlessly and plug and play at least thirty, including an Ed Roman custom job, a Gibson Jimmy Page Les Paul, a jet-black Gretsch English Gentleman like George Harrison played, a Johnny Ramone Signature white Mosrite, a flametop Paul Reed Smith Hollowbody Archtop, and a Hamer that Slash played in concert. The one I fall in love with is a Gibson '57 Les Paul Goldtop Darkback Reissue. Allman played an original of the same model. With its antique gold luster, the fucker could pass for a piece of art. Feels like butter in my hands. I start playing "Layla," interspersing licks from Clapton and Allman. I get lost in it. It's like I go somewhere I've never seen. I'm surprising myself. For the first time, I'm feeling it—in the marrow. Now I know why John Mayer makes all of those goofy faces. He's feeling it. His marrow's boiling over. Maybe he's all right after all. When I finish, I hear applause, whistles. Open my eyes. I've drawn a crowd. I'm a guitar hero.

The Gibson is like Excalibur. Gotta have it. Four thousand bucks out the door. If I don't kill myself, I think I'll buy it when Father Demtrius's check clears.

By dusk, Vegas is in my rearview mirror. I'm driving on autopilot. My mind is a cluttered mess. I have a choice. Need to think. Need to drink.

Fill up in Barstow—same pump as last time—and hit the Slash X Ranch Cafe again. Place is different at night. Last time, in the afternoon, it was practically empty and I sat by myself and bawled like a baby. This time, it's packed with blue-collar shitkickers downing bottles of cheap beer and shots of bottom-shelf bourbon. The same barstool from last time is open, though. Right under the guitar-playing mannequin that looks like Skeeter Jackson. I order a Bud draft and a shot of Wild Turkey. Pop a Vicodin.

Seven rounds later, I'm good and drunk.

Clapton's version of "Crossroads" plays on the jukebox. I get a chill. This seat—this exact spot—is my personal crossroads. While Clapton sings the blues, I live them. I have a choice. And I'm going to make it right here.

ISSUE 1:

If I do it—how? Don't have a gun. Don't have sleeping pills. Got a shitload of Vicodin. Could try to mix it with booze and antihistamines, but I don't know if it's foolproof. Have a sharp knife, but the thought of all that blood. Could buy rope at Home Depot, but too scary, too painful. No way I'm taking a flying leap. I have a recurring nightmare where I fall off a bridge. Heard freezing to death is a good way to go, but quite the chore in Southern California. Maybe I can sneak into a freezer somewhere. There's carbon

monoxide. Could pull over somewhere deserted.
Block up the exhaust. That'd work.

I keep drinking.

Issue 2.

Thinking it through. If I'm nothing else, I'm an ana-
lytical decision maker.

I grab a bar napkin and bum a pen off the bartender. Two columns. Pros and Cons. Pro column is short and easy: being with
Donna and Ollie. That's all I can list. I have no idea what lies beyond
that door. Donna's right—maybe the slate gets wiped clean. Maybe
we all go our separate ways. Maybe I'd be punished and taken away
from them. The only thing I could say for sure is without a body
tethering me to earth, I could step across that threshold into the
unknown with them.

Cons
1. Ned would be majorly pissed.
2. I'd miss Ned.
3. Would be up to Ned to find me on the other side. I've
   seen enough to know you can't predict where the universe will dump you if you refuse to exit through your
   door. What if I end up in one of my old foster homes in
   Colorado or one of my old apartments or any one of the
   dozens of bars I frequent? What if he can't find me?
4. Donna and Ollie would be stuck in the trap until Ned
   finds me. Could take months. Years. They might go stir-
   crazy, or worse yet—forget me.
5. No guarantee I can stay with Donna and Ollie.
6. Wouldn't get to see the Circle Jerks at the House of Blues
   or U2 at the Rose Bowl.
7. What if I end up in hell? I don't think I'm that bad, but
   who knows? It was a mighty crowded place.

8. Even if I can stay with Donna and Ollie, I damn well might fuck it all up somehow. Usually do.

9. I'd be dead. I write the word again in caps and underline it.

10. <u>DEAD</u>.

I think about Rita Merrill and her son, Danny. Danny died at the age of twenty-two. Never even really got started living. That's sad. Then there's Rita. Lived a long time, maybe too long, but at the end of the day, she died alone and her lifetime of memories are packed in boxes and on their way to nowhere. That's sad, too.

I don't know.

I glance around me. Through a boozy fog, I watch a bunch of rednecks laughing, drinking, tapping their cowboy boots to blue-grass music. It's fun to get fucked up and listen to music. Road trips are fun. Business is picking up. Maybe I do want to play in a band. I reach down, touch my backpack resting at my feet, nudge the soul trap, and remember Donna's words: *"You have life. And it's a precious gift."*

I think she's right.

I know she's right.

Bottom line. I'm not done living yet. Not by a long shot.

The choice is made.

But, then again, when the hell did I ever listen to myself?

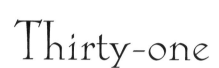

Thirty-one

I hear the Beatles' "Paperback Writer" and open my eyes. Donna and Ollie are dancing in the center of the diner. I startle them. They rush over and hug me.

"I'm so glad you're back," Donna says.

"Me, too." I say, kissing her on the cheek and squeezing her hand.

"I'm sorry about what happened when you tried to show us Las Vegas," she whispers to me.

"It's okay."

Ollie nudges me. "Here you go, kemosabe," I say, handing him back his badge.

"Thanks, Kane." He pins it on carefully and gallops around in a circle. He stops, looks at me. "What are we gonna do today, Daddy?"

"Ollie, you shouldn't call Kane that," Donna tells him.

"It's all right," I say. "I don't mind."

Ollie smiles and play-punches me. Donna nudges him. "Ollie, go play over by the jukebox."

"Why?" Ollie asks, suspicious.

"Because . . . I need to talk to Kane," Donna says softly.

"But, Mom . . ." Ollie argues.

Donna cuts him off and gets firm. "Heaven's to Betsy, Ollie, mind your mother."

"Okay." He slinks away toward the jukebox, head down.

When he's out of earshot, I say, "Nice punch." Donna smiles. "I'll bet that felt good."

Donna looks scared. "That was Alastor, wasn't it?" She leans and whispers in my ear, "He came for me, didn't he?"

"He came for Nick," I assure her.

She looks surprised, relieved. "What happened?"

"Nick's the new tenant in your old place," I tell her.

"Dead?"

"And it wasn't pretty."

Donna looks at her shoes, her hands, then me. "Good," she says. "Then it's really over." She pauses and it hits her. "It's time to go, isn't it?"

I fight the words. "This is good-bye." I soak up her face. "I can't join you."

She smiles, touches my cheek. "I know."

We look at each other. I'm the one with tears in my eyes.

"Where are you sending us, Kane?"

I look at that door and tell her the truth. "I don't know for sure, but it's gonna be a far cry from where I found you."

"You think so?"

I'm choking up. "Baby, you paid your dues. If there's a heaven, there's a mansion with your name on the mailbox."

Now Donna's eyes fill with tears. She holds me close and whispers, "I wish there was a way."

"Me, too," I whisper back. "But look at us . . . what a pair. I live on Yucca Street with one foot in jail, and you're dead."

Donna chuckles through tears. "That is a problem."

"Maybe we'll get lucky and there'll be reincarnation," I offer.

She pulls me close. "I'd find you."

"Come on," I joke. "You'll forget all about me as soon as you track down Elvis."

Donna doesn't laugh. "I'll never forget you, Kane. Never," she stresses. "In this life or the next, I'll think of you." My knees go weak. She pokes me in the chest and her voice cracks with emotion. "You didn't even know me and you came and got me away from him. Maybe you did that for Ollie, but it really doesn't matter."

She stares off, remembering Alastor's lair. "No, sir. Elvis has nothing on you."

I reach inside my shirt and take off my lucky necklace. I pluck the Saint Christopher medal from the chain, place it in Donna's hand, and squeeze it shut. "Take this," I say, "for a safe journey."

Ollie's no dummy. He knows what's going on and marches toward us. "We can't leave, Mommy," he begs. "We're a family now."

Donna stops him. "We have to go, Ollie."

Ollie's on the verge of a tantrum. "We can't go without Kane," he shouts.

Donna looks to me for help. "Let me talk to him," I say.

I kneel down, try to calm Ollie by rubbing his shoulders. "Hey, Ollie Ollie Oxen Free," I say.

Ollie tries to be playful, but can't. "Hey, Kane, Kane, the big fat pain," he says, wiping tears away.

I look him in the eye. My voice cracks worse than when Peter Brady hit puberty. "You make me very happy. And very proud."

Ollie gives me the warmest of smiles. He's been waiting to hear that from a man his whole life.

"I love you, Kane," he says, beaming.

"Me, too." I'm fighting tears.

"Will I ever see you again?"

"I hope so," I say. "I hope I see you both."

Ollie glances at the door. "I'm scared," he whispers.

"Nothing to be afraid of," I assure him. "You'll make new friends. You'll never be alone again."

He's not sold. Still scared. I give him a squeeze on his shoulder. "Now it's time for you to be the Lone Ranger, Ollie. You have to take good care of your mother."

"Okay," he says standing a little taller, straightening the badge pinned to his shirt. "I'm ready."

Donna pats Ollie on the head. "Let's go, honey."

Donna whispers one last thing to me: "I love you." She hurries across the room with Ollie before I can say it back.

The lever appears at my side. As I touch the crystal handle, I hear Ollie tell his mother excitedly, "Don't worry, Mommy, I'll protect you."

Goddamnit, this hurts. Desperation. *Come on, think, Kane. There's got to be a way to make this work. Think!*

I'm frozen, staring at them. They're staring back—waiting, wondering. I clutch the lever. The crystal handle is cold.

Game over. Dragging this out another second is torture. I pull. The door creeps open. A cool, penetrating blue light and calming vibrational tones. Voices beckon them forward. Through the foggy blue light, I make out two figures—Rita Merrill and her son, Danny. Then I hear the instantly recognizable voice of the Lone Ranger boom, "Follow me, my faithful companion."

Donna and Ollie rise and are pulled gently into the light, into the welcoming arms of Rita and Danny. Donna blows me a kiss. The image sears in my brain.

Their voices reverberate even after they vanish. Ollie giggles his way to the other side. "This'll . . . be . . . fun," are the last words I hear. His voice reverberates even after they vanish.

And all goes silent.

I don't linger when my exit door appears. Too lonely here.

I come to, covered in sweat, flailing, gasping for breath.

"Take it easy, Kane," Ned says, looking down at my face. "You're back."

Struggle to catch my breath. An uneasy silence between us.

Ned helps me off with the helmet, goggles, and wires, and puts a cold cloth on my forehead and checks my temperature. "I don't know what to say. That was a tough one, buddy."

I'm quiet. When Ned tries to leave my side, I reach out and grab his hand. "You know what sucks?" He shrugs. "That's as close to happiness as I'm ever going to get."

He understands. "Relax a little bit. Then we'll go grab a beer or twelve. Toast to a job well done."

"Nah," I grunt, stretching my limbs. "I just need to be by myself right now."

"Get some sleep."

"Yeah."

Ned packs up and leaves. I've never felt more alone. Before I went in to say good-bye, I invited Eva over, but she blew me off again. Looks like our little partnership is up shit's creek.

My chest is killing me. Feels like someone put a cigarette out through my shirt. Examine myself in the mirror. Pull my lucky necklace off and notice the Saint Christopher medal is gone. Skin is burned crisp on the spot where the medal rested against me. It'll leave a nice permanent scar. No explanation for that one.

I fasten Ollie's badge to the necklace where the medal used to be.

Then I turn on the equipment, plug in my guitar, and begin recording the guitar solos in the "Layla" finale. I can do this. It's all about feeling it—letting go. I start out stiff, but an hour in, I'm nailing the Clapton parts—bending strings until they almost break, all my body's energy focused on the tips of my fingers, playing notes that I never knew were on my guitar. I'm way beyond surprising myself. Clapton: done.

Take a walk around the neighborhood. Jack myself up on bad coffee at 7-Eleven. Eat a grimy meal at Roscoe's.

Go back, don my glass finger slide, and channel Skydog Allman. Technically, his parts feel easier, but it's all about the slide. Your body can't get in the way. Neither can your brain. Your spirit has to slide that slide. I struggle with it for a while. Slowly, it comes, not at once—in tiny bite-size segments. I lose myself and three hours later, after I finally nail that final, unforgettable sound—the bird chirp—I know I have enough decent files assembled to piece it together digitally.

Duane Allman was a guitar genius at twenty-three. Un-fucking-believable. A year later he was dead. Motorcycle.

It's a precious gift all right.

Another walk, this time down Cahuenga to Sunset across to Vine and back up to Yucca. I skip the coffee this time. Open a fresh fifth of Jameson back in my apartment. Time for the vocal track. Need to be good and loose.

I start with the howls of anguish. They're easy.

I print out the lyrics. It's not like I haven't heard them a million times. But when I fall in love with a song, it's almost always about the music, rarely about the words. For me, the words in "Layla" have always been drowned out by the brilliance of those two guitar icons. Those words never really sank in. Until now.

I pipe the song in my headphones and record myself singing along. The whiskey has limbered me up. The words are flowing. They start to reveal themselves in new ways. The words ring true.

I tried to give you consolation
When your old man had let you down.
Like a fool, I fell in love with you,
Turned my whole world upside down.

Layla, you've got me on my knees.
Layla, I'm begging, darling please.
Layla, darling won't you ease my worried mind.

Let's make the best of the situation
Before I finally go insane.
Please don't say we'll never find a way
And tell me all my love's in vain.

I'm on my knees. Singing the blues. For real. I could front a band singing like this. I glance over at the album cover. I glance over at a photo of Donna on the floor. It's her. It's all about me and her. I got obsessed with the song just before all this began. "Layla" was a storm cloud approaching, a harbinger of what was just around the corner.

Jung's synchronicity fucking with me again.

One take. That's it. I know I'll never get that feeling of revelation back in my voice. And that's what makes it real.

I drink half the bottle of Jameson. Doze off for a couple of hours. Wake up with a dull headache, head straight to my Mac, and launch Pro Tools.

It's maddening. Whiskey. Coffee. More whiskey. I tweak for what seems like an eternity. Playback after playback.

Sixteen hours later, it's done. It's the hardest I've ever worked on anything in my life. At least on this side.

I collapse on the sofa. I stare straight ahead. There they rest— my Fender and the soul trap side by side.

I muster the strength to stand. I grab the trap, take it into my room, lock it in its box, place it in its hiding spot behind the wall in my closet, and cover the opening. May it rest in peace.

I'm done with it.

All of it.

Fuck it.

I'm joining a band. No—I'm starting a band. Just as soon as I wake up.

Must sleep or die. I drop on my bed.

Maybe I'll get lucky and see Donna and Ollie in a dream.

Thirty-two

Eighteen hours later, my iPhone rings and I'm roused from a dreamless slumber. So groggy, I slur like a stroke victim. "Hello?"

An angry man berates me. "You gave me your word, Kane. You broke your promise."

"What?" I stammer. "Who the fuck is this?"

"Father Demetrius—and watch your language." He's panting in anger. "Why did you betray me?"

I sit up and reach for the light switch. "I don't know what you're talking about."

"It's in the *Times*," he snaps. "Bold headline:

PRIEST CALLS IN CONVICTED GHOST HUNTER

They've made fools of us both. Do you know the trouble this causes me with the archdiocese? I'm not paying you a dime!"

Feels like I'm dreaming, but I'm not. "Look, I have to call you back,"

"You should be ashamed of yourself," he berates me. "I trusted you, Kane."

Priest is testing my patience. I'm ready to give him an earful. "Just let me find out what's going on. I'll call you back," I snap.

I hang up, jump out of my bed, throw on my clothes from yesterday, and run to the newsstand on the corner of Hollywood and Highland. A sense of dread builds as I get closer. A bad, fucking feeling.

Grab the paper. There it is, page one, section B—the whole story. Under the name B. J. Cross. Feel like I'm standing naked as traffic rolls by.

I can't believe it. What am I saying? Of course I can believe it. What did I expect? How stupid could I have been?

I toss the paper on the sidewalk and stagger back to my apartment in a daze. Round the corner on Yucca. Eva's waiting in front of my building. She's a wreck, but, as always, totally put together. I ignore her. She grabs me as I pass by. "Kane? Kane, you have to believe me. I didn't do it."

Don't want her looking at me. Feel like Oz trying to scamper his way back behind the curtain. "Get away from me." Comes out more sullen than angry.

She's in tears. "It was another reporter—the guy I was seeing. When I broke up with him, he got jealous. Went ballistic. Got hold of my notes—in my apartment—and did a hatchet job on you."

Now it pours out hot and angry. "And you knew nothing about it?" I shout in her face.

"I swear I didn't," she cries.

"And you expect me to believe that?"

"Yes," she says adamantly.

"You're a liar," I yell in her face.

Her defenses are going up. "I've never lied to you."

"Bullshit."

"I've never lied to you," she repeats. "More than you can say for yourself."

"Don't try to change the subject," I snap.

"You looked me in the eye and lied right to my face. And you're going to lecture me about honesty?"

I'm a second away from punching the wall. Breathe deep. I bury my head in my fists. Do I believe her? The answer comes in a violent wave of rage I haven't felt since that last foster home. Gotta seal Pandora's box tight and bury it so deep it can never be unearthed.

Eva's the enemy. The devil with a perfect ass.

Hurt her.

The last traces of nice guy burn to ash. I am my reflection in hell.

I unload: "You're a tabloid hack. You are the lowest form of scum in this town. Why don't you go chase Lindsay Lohan or Britney Spears?"

Them's fightin' words. She goes from crying to pissed off in milliseconds. "That's not fair," she says. "I'm a journalist."

I get right in that pretty face. "You're a two-bit muckraker."

"I'm a newspaper reporter. And I've got talent. Something you know nothing about."

I laugh in her face. "You're sitting on the only talent you have."

She slaps me square in the face. "Pig."

I offer the other cheek. "Do you know how pathetic you are?" She's raging, waiting for me to answer my own question. "You were jealous of a ghost."

"No, I wasn't," she snaps.

"Bullshit. I wouldn't fuck you, so you went for the jugular. I just said good-bye to a woman—a woman," I reiterate, "who had more guts, more soul, more heart than you'll ever have."

"You're wrong," she shouts in my face. "But you're too scared, too alone, too drunk half the time to think clearly or trust anyone." I look away. "That's the real story." She waits for me to respond, but I don't. That one stings.

"Get out of my sight," I say, sullen again. I push her aside and duck into my building. She doesn't follow.

Pace around my apartment. Need to burn off steam. Need to walk. Watch out homeless. Tourists. Stray cats. Something's gonna get the shit kicked out of it.

Pound the pavement, breaking a sweat. My phone keeps ringing. It's Ned. He's gotta be freaking out. He's leaving me messages. Too fucking bad. I'm done with him, too.

On my way down Hollywood Boulevard—not far from the Chinese Theater—I glance down and notice the star on the sidewalk— Clayton Moore: the Lone Ranger. Now I'm seriously ready to get my drink on.

I may not be able to drown my sorrow, but I'll sure as fuck teach it to swim.

I opt to self-medicate at the Frolic Room. As soon as I enter, Gabe, the bartender who annoys the piss out of me, holds a fifth of Jameson aloft and yells all cheery, "Behold, Kane, I bring you glad tidings of great joy."

I take my usual seat in the corner stool by the mirror.

"Read about you in the paper," Gabe says, starting in. "Dude, I didn't know you were a ghostbuster. What'll it be?"

"What else?"

Gabe pours a shot of Jameson and I down it as soon as it's in the glass. I slam the shot glass down. "Another."

"No beer, huh?" Gabe asks.

I shake my head.

"One of them days, huh?" he asks. "What—ghosts not biting?" He laughs.

I want to bitch-slap his doughy face. "Go eat some more carbs," I say, waving him away.

Gotta calm down. Have a shitload of drinking to do. Can't get eighty-sixed. I get up and walk to the jukebox. Seven songs already in the cue. I flip back and forth between the albums. Stuff is missing. New crappy stuff in its place. My temper flares. How dare they touch my jukebox. Where's that song?

"Where's Ritchie Valens?" I yell to Gabe.

"In the cemetery . . . didn't you see the movie?" Gabe laughs at himself again.

"Put him back," I demand. "Do you hear me?" Gabe shrugs it off. "I wanna hear 'Donna,'" I shout.

A drunk at the end of the bar pulls his head out of his vodka and starts singing. He can carry a tune:

> *I had a girl,*
> *Donna was her name*
> *Since she left me*
> *I've never been the same*
> *'Cause I love my girl*
> *Donna, where can you be?*
> *Where can you be?*
>
> *Now that you're gone*
> *I'm left all alone*
> *All by myself*
> *To wander and roam*
> *'Cause I love my girl*
> *Donna, where can you be?*
> *Where can you be?*

Gabe applauds. The drunk looks at me.

"Buy that bum a drink," I say. I return to my barstool, slam down another shot, and bang the glass on the bar.

Gabe pours another. "On the house," he says. Bullshit. Nothing in life is free. Here it comes. "You know," he says, leaning in, "they say Marilyn Monroe's ghost haunts the Roosevelt Hotel's lobby mirror. And there's supposedly a ghost in the mausoleum at the Hollywood Forever cemetery. You know why ghosts are here, right?"

I don't answer.

"They're just a little lost," Gabe finishes. "It's easy to get lost when your soul aches. Right?"

I study Gabe from the waist up and imagine where I'd stab him first. "As God is my witness," I growl, "if you say the word *ghost* again, I will find a way to drown you in my shot glass."

I'm twitching. When Justin Timberlake comes over the speakers, I snap. March straight over, unplug the jukebox, and reset it. Play one song and return to the bar. The Doors—"Roadhouse Blues." Jim Morrison, member of Club 27, belts it out. I toast to the Lizard King, down my Jameson, and pound the shot glass on the bar.

"Your gonna break that glass," Gabe shouts. "Take it easy, Kane." He wipes the bar. Walk away, asshole. But he doesn't. "What's troublin' ya?" he asks. "Tell me. I'm a good listener. I can help."

Irish whiskey on an empty stomach. Recipe for a bare-knuckle fight.

"Mind your fucking business," I warn him.

"This bar is my business," he says. "Guys like you are my business." He starts to walk away but turns back. He's begging for an ass-kicking. "You know, you're starting to hang out here too much, Kane. You seem like a haunted guy . . . no pun intended." He laughs. I'm gonna blow. Assault and battery. Back to jail. Who cares?

I fidget. Knock *The Lone Ranger* theme on the bar. My heart races. Down goes another shot and everything gets rubbery. I'm drunk.

"You're gonna end up with a drinking problem," Gabe continues. "I've seen it happen a million times. At least a million."

Clear my throat. Try to meditate. Sorry, Buddha. Not today.

"I've got you pegged, Kane," Gabe says with a smirk on his fat face. "You know what you need?" He waits for me to answer, then says, "You need a wife and kid to tame your savage soul."

There goes the camel's back. I'm out of my barstool and squeezing Gabe's throat. His eyes bug out. I growl in his face—possessed. "You can go to hell."

Gabe is walking on the moon without a helmet. Absolutely no air. He'll be dead in less than a minute. I picture my prison cell. Ease my grip a hair. "Let . . . go," he pleads.

The drunk has one foot out the door, ready to yell for help. I let go and shove Gabe. He flies backward into the bar and then falls on his ass. The force knocks a bottle of Patron off the shelf. It smashes on the floor. Gabe gets up slowly, a big wet spot on his pants. Hope it's from the tequila.

"Chill," he says.

I'm turning back from werewolf to man. The drunk returns to his barstool. Gabe shakes it off and grabs his broom.

"Whatever's wrong—it'll get better," he says as he sweeps up the glass. "You can't have a rainbow without the rain, Kane." He laughs at himself yet again. "Hey, that rhymed."

Some guys never learn.

"Shut up and pour," I say.

And he does.

Acknowledgments

There are a number of people I would like to thank:

First, my mother, Jean Lennon, who prayed this book into being. I am so lucky to have you. Thank you for all that you've done for me.

Peter Steinberg, for all that you did to make this happen. You helped in so many ways. I've been waiting forever to work with someone like you.

Emily Bestler, for taking on this project and for your incredible editorial direction. And thanks to Judith Curr, Laura Stern, and everyone at Atria Books. I am so proud to be published by Atria.

Dave Warhol, Kane Pryce's godfather. Thank you for having enough faith in *Soul Trapper* to develop it originally as an iPhone app. You and everyone at Realtime Associates, Inc., are a joy to work with.

Fellow author Lisa Wood Shapiro, for all you did to help and for all the years of friendship and encouragement.

My early readers, for your input and useful suggestions: Lee Ann Lennon-Costanzo, Dave Warhol, Seth Shapiro, Shirl Porter, Michael and Kimberly Bross.

Acknowledgments

Julie Sessing and everyone at Sessing Music Services, for all your help.

Matthew Snyder at CAA, for your support and faith in *Soul Trapper*.

Doris Huertes, Ivana Ezrol, and Nicole Radish, for taking good care of my daughter during crunch times.

My large and loving family and all my friends.

My late sister, Janet, who loved ghost stories as much as I did. I often felt her presence, nudging me along in the wee hours when this book was largely written.

My daughter, Olivia. Kane Pryce was born a few days after you were, during a late-night bottle feeding. You are my muse and my lucky charm. Daddy loves you.

And finally, my wife, Laura, who has carried too heavy a weight for too long while I've wandered (sometimes aimlessly) like a Bedouin across an uncharted career wilderness. And thank you for your mad editing skills. You are responsible for whipping this book into shape.

Printed in the United States
By Bookmasters